For Frank

Acknowledgments

My friend Mitch Heiserman once told me about something strange going on in his neighborhood. Neither of us knew it at the time, but that story would eventually inspire this one. Thanks, Mitch.

Three talented writers, also wonderful friends, stuck with me through multiple drafts. Bill Tate, David Hansard, and Ginger Calem, thank you for helping me find the story I wanted to tell.

Mike Pace, Robert Little, Chad Randall, Zenaida Davis, Kelly McDonald, Ron Worley, and Josephine Wagner straightened me out on the technical facts. You have fascinating jobs and I appreciate that you shared them with me.

Victoria Skurnick and Barbara Peters are sharp, strong women who worked hard to polish both the story and its writer. The manuscript is finished, but I remain a work in progress. I'm lucky to have you.

Robert Rosenwald, Jessica Tribble, and Nan Beams at Poisoned Pen Press make publishing miracles happen for me every day. I couldn't ask for a better team.

To my friends in the Brazoria County Library System, thank you for giving me a quiet place to write and an endless supply of good books.

Finally, I'm reminded of the adage, "Home is where your story begins." Tey, Jill, Lindsay, and Sam, my best stories unfold with you.

Chapter One

Claire Gaston's amber hair rode flat against her head, giving the impression she'd just climbed out of bed. Any make-up had worn away too, yet she still looked closer to forty than her real age—which I knew from her file was fifty-three. In any case, Claire was twenty years my senior, had spent a day and a night in the clink, and still looked better than I did after a comfortable night of sleep and a shower.

We picked up telephone handsets on either side of an opaque window in the jail's visitation room, and I tried to ascertain whether she regarded me with hope or just curiosity.

"I'm Emily Locke," I said, "part of your defense team." I smiled, trying to convey that I withheld judgment, even though I wasn't sure that was true. "Sorry about the circumstances."

She leaned forward and rested her elbows on a countertop that extended away from the dividing window. Richard Cole, the private investigator I worked for, often said that it was a good practice to mirror a subject's body language during interviews, so I did. My forearms ended up in something sticky.

"Are you the investigator my lawyer hired?"

"I'm that investigator's lackey."

She tipped her chin up but didn't speak.

"Hope you don't mind." I pulled a folded paper from my purse. "I brought a list of things to clarify. My boss is painfully deficient with specifics."

"What every woman looks for in an investigator."

"Actually, he's very good. We just work differently."

Claire surveyed the tiny countertop on her side of the glass and brushed invisible debris onto the floor. "Ask away."

"Let's start with your kids."

She inhaled and seemed to hold the breath. "They're all I think about."

"Who's keeping them?"

"My parents." Her gaze fell. "Even though they're too old to be caring for kids." She traced imaginary shapes on the countertop with neatly manicured fingers that reminded me of my best friend Jeannie's hands. "You probably know I'm in the middle of a divorce."

She glanced up long enough to see me nod.

"Daniel's not their father. My second husband, Ruben, moved back to Argentina last year. Our custody fight was…I'm ashamed of it. And now with me here—" she looked around our tiny, divided cubicle— "he'll come back and take them away, I know it. I didn't kill Wendell Platt. You have to help me prove it before Ruben swoops in and disappears with the boys."

"It would help me to understand what's going on with Daniel."

Claire leaned back and crossed her arms. Richard would have said I'd put her on the defensive.

"What does he have to do with this?"

I cupped my chin in my hands and watched her for a moment, trying to figure out if she was angry. "Police are reconstructing your day on Thursday, trying to figure out where you went and what you did before Dr. Platt's murder. I hear you and Daniel had quite a fight."

She straightened and opened her mouth to argue, but I raised a hand and continued. "We've all said things we didn't mean, don't worry. The trouble's that the police want to interview Daniel but can't find him. You were the last person to see him and witnesses say you were enraged. It doesn't help to have extra suspicion directed at you."

"No one can find Daniel?"

I shook my head. "Know where he might be?"

She shook her head in return.

"Why the divorce?"

Her shoulders relaxed, like she was resigned to surrender her privacy as well as her marriage.

"Neither of us could be faithful."

My stomach flip-flopped, but I stayed quiet. Richard said sometimes people will volunteer extra information if you give them a chance.

This didn't turn out to be true for Claire. After a few moments, I asked her to continue.

"It's complicated," she said. "For years we've talked about parting ways. Last month I finally filed."

"What was your relationship with Platt?"

Claire shook her head, more to herself than to me, and screwed her face into a queer sort of smile that could only be described as sarcastic. I was considering how to rephrase when she surged toward the glass and banged it with her fist, sending me back in my chair so violently its legs scraped the linoleum.

"I've never met Wendell fucking Platt!"

All I could do was try to control my breathing.

"Never met him," she said. "No one believes me."

She settled back into her chair and I tried to convince myself that the person in front of me was the same woman from thirty seconds ago.

"He was murdered in his home," I said. "Your fingerprints were at the scene."

"Worse, honey. They were on the weapon."

Perhaps reading my incredulity, she added, "Don't tell me. Your boss left that out."

"How do you explain your prints on the weapon?"

She squinted at me and the vibe I got was borderline venomous. "That's what I'm paying *you* to do."

I pressed my fingertips to my temples. "If you never met him, I assume you were never in his house?"

She combed her fingers through her hair so severely I thought she might yank out a fistful of highlights. "I already told all this to Mick Young."

The name elicited a visceral adrenaline surge—the kind brought on when something's wildly wrong.

I made a point to keep my tone calm. "You're represented by Brighton and Young?"

She looked at me quizzically. "Of course."

That explained why Richard had been sketchy about her case. His omissions made me look like an idiot, so now I was doubly miffed. But nothing good would come of showing that to the client, so I pushed it aside and put on my best professional show.

"I apologize for the lack of communication in my office," I said. "Your case is important to me and I want to get the facts straight. Please tell me about Thursday, starting from the beginning."

She regarded me for a drawn out interval and I felt the discomfort of being on the receiving end of a silent stare.

"Do you have kids, Emily?" she finally asked.

If she did kill Platt, I certainly didn't want her to know about Annette.

But then she added, more gently. "I need to know. Please."

"Why does that matter?"

"Because I didn't kill anyone. And if Young can't prove I'm innocent, my kids will go to a man who shouldn't have them. Ruben isn't capable of putting the boys' needs in front of his own. It's terrifying to imagine and hard to explain to someone who's not a parent."

Her fears resonated with me, but I wasn't ready to share that. "Tell me about Thursday."

She tucked her hair behind an ear and edged forward, resting a forearm on the little countertop again. I promised myself I wouldn't flinch if she had another outburst.

"Thursday I got a tip about a dog and went to check it out."

Before I could ask, she added, "I'm in an animal rescue group."

Claire seemed more likely to wear an animal than rescue one. I wondered what else about her I might have misjudged.

"When I got to the address, something was off."

I tried to conjure the image of Claire skulking into bad neighborhoods, retrieving mutts. Pet rescuing sounded like a dirty, hands-on job, ill-suited for her.

"Most of our rescues are from poor, rundown areas. The address for this dog was in the Heights."

That *was* weird. Houston Heights, better known as simply the "Heights," was a quaint, historical community in north central Houston. Noted for meticulously maintained period architecture and its artist community, it didn't seem the place one would expect neglected pets.

"I knocked, but no one answered the door."

I wondered what she might have said if someone had. *Hi. I heard you're mean to your dog so I'm here to take it away?*

"I looked through the windows and didn't see anyone so I went around back. There was one of those wooden privacy fences. I went through the gate. It wasn't the backyard of someone who can't afford to feed a dog, believe me. But I thought there was a hurt animal inside so I had to check anyway."

"You broke in?"

"I didn't have to. The back door was open a smidge. I knocked and shouted inside, but no one answered. I whistled for a dog, but none came. I should have stopped there."

You should have stopped at the gate.

"But I went into the kitchen and called for the dog again. When I didn't see signs of one, I left."

"That's why your prints were at the scene."

"Front door, back door, and windows." She considered. "And countertops, I guess."

"They ID'd you pretty fast. You have a record?"

Claire shook her head. "When my boys were little, I worked at their elementary school. They fingerprinted everyone they hired."

That made sense. She'd still be in the system.

"So what do you think happened? You think Platt was already dead in the house when you showed up?"

"I think it happened after I left."

"Why?"

"Because I don't think he had a dog."

"What?"

"Somebody went to a lot of trouble set me up."

I thought of my friend Jeannie again. She'd have loved the element of scandal.

Claire continued. "I got summoned to a rescue and when I got there, there were no signs of a dog—no poop in the backyard, no bowls on the floor. My fingerprints were on the inside and outside of the house and even on the screwdriver lodged in his trachea—a tool that came from my own garage."

Inwardly, I winced. The bit about the screwdriver was news to me, but I didn't dare show it.

"So I asked myself…who hates me enough to go to all the trouble? Don't get me wrong. Plenty of folks would leave me off their dinner party lists, but it would take real *hate* to pin something like this on a person. And I keep coming back to Diana King."

"Who's she?" I'd been tailing Socialite Diana around Houston for two days, but Claire didn't know that. "What's your relationship with her?"

Claire pursed her lips and gazed upward as she considered how to answer.

"The better question is what's my relationship with her husband."

I blinked. "Oh."

"Chris did a lot for me last year. We developed a comfortable rapport that developed into friendship and eventually," she shrugged, "an affair."

I leaned forward again, into the same sticky residue I'd forgotten was on the damn counter. "What does that mean, 'did a lot for you'?"

She touched her nose and forehead, then counted silently on her fingers. "Nose, brow, boobs, thighs, ass."

"Excuse me?"

"He was my surgeon."

I nodded, buying myself a moment to let the new information gel.

"So you think Diana King has framed you for a murder as revenge for your affair with her husband."

"Yes."

"Why not just kill you?"

Claire moved her mouth into a peculiar combination of a pout and a snarl. I got the impression she'd never considered the question. She shook her head by way of response.

"Do you know a reason Diana King would want Platt dead?"

"No."

"Then I agree with you. This set-up was an awful lot of trouble and risky too. Maybe we should think about who else wanted Platt dead and you in trouble."

"It was Diana."

"I'm only saying—"

"That tip about the dog came on an anonymous note in my gym locker. I belong to a private club. It'd be hard for anyone but a member to leave a note that way."

Her mind was made up.

"You still have the note?"

She shook her head. "The police asked me that too. I remember putting it on my kitchen counter, but after that, who knows. Maybe the cleaning lady tossed it."

After a bit, I thanked her for her time and left.

Claire's interview raised more questions than it answered and my mind was busy sorting and filing critical pieces. One nugget had me hot for an explanation, and it had nothing to do with finding Platt's killer. I dropped into the driver's seat of my now hundred-and-twenty degree car and headed for Richard's office so we could talk about Mick Young.

Chapter Two

More hurt than angry, I slumped into a visitor's chair across from Richard's desk, my keys still in hand. "You didn't tell me who we were working for."

Richard looked over the rim of his coffee mug and paused mid-sip. Even behind his spectacles, the dull shadows beneath his eyes were unmistakable. He set down the cup, rolled away from his computer monitor, and made no excuses. "It's not relevant."

"It's relevant to *me*."

He glanced at a picture on the corner of his desk. If I hadn't been so focused on his eyes, I'd have missed it.

"Linda wanted you to tell me, didn't she?"

His silence said it all.

"Smart men listen to their wives." I turned my keys, one at a time, around the circumference of my key ring, listening for the metallic clink as each landed on its neighbor.

Richard removed his cheater glasses and dropped them into his shirt pocket. "Unlike Tone Zone," he said, with obvious distaste for the health club we'd been watching, "I can't afford to turn away business. I considered telling you. Decided it would cloud your judgment."

Morning sun was bright behind him and his tired eyes and graying hair phased in and out of focus depending on which way I leaned.

"My judgment's clouded more because you lied."

Only months ago, Mick Young had defended the people responsible for destroying my family.

Richard took a breath as if to say something, then let the thought pass.

"I interviewed Claire this morning and looked like a fool because you didn't tell me."

"You were supposed to keep tabs on Diana King," he said. "Leave Claire to me."

"I wanted to form my own opinion about her."

"That's irrelevant. Diana's your assignment."

"My impression's relevant if I'm going to invest personally in this case, Richard. That's the difference between you and me." I rose and strode toward the door.

"Don't judge Claire based on Young's other clients," he said to my back.

I spun to face him. "*You* don't get to decide what I can handle."

"Look how upset it made you!"

"This isn't about Young. It's about you not trusting me. Underestimating me. Being a jerk."

He stood. "It's not about Young?" The words sounded more like a challenge than a question.

"I don't care what you believe. You're not my shrink and you're not my father. And effective immediately, you're not my boss anymore either. Find somebody else to insult and psychoanalyze."

I turned and walked away.

"Come back," he said behind me. "Let's finish this."

I didn't stop to answer, just shoved open the door and left, taking all my irrelevant opinions and unfounded overreactions with me.

I did something new on my drive home—turned off my radio. So much noise was in my head that I couldn't stand anymore. Mick Young had recently defended murderers, kidnappers, and world class racketeers and, as far as I was concerned, that made him unconscionable. By association, I brooded over what that implied about the character of his newest client.

For all I knew, Young himself might even be part of the same criminal ring—still at large—that he'd recently tried to help. The FBI had chased that group for years and was still after its splinter groups today. I knew firsthand that its members were steeply networked into all sorts of professions. Having an attorney in the mix certainly couldn't hurt.

No, I told myself. Everybody who came in contact with that group was not necessarily linked to it. I forced the idea aside.

Shortly before eleven, I let myself into my apartment, half expecting Jeannie to be nestled in Annette's pink princess bed where I'd left her two hours ago. Instead she was unpacking shopping bags strewn across the sofa and loveseat, her suitcase open at her feet. I smelled toast and coffee.

"I meant to shop for your birthday," she said, "But I ended up shopping for myself. Happens."

She removed a cashmere sweater from a bag, folded it neatly, and added it to a stack of other new merchandise in her now very-full bag on wheels. "Saved you some brunch though."

I looked over her new clothes. "You got an early start."

"The boutiques were calling me."

I dropped my generic purse on the coffee table next to her Louis Vuitton tote. Unbuttoning my sleeveless blouse, I headed for the hall. "I need a run to clear my head."

"Silly girl," she said. "Coffee clears your head, not exercise."

When I didn't answer, she followed me into my bedroom. "If you're going to run, you might as well do it at that fancy club, right? Get the 4-1-1 on Diana King?"

I pulled on a dirty pair of shorts and an ancient tank top. "I'm not in the mood for your jokes."

Claire's and Diana's hoity-toity, women's only gym had denied my membership request on the spot. When I'd tried to join, the front desk attendant, Starr, took a little too much pleasure in explaining that membership was by invitation only. Her sideways glances at my clothes and hair translated the euphemism for me: I wasn't rich or pretty enough.

Jeannie disappeared for a moment and returned with a luxurious envelope. She extracted the card inside and presented it with a flourish. Pressed flowers adorned the paper, through which a sheer ribbon had been woven. It looked like a wedding invitation.

I read its message, incredulous. "They let *you* in?"

"Of course. And now you'll be my guest. Happy?" Her self-indulgent smile said she certainly was.

"No," I said. "I'm pissed."

"We have appointments at one."

She vanished into the hallway.

I knelt on the floor and reached under my bed for a stray running shoe. Behind it I found an abandoned bowl of goldfish crackers and a cow flashlight that mooed when I grabbed it. "What kind of appointments?"

She hollered from the kitchen. "Nails!" A cupboard slammed.

My irritation edged up a notch. I laced up my shoes and reminded myself she was only trying to be nice. Then I got an idea and, still on my knees, reached for the phone.

Richard sounded relieved to hear from me. "I thought you might call."

"I'll help with your case."

"Good! That's—"

"On my terms."

He hesitated. "But you're not—"

"Yeah, I know I'm not. But that's my condition. Unless you plan to suddenly go transgender, I'm your only ticket inside that gym. You need me."

Jeannie reappeared with a cup of coffee and set it on the floor next to me. She watched, impassive, and waited to openly eavesdrop on whatever was being said.

"I thought you said they wouldn't let you in," Richard said.

"I'm in now. Yes or no?"

Jeannie smirked.

"How'd you get in?"

I didn't answer.

"What 'terms' do you mean?"

"I don't want to follow Diana anymore. It's boring."

"I'll find somebody else."

"And I want to attend any meetings with Mick Young."

He was silent.

"Richard?"

"That's a bad idea."

"You need somebody on the inside of that club."

He muttered something. I thought he called me stubborn.

"I'm sorry, was that a yes?" I said.

"Good luck at the club." He clicked off the line.

I passed the phone to Jeannie, who returned it to my night stand, and then I leaned back against my box springs and mattress.

"What's up?" she said.

"I went to the jail."

"Cool."

"Not really. Claire Gaston's kind of...I can't figure her out. She's represented by Brighton and Young."

Jeannie's lip curled in obvious disgust.

"Richard didn't tell me," I added. "I found out during the interview. Found out a lot of things he left out."

She sat on the floor across from me. "Men and details," she said. "Like men and condoms. They only use them if they have to."

Too distracted to smile, I only shook my head.

"I'd have a real problem working for those guys," she added.

"I guess Mick Young will defend anyone. Still..."

I pushed away the thought and raised the coffee to my lips, blowing on it and watching tiny ripples.

Jeannie used her long fingernails on one hand to push back cuticles on the other. "Keep going."

"Hard to say. Something about her is definitely off but I think she might be innocent."

"Sweetie, you're a wonderful friend and you're freaky smart. But you're also the most gullible person I've ever met."

I let my head fall back and watched dusty ceiling fan blades go around in slow motion. "Yep."

She stood and patted me on the head on her way out. "This is why you're not having sex."

"Because I'm gullible?"

She didn't answer.

I lumbered to my feet, bringing my coffee along, and found Jeannie in the living room, digging through her purse. She produced a lighter and a pack of Salem Lights and went outside. I followed, appalled that anyone would endure triple digit heat and 88% humidity for a smoke.

When I closed the door behind me, it shut louder than I'd intended. "Tell me more, Dr. Ruth."

Jeannie settled into the wooden rocker my neighbor Florence kept on the landing between our two apartments. She took a long drag. When she exhaled, she twisted her lips so the smoke would go off to the side. "Does it bother you more that you're working for the scum who defended that ring, or that you're falling for a man who was embroiled in the whole mess?"

"This has nothing to do with Vince."

"Of course it does. I'm not saying it's the bulk of what's bothering you. Just pointing out that your professional life and personal life are mixed now."

"I just told you that. Because this new case is Mick Young's."

She examined the cigarette between her ivory fingers, then suddenly her gaze jumped to me. "How long after you met Jack did you go to bed with him?"

I looked at her, aghast. Vince and I had been on the cusp of something since March, and Jeannie was beside herself with worry because four months had passed and we hadn't slept together. I didn't see what it had to do with my late husband or how it related to Claire Gaston's case. She mistakenly interpreted my silence as agreement.

"You see my point then. If it weren't for Vince's family tree, you guys would be a done deal by now."

"That has nothing to do with work. And you oversimplify. I'm in a new city...I've made a career switch. There's Annette now. Vince knows I'm working through a lot."

I left out the worst, that the fourth anniversary of Annette's kidnapping and Jack's murder had passed only days ago. This was the first year I hadn't visited his grave, back home in Cleveland, on July seventh.

"He respects your situation, yes. But trust me. Even a saint runs out of patience at some point. It's time."

"Easy advice coming from a woman who's slept with more men than I've ever talked to."

She leaned so far back in Florence's rocker that its runners pointed up. A broad smile played over her shimmering lips and I wondered which of her past lovers she'd flashed back to. "That wasn't meant as a compliment."

She ignored me. "Thinking about Mick Young has already ripped open the March wounds again, fresh and bloody. Poor Vince is going to pay for it. If you were too confused to sleep with him before, there's no way he's getting action now."

"He had nothing to do with all that. Those are two separate things."

"Says your rational mind. It's your subconscious that worries me."

"You're a fruitcake." I opened the door to my apartment. Jeannie explaining psychology was like a child dabbling in taxes.

Chapter Three

That morning I spent an inordinate amount of time on our drive to Tone Zone mentally rehearsing what I'd say if Starr refused to let me in again. Thankfully, the desk attendant was a new girl who waved me in when Jeannie flashed her temporary membership pass and introduced me as a guest.

I hastily filled out a name-address-phone number card and Jeannie tucked her fancy membership pass into her bag.

"I don't see why they make you bother with that card." Jeannie crossed the lobby and headed for a wide corridor across the room. "It's not like they want to recruit you."

Before I could answer, she stopped and looked around, confused. "I have no idea where anything is."

Tone Zone's floor plan was sectioned into specialized fitness studios that opened off a series of serpentine halls. We found a sign directing us to Yoga and Pilates, Indoor Cycling, Cardio and Strength Training, Aerobics and Kickboxing, or Dance. Below it, a wall-mounted map showed our current location relative to larger facilities like racquetball courts and the indoor pool.

Jeannie tapped a glittery, salmon-colored segment of the map, representing the spa. "I'm there."

I read the list of available services out loud. "Tanning, massage, waxing, facials, body treatments, manicures, pedicures, permanent make-up, lash extensions, and hair." Underneath each item, more specific services were listed in smaller, curlicue letters.

"This is wrong on so many levels," I said. "The spa takes up more than half the square footage of the building."

"So?"

"People need exercise, Jeannie. Not lash extensions."

"These people need lash extensions."

"I hate that glittery map and those stupid curly letters."

She grabbed my shoulders and spun me to the left. "Treadmills are that way. Go melt your inner grump. When my friend Emily comes back, tell her she can find me relaxing in the spa, admiring long lashes."

Wordlessly, I trudged down the hallway in the direction she'd indicated.

Behind me, she said, "Remember to meet at the nail salon a little before one."

I checked my watch—11:45—and waved acknowledgement without looking back.

The corridor I thought would lead to the Cardio and Strength Training Room dead-ended at a smoothie bar, where a woman waited for someone to blend her drink. A form-fitted singlet clung to her narrow waist; little shorts with stripes on the sides showed off her solid butt and thighs.

"Excuse me…"

She turned, dabbing a thick, white towel at her temples. Sweat had broken through her foundation make-up and the towel was spotted with little streaks of beige. One of her penciled-in eyebrows had wiped away. I tried not to stare but that was impossible.

"Can you tell me where to find the cardio equipment?" It also bothered me that the tint on her face didn't match the natural skin tone on her neck.

Dark eyes, slightly pulled up in the corners, made a quick pass over my clothes and hesitated at my shoes, still caked with mud from my last run.

Behind her, the blender stopped. She turned her attention to the girl behind the counter without answering me. Then, with no payment or "thank you," she picked up her drink and stepped away. The club probably ran a tab for its members, I figured, but I couldn't come up with an excuse for not saying thanks.

She nodded toward the hallway behind me, as if offering to show me the way, and I followed, hoping I hadn't misinterpreted.

After what felt like minutes, but was probably ten seconds, I buckled under the oppressive silence. "This is my first visit."

She strode forward, about a step ahead of me, and carried her lime green smoothie without taking a sip. We came upon a set of double doors inset with glass, through which I was relieved to see treadmills and elliptical trainers lined up on one side, free weights and nautilus machines on the other. With her available hand, she opened the door.

"We're a first-rate club," she said, as I passed into a room that smelled like hand sanitizer. "Please observe the other ladies' attire and adjust your future clothing choices accordingly."

I could only nod, not having been reprimanded for dress code since grade school. I wanted to say, "Please observe the other ladies' eyebrows and note that everyone has two," but I refrained. Smoothie Nag retreated into the hall and I went toward the free weights because they were in the corner of the room furthest away from everyone. Dumbbells were arranged in racks along a mirrored wall. I used the mirror to survey the clientele behind me while I pretended to plan a workout. I didn't care about being chewed out by a snob, but she'd made me curious.

I counted four coordinated athletic sets, two tennis dresses, and a bicyclist's jersey with black spandex shorts. The women around me commiserated about whatever rich people talk about. Jealous and snubbed, I dismissed them all as lightweights who only came to gossip, not sweat. In a moment of self-righteousness, I loaded up a bench press bar and got started in the squat rack using an inclined bench. The first set felt easy but the second took some work. I was digging deep, feeling hot, by the third.

"Whoa there, Chief." Jeannie stared down at me from what would have been a spotter's position.

I racked the bar, breathing hard. "Where'd you come from?"

She moved around the rack so I could see her better. She bore the distrustful expression of a parent who has caught a child raising a crayon to the wall. "What's going on?"

"You interrupted my set. That's what."

She leaned closer and lowered her voice. "Parsley."

"What?"

"When you're having a meal and there's a little sprig of parsley on your plate?" She gestured demurely as if presenting a dinner entrée. "Nobody really expects you to eat it. It's a garnish."

I squinted at her.

"Free weights are a garnish in a club like this." Her voice was still low, conspiratorial. "You're sticking out like a sore thumb."

I glanced around and two heads snapped to look away. When my gaze came back to Jeannie, she actually looked sympathetic. "At least while you're here…be a girl. Use the nautilus machines."

I came back to a seated position on the bench. "I don't see why they would have—"

She raised a hand and cut me off. "Be a girl."

"What's the point of—" I scanned the women around me, not really caring if they noticed. "The only push ups around here are in their bras."

A nearby wall-mounted rack offered paper towels and disinfectant spray. I used them to wipe my bench while Jeannie checked herself in the mirror.

"Anyway, you looked manly. I mean, besides the free weights. You had the red face and intense breathing thing going on. Do you always do that or were you channeling some kind of inner rage?"

"Aren't you supposed to be trying on lip gloss or something?"

"Here." She held out a brochure. "You should decide what kind of manicure you want before you show up for the appointment."

I glanced at it. "French, paraffin, luxury, hot stone, spa… Like I care."

She regarded me a moment. "That *was* an inner rage I walked in on. What aren't you telling me?"

"Nothing you don't already know. I was thinking about Mick Young, wondering if he's a normal attorney or if he's dirty like his old clients. Claire's case might be my ticket to finding out."

"If there's *any* chance he's involved with those people, you should stay as far away from this case—and that gang of low-lifes—as you can. You know better."

"They stole my family."

I felt my heart rate jump. Jeannie pulled her eyes off mine and nodded to a passing gym patron. Remembering where we were, I did the same. I was already the unwelcome visitor with ghetto clothes and a manly workout. No sense adding "rude" to the list.

"We'll talk later," I said. "I'm going to run."

She left as unobtrusively as she'd arrived. I found a treadmill and skipped the warm-up, opting to get straight to business. I locked in a brisk pace and added a slight uphill grade. When my breathing caught up, my mind wandered back to the issues that had brought me in the first place.

Imaginary conversations with Richard played out in my head. In one, he accused me of being immature, so I quit my job a second time and went on to single-handedly prove Claire's innocence or guilt. The guilty ending was especially satisfying because I got to lord over Richard that he should have known better than to work for Mick Young.

"You look hard core," said a voice beside me.

Startled, I grabbed the handrail. The display said I'd been running for thirty-six minutes, which was news to me.

"Sorry." It was a twenty-something brunette. She carried a squirt bottle of disinfectant and a large stack of paper towels like the ones I'd seen in the rack by the weights. "You were away with your thoughts." She stepped onto the belt of an unoccupied treadmill three machines to my right and sprayed its keypad and handrails.

"I was daydreaming about telling off my boss."

She laughed, wiped the equipment down. "You're new. What's your story?"

I huffed through a few more strides, then dropped my speed to six miles an hour. "You're normal. What's yours?"

"I guess that's a compliment." She moved one machine closer and repeated the disinfecting routine. "A friend got me this job. I couldn't afford to come here otherwise."

"Let me ask you something." I dropped to five-and-a-half. "Am I the only one here who's willing to exercise without make-up and cutesy clothes?"

She moved to the machine adjacent to mine and squirted and wiped its panel. "Yes." When it was clean, she squirted it again, something she hadn't done previously. "Guess this isn't your natural habitat. I'm Kendra, by the way."

She stepped down and circled behind me, resuming her duties on the machine to my left.

I introduced myself. "My natural habitat is a two-bedroom apartment and a thirteen-year-old car, not leather sofas and smoothie bars. This place was my friend's idea. I'm a *guest*."

Kendra didn't miss my sarcasm. She checked the mirror in front of us to be sure no one was near. "Most of these ladies are nice once you find something in common with them." She gestured to her own outfit, a sporty turquoise top with matching yoga pants. "I can't compare plastic surgeons or nanny services with them. Instead I try to look the part."

I dropped to four miles-per-hour and switched from a jog to a fast walk. "Sorry," I said. "I didn't mean to include you in my rant."

"No, what I meant was…after I made an effort to fit in, most of them warmed up to me. Try it next time."

"I hope there'll *be* a next time." I dropped my speed to a slow walk, catching my breath and thinking ahead to the manicures Captain Vanity had arranged. "My friend made salon appointments for us, but I left my house in a snit and forgot my shower bag and clothes. Should I cancel?"

Kendra waved away the question. "Toiletries are provided by the club and I'll loan you my extra clothes. Follow me."

I protested, but Kendra insisted. It felt good to have an insider championing for me. She loaned me linen Capris by Liz Claiborne and a paisley, cap-sleeve shirt by Calvin Klein. After changing, I joined Jeannie in the nail salon, where she waited in an overstuffed chair, flipping through the new issue of *Elle*.

When she spotted me, she cast the magazine to a side table and click-clacked on her too-high Gucci heels to meet me before I entered into the salon.

"That's an improvement," she said. "Where'd you get the clothes?"

She was suspiciously giddy and I wondered if she'd been around the acetone fumes too long. "Why are you so chipper?"

"Wendell Platt's funeral is this afternoon," she said. "Isn't that *perfect*?"

Only Jeannie.

Chapter Four

Maybe it was the tough work-out or all the junk in my mind. It could have been the volatile organics in the salon's air supply. When I settled into the high-backed leather recliner, my hands propped on individual velvet pillows, I relaxed and drifted off a little, alternately planning outings for Annette and thinking about Vince's gorgeous smile. At one point Jeannie's idea to sleuth at Platt's funeral drifted by, but my manicurist's warm hands smothered my own with intoxicating peppermint exfoliant and the thought evaporated.

I let myself enter a quasi-dream state, mistakenly convinced I could ward off a full-blown nap. But an indeterminate amount of time later, I woke to find my manicurist applying an acrylic tip to my right ring finger. Two more, and both hands would look femininely fake and elegant, like Jeannie's.

From the chair beside mine, Jeannie watched me take in the unexpected acrylics. "My treat."

"Thanks, sort of." It was a stretch for me to agree to just have them painted. To the manicurist, I added. "No offense, they're lovely. Just not *me*."

She smiled. "First time?"

I hesitated. "Second."

I told her about the grandmotherly Asian woman who'd painted my nails on my wedding day. She'd sung along to Billy Joel's *My Life*, which was playing on the salon's radio, while working on me. The twist was that she'd used the lyric "my lice" by mistake, a flub that still made me smile whenever I heard that song.

When my hand was finished, Jeannie smiled her approval and paid. We walked to my car.

"Do I have a glow?" she wondered out loud. "I spent twenty minutes in a tanning bed."

"You always have a glow. It's annoying."

"The tanning salon matron—she really was a matron—was a patient of Platt's. Said the funeral's at 4:30 at Something Gardens. Serenity Gardens? Eternity Gardens? Whatever. We'll look it up on-line."

"It's a funeral, not a rock concert."

"Everything's on-line."

"How'd you find out she was a patient of Platt's?"

"Lots of those women were his patients."

I tried to pick my keys out of my purse but my fingers didn't feel like my own anymore and the fake nails kept getting in the way. "Lots of them?"

"That's what the tanning lady says."

We arrived at my car and went to our respective doors, the afternoon sun beating down on us. I finally retrieved my keys but accidentally dropped them.

"Damn it, Jeannie. I can't do anything with these nails. Take them off." I held out my hands, impatient.

"No can do. Get used to those babies." She walked around to my side of the car and palmed the keys off the gritty concrete in one smooth motion. Her fakes were even longer than mine, but she was well-practiced. "I'll drive, Whiner."

We returned to my apartment so I could clean up and get into my own clothes. Jeannie hollered through the bathroom door that Platt's service would be at Tranquility Gardens and that I should never doubt the power of the Internet.

Annette's Batgirl towel, still wadded on the rack, stopped me for a moment as her belongings sometimes did. She was away with Nick and Betsy Fletcher this week, spending time with the couple she'd grown up knowing as parents. We'd finally been reunited in March, when the crime ring responsible for her abduction was busted, and after only a few months, my home already felt incomplete without her. A familiar, lonely ache resurfaced.

Missing her, I dried my face with her little towel instead of mine.

Floral wreaths were positioned throughout the Remembrance Hall at Tranquility Gardens Funeral Home and Cemetery, but all I could smell was carpet shampoo. Pews, stained glass, and a vaulted ceiling suggested the hall was designed to resemble a chapel, although it was devoid of any religious decorations.

Jeannie and I paused with a small group to reflect on a photo collage featuring Platt throughout his fifty-six years. In the largest image, centered among the others, Platt relaxed on a park bench, one arm casually draped on the back rest. He wore a Hawaiian print shirt and seemed jovial and carefree. His photographer had caught him laughing.

Piano notes floated softly in the still-filling hall and a woman ahead of Jeannie turned and handed her an ornamental pen. The guest book waited ahead on a podium, past the photographs. Before I could stop her, Jeannie stepped up to the book and signed our condolences. I regretted she'd left a record of our attendance but wasn't about to scratch anything out of a family's funeral book.

We slid into the last pew, trying to blend into the background. I studied passing faces, most tired or distracted, and felt guilty for coming to the service of a man I'd never met.

As the room filled, Jeannie and I recognized several people from Claire's gym. She tapped me on the knee when the tanning matron arrived. I pointed out Kendra, who'd loaned me the clean clothes. Then we huddled together and whispered ferociously when Diana King showed up on the arm of a man we presumed to be her husband. Diana's ash blond hair was swept into a classy French twist, stabbed through with a rhinestone chopstick. She walked within a yard of me and I caught the scent of her lush perfume.

"Danielle Steele," Jeannie whispered. "Hundred bucks for a bottle this big." She indicated something the size of a salad mushroom.

Diana's companion ushered her into a pew near the front and soon the officiant began.

Turned out, the speaker had never met the late doctor, so any personal accounts I'd hoped to glean were absent from his eulogy. We did learn some generic information, though, like that Platt had survived his wife of twenty-one years and that the couple had never had kids. After her death, he'd become an avid hiker and bird watcher who preferred to pass his spare time in quiet solitude.

Friends and family were invited to the speaker's podium to share memories, but only two stepped forward—an uncle and a co-worker—with long, awkward pauses preceding each.

"I'll be *pissed* if no one gets up to talk about me," Jeannie whispered.

"You'll be dead," I whispered back.

"Especially you," she said. "*You* better say something really good."

When the service ended, our back row seats helped us make a quick exit, and Jeannie headed outside for a cigarette. I stopped at the ladies' room, where a tall, austere brunette I hadn't noticed earlier touched up her lipstick at the mirror. It was Smoothie Nag from the club.

Her dark eyes, corners taut as ever, met mine in the mirror and she rubbed her wine-colored lips together. When she glanced down to cap the lipstick, I ducked into a stall and locked the door. She washed her hands, pulled down a paper towel. I heard it crumple and listened for the door, but it never opened.

When I came out of the stall, she was waiting. "You're the one from this morning. How'd you know Wendell?"

Hiking or bird watching would have been safe answers, but I decided to go with something more likely to resonate.

"I was considering surgery."

She cocked her head and evaluated me. "Your nose?"

Smoothie Nag, I hate you.

I forced myself to nod. "We'd consulted a few times. I felt comfortable with him."

She studied me so long my palms moistened.

"Chris is quite good too," she finally said. "Try him."

"Chris?"

"Wendell's partner, Chris King. Remarkable man." She pulled open the door and passed through it with the same indifference I remembered from the gym.

I was left alone with the faint scent of her expensive perfume and a sinking feeling that the name King was no coincidence.

Chapter Five

After the graveside service, we puttered along the winding cemetery road at five miles per hour, looking for the exit. A familiar car approached, its driver's side window down.

Jeannie leaned forward. "Is that—"

"Richard." I rolled down my own window and leaned on the sill. We stopped alongside him.

"Whatcha doin' here, Big Guy?" Jeannie asked.

Richard leveled a look at me, then pulled his eyes away and answered. "Shadowing Diana." He paused. "This is how you spend your day off, Emily? At a funeral?"

"Funeral's nothing," Jeannie said. "Earlier she went to the jail. Then that fancy gym." She nudged my shoulder. "Show him your nails."

I pulled my arm back inside the car. "Diana's husband and Wendell Platt had a surgery practice together. Did you know that?"

He shook his head.

"What happens to a business when a partner dies?" I asked.

Richard tapped his steering wheel. "I guess Platt's share goes to his heirs."

"Ooh!" Jeannie piped up, as if answering a trivia question. "No wife, no kids!"

By way of clarification, I told Richard what we'd learned during the eulogy.

"He must have left his share to somebody," Richard said. "The question is to who."

Jeannie pointed at him. "To *whom.*"

Richard ignored her and squinted at something ahead of him, behind us, in the distance. "She's leaving." He took his foot off the brake and idled forward. I watched in my rear view mirror as he slowly caught up to Diana's departing Mercedes. My cell phone rang.

"I've heard of buy-sell life insurance policies," Richard said. "Something about buying life insurance on your partner."

"I'll look into it."

"Into what?" Jeannie asked.

"Ever heard of a buy-sell life insurance policy?"

She shook her head. "We'll Google it."

"You won't believe this," I said, climbing into the passenger side of Vince's old pick-up. "She's gone."

It was an old-style truck, the kind without an extended cab. Jeannie made Vince drive whenever she could, reminding him each time how much she liked cowboys and their trucks.

I shoved my hip into hers and forced her to scoot over, not wanting to spend another minute outside. The heat was so oppressive my clothes were already sticking to me after the short walk across the lot.

"Gone, like out on bail?" Vince asked, reversing out of our spot. He and Jeannie had agreed to stop at the jail on our way out for Mexican.

"No. Transferred to County."

Jeannie whistled. "She's hating life tonight."

"So am I." My boss was hiding things. Our client was hiding things. "I asked Claire for a reason Diana would want Platt dead and she didn't suggest one."

"You're assuming Diana's responsible then?" Vince said.

"I'm not assuming anything." I leaned forward to look at Vince around Jeannie. "But don't you agree it's weird she didn't tell me Platt was linked to Diana's husband?"

"She's a liar," Jeannie said. "Liars leave stuff out all the time."

Maybe Jeannie was right. Still, Claire intrigued me and I spent the remainder of our short drive trying to figure out why.

"Is it her money?" Vince asked. "Her looks?"

Certainly, her wealth and beauty fascinated me, but those weren't the lures that continued to draw me in.

"It's the type of parent she is, I think. To me, it seems incongruous that a woman who cheats could be a good mother. Yet, somehow I believe she is."

"A murderer can be a good mother," Jeannie said. "Take self-defense, for example."

I didn't have the energy to point out that murder and self-defense were different things.

Vince flipped his turn signal and pulled into the parking lot of Pepe's.

"If there are acceptable reasons for murder, you should ask yourself if there are acceptable reasons to cheat."

"Cheating's never okay," I said, a little too quickly.

Vince took a spot near the multi-colored stucco building, stopped the engine, and shrugged. I wondered if the shrug meant he had no opinion or that he thought cheating was allowed in some circumstances.

I didn't ask.

During the meal, Jeannie sat across from us in a booth and the three of us ate enough fajitas and enchiladas to serve a party of six. In the company of my two most favorite people—well, grown-up people—I tried to relax and enjoy the moment, but couldn't completely do it. Annette was away. My relationship with Richard was strained again. Vince was wonderful, but he communicated in undertones I couldn't figure out. And Jeannie had come all the way from Cleveland to celebrate my impending birthday and I thanked her by hauling her around to do job stuff.

"The waitress is too slow," she said. "I'm going to the bar for another margarita. Want anything?"

Vince's beer was nearly full and I'd hardly put a dent in my own margarita. I shook my head and she slid from the booth, giving us a too-close view of her cleavage as she stood. Maybe just too close for me.

I drummed my nails on the table, playing with new clicking noises I was never able to make before. Vince took my hand.

"These are new."

I extended my fingers and evaluated them. "Like wearing a thimble on every one. Dialing's impossible and buttons are the devil."

He laughed. "What were you thinking?"

"*Me?*" I nodded toward the bar. "I fell asleep in the salon's shiatsu chair and Miss Diva had this done before I woke up."

He raised my hand to his lips and kissed it, smiling to himself. Then he chuckled.

"What?"

"There's more coming."

"More what?"

"Spa treatment…things."

"No there aren't."

"Yes there are. She told me."

"Told you when?"

"At the jail, when we were waiting for you."

I drummed the fakes again. They were really good for that.

"I won't go."

Vince took a swig of beer. "I'm staying out of it."

Then he set his glass down and pulled me into the tight space around him that smelled like nautical cologne and sawdust, which I loved. "Got a question for you. How about, before kindergarten starts, we take Annette on a trip? Nothing huge. Maybe the Alamo. Or Sea World."

I glanced at the bar, wishing I were wired so Jeannie could tell me through an earpiece what to say. But she was talking to a man of her own, too busy flirting to throw me a lifeline.

Connecting with Vince was still hard and I often associated it with the awkwardness of teen dating. Much as I liked him, I couldn't figure us out. "I…Here's the thing—"

He raised his free hand in a don't-get-me-wrong gesture. "I meant, only if you're comfortable. Maybe I shouldn't have—"

"It's fine." I nestled in closer and took his hand. His eyes were such a deep green that they almost looked brown under the dim lights. And they bored into mine so intently it was clear we were having two conversations. More undertones. "I'm glad you brought it up."

He waited for me to go on, stroking the top of my hand so gently with his thumb that I barely felt his touch—yet only felt his touch—both at the same time.

"I'm terrified of failing her," I said. "We hardly know each other. I want her love and don't know how to get it."

"That'll come," he said. "It gets better all the time. You said so yourself."

"But in her mind, I'm still the one who separated her from her parents. It's incredible she doesn't resent me. I couldn't live with myself if she started to believe anyone else comes before her."

He nodded. "I think you're too hard on yourself. But I understand where you're coming from."

"For the record," I said, "If things were more stable, I'd go on that trip. I'd go on lots of trips with you."

He gave me a delicate and lingering kiss. "Then when they are, we will."

Chapter Six

"I said I never met him, not that I never heard of him." In the city jail, Claire had worn her street clothes but, at County, they'd been traded for a standard-issue orange jumpsuit with a loose cut that hid every curve on her slender frame.

"Did you know that Platt and King co-owned the Westside Cosmetic Surgery Center?" Afraid of the microbes I knew were there, I kept the visiting room's scummy telephone handset a couple centimeters from my ear.

Claire's eyes, flat and tired, had sunk into a complexion that lacked yesterday's vibrancy. The pane separating us was so gritty I thought maybe its opaque glass was partly to blame for her weathered appearance.

"Of course I knew," she said. "I've been a patient there for years."

"Why'd you withhold that yesterday?"

"I didn't withhold anything."

"Now two things trouble me."

With her free hand, she massaged her temple in a gesture that hinted at impatience.

"You suggested you had no connection to Platt. And you didn't disclose that the woman you *say* set you up is *married* to his business partner."

"I don't have a connection to Platt."

"But you knew—"

She raised her free hand to cut me off. "And I assumed the partnership was common knowledge. My attorney has all that background."

When I didn't answer, she narrowed her eyes. "Who are you to judge me?"

"I haven't judged you."

"You were in the papers. The out-of-towner who helped the FBI bust up that crime ring last March. You killed a guy."

"Those people had my daughter."

"You let them take her away from you."

"I...*let* them?" I fought to control my anger. She was either misguided or cruel. Racketeers had kidnapped my baby when they killed my husband—I thought I'd lost them both—and then they sold her to an unwitting couple desperate to have a child. Even helping to bust them hadn't made things right. Annette still thought the Fletchers were her parents, and Jack's death would forever leave a void. But I couldn't let my thoughts go there now. I needed to focus on why I'd come.

I stared at her through the glass. "Did you kill Platt?"

She smacked the pane. "No. A thousand times, no."

I regarded her for a moment. The strange Jekyll-Hyde feeling was back and I couldn't figure out what it was about this woman that made me alternately think she was innocent, then nuts. "If you knew that about me, why'd you ask yesterday whether I had kids?"

She shook her head. "I didn't know yesterday. My mom looked into you. She visited me last night before my transfer. Told me about the news articles she found."

"The people responsible for kidnapping my daughter also killed my husband," I said. "They tore apart dozens of families and took uncounted lives. Your attorney defended them. So I ask myself, if he took *their* cases..."

She finished. "Would he take anyone's? Probably. But I'm not guilty."

I checked my watch. Visits at County were limited to thirty minutes and we had four left.

"Got somewhere to be?" she asked.

"Your gym, actually."

She raised her eyebrows, amused. "The shark tank."

"We're still watching Diana." I paused. "When's the last time you were there, by the way?"

"Thursday. Why?"

I shook my head. "Just curious." Then, in an inexplicable moment of courage, I added, "Mind if I take a look around your house?"

She shrugged. "Look all you want. Hide-a-key's near my bathroom window. Alarm code's 0606-star, my youngest's birthday."

I didn't know what I expected to find at her house, but Claire's cooperation swayed me back slightly toward the Dr. Jekyll end of her personality spectrum. "Thanks."

"As for the club," she said, surveying my faded, off-brand tank top. "Help yourself to my closet. Might give you a head start toward fitting in."

Something told me Claire paid more for a top than I paid for a week's rent.

"I wouldn't feel right sweating in your designer clothes."

"Standing offer," she said. "Think it over."

◇◇◇

While I was at County, Jeannie power shopped at Houston's Galleria, browsing expensive stores and probably buying more stuff than she could afford. She sounded a little disappointed when I called to say I was finished at the jail, but when I told her my plans to visit Claire's house, she perked right up.

"Bring me," she said. "That place will be *nice*. And what's this business about borrowing her clothes?"

"Calm down," I said. "Cocktail dresses and four-hundred dollar shoes weren't part of her offer."

"I've barely put a dent in the second floor of this fabulous mall," she said. "What time are we going to Claire's? We have appointments at noon."

I remembered Vince and his half-laughing warning. "Pedicures?"

"Negative," she said. "Highlights for me. Wax for you. And, listen, before you—"

"No."

"—refuse to go, the waxer is—"

"*No.*"

"—Diana's daughter."

I hung up.

She called me right back. "I met her during a smoke break at the funeral yesterday. Start thinking about what you'll say."

I didn't want to think about hot wax anywhere on my body, much less what I would say to the daughter of a potential murderer as she applied it to me.

"Back to our plan," I said. "Richard got some police cronies to take over Diana's surveillance…sort of a second job thing, I guess. That freed him up, but I'm still too edgy to include him at Claire's. How about we meet at her house and stay until it's time for your appointment—"

"*Our* appointment*sss.*"

"—Then we'll head to Tone Zone and see what we can learn. Diana usually goes around lunchtime. We may cross paths."

It took some prodding before Jeannie would agree to skip the rest of the Galleria, but the prospect of seeing the inside of a decadent River Oaks home was too much. Finally she broke down and asked for directions. We agreed to meet at Claire's.

I arrived in the neighborhood first. My slow drive through one of the oldest, most affluent communities in Houston was strangely quiet. Except for the occasional dog walker, everyone seemed to be cocooned in stately mansions that ran the gamut from old Tudor to Victorian to contemporary, and service vehicles on every street underscored the upkeep required to maintain appearances. Trucks and trailers for various landscape architects and vans belonging to general contractors, sprinkler services, and painters reminded me how much additional cost, beyond the inconceivable mortgages, an upper crust lifestyle demanded.

Enormous oaks, easily over a hundred years old, towered overhead forming an arboreal tunnel for passing motorists like me. In their shade, some homeowners had suspended children's swings in front yards, their ropes often tied off from perches as high as twenty or thirty feet. The maturity and abundance of these trees, many with trunks covered in lush ivy, certainly made an impression, but to a grassroots Midwesterner like me, the shock value was in homes large enough to be hotels. Evidently, Monday was trash day because residents had deposited recycle bins on their curbs, a detail that somehow humanized them for me.

In Hollywood, I'd once paid forty dollars for a tour of the stars' homes and been disappointed to find so many of them obscured from public view by high and thick shrubbery. By contrast, Houston's elite proudly shared sweeping views of their estates, opting instead to simply keep their front drapes drawn and, where applicable, their gates closed.

I passed three properties in a row, all some variant of the White House, before finding Claire's cul de sac which, like everything else in the neighborhood, was super-sized, more like a traffic circle on steroids. Wide, tall, and deep, Claire's house was clearly spacious, but I was relieved it wasn't as sprawling and over-the-top as those on nearby White House Row. I eased my car around a laundry service van and pulled into her extended drive, which curved to the right and ended in front of a three-car detached garage with an upstairs apartment I thought might be some kind of guest quarters. The garage was connected to her house by a covered breezeway, beyond which a wooden play-set, so large I thought it might be a commercial model, was nestled in the shade of four sprawling oaks near a lacrosse goal. Further back, an empty dog kennel reminded me of her love of animals.

The hide-a-key was where she'd described and I rehearsed the alarm code in my mind twice before pushing open the back door and keying in the numbers. I stepped into her kitchen, past a heap of muddy sneakers that clearly belonged to boys, and was momentarily awestruck. My entire apartment would have fit in her kitchen and dining hall. I shut the door and got to work.

At yesterday's meeting, Claire had said she'd left her anonymous note on a counter. But, she'd also mentioned a cleaning lady and I knew the police had been through there too. If there ever was a note, it was gone now. The only item that caught my eye was a stainless steel plaque left discreetly in a corner nook that said, "Pets leave paw prints on our hearts." Draped over its corner was a worn leather collar with a tag that said, "I rescued a human."

I crossed to her two-sided stainless refrigerator and studied the photographs and notes stuck there. A series of wallet-sized school pictures showed two boys evolving over what I assumed to be the last three years. Both had darker coloring than Claire, caramel skin and brown eyes, not green, but the bone structure and expressions were all hers.

A pocket calendar, held in place by a magnet from a local private school, was open to July and its date boxes were crossed off through last Friday—when Claire had been served with her search and arrest warrants and taken away. The little squares were too small to write down anything descriptive, but Claire apparently used initials and abbreviations to remind herself about upcoming plans. July had various entries for *P, J* and *KT* with times beside them. I flipped back to June and saw more entries for *J,* a few for *P,* and a smattering for *K.* May had two *Js,* no *KTs,* and three *Ms.* May was also thick with *Ks.*

I gave up on the alphabet soup but suspected it might be useful so I took the calendar and dropped it into my bag. Around the corner, her neutral beige living room displayed artsy, wall-mounted shadow boxes that contained some kind of dried flowers. Drapes made from the same burgundy and gold chenille that covered the throw pillows were open, unlike her neighbors', letting morning sun fill the first floor. I ran a finger over a soft, fancy sofa pillow and marveled over the effort that Claire—or more likely, her decorator—had put into the room.

A set of French doors, open on the other side of the foyer, led to a home office and I walked inside. Her computer was conspicuously absent from its spot on the desk, but the keyboard and mouse had been left behind. The desk faced the door, and I walked behind it and took a seat, staring across the foyer into the bright, super-coordinated living room, imagining for a moment that the house were mine. My attraction, I realized, was directed toward the home's tidiness, not its pricey artifacts.

I started pulling open drawers. Bills and receipts, some dating back ten years, were tucked in hanging folders. She seemed a compulsive keeper of owner's manuals—vacuum cleaner, dish washer, electric toothbrush, DVD player, cellular phone. Three models of cell phones, actually. From her files, I learned Claire's kitchen cabinets and countertops were replaced in May and that Daniel's Z4 was due for an oil change, though I doubted she cared. There were investment portfolios and 529 plans, copies of her parents' living wills and power-of-attorney forms, and tax returns dating back through her last two marriages. I spent twenty minutes browsing paperwork but found nothing to tie Claire to Platt, or to anyone other than her family.

Her bookshelf had a collection of romance paperbacks, the sort of books Jeannie liked to read, as well as a collection of fitness magazines, photo albums, and a dog-eared copy of *How to Move On—After He Moves Out*, which struck me as odd since Claire had initiated her divorce.

My cell phone rang. It was Jeannie.

"Just turned onto her street," she said. "Brought you a latte."

"Right after the laundry service van." I started up the custom curved staircase. "The back door's unlocked. I'm going upstairs."

Over my shoulder, I watched through an ornamental foyer window as Jeannie's rental car rolled up the drive. She headed toward the back of the house, where I'd parked my old Taurus. I continued up the steps, headed for the master bedroom. Soon, the back door swung open, then shut, and Jeannie hollered out, "Helloooo?"

I leaned over the balcony. "Nice digs, huh?"

"Hell yeah."

"Come on up."

"In a minute. I'm starving."

I wondered what that had to do with coming upstairs. "You're *not* going to eat her food."

"*She's* not gonna."

Suction broke as she yanked open a refrigerator door and I turned away from the banister. Arguing was futile.

Then, Jeannie screamed and there was a crash. She screamed again and I raced down the stairs.

Chapter Seven

In the kitchen, I found Jeannie backed up against Claire's granite island countertop, two spilled coffees and a broken dish at her feet. She stared, wide-eyed, into an open freezer and pointed.

I rounded the corner, stepping around puddles and glass. Jeannie curled her lips into a disgusted snarl and pulled her eyes off whatever she'd found. "This lady's a freak."

Fog whirled in front of us and I gazed, disbelieving, into the freezer. Nestled on a shelf of its own was a set of vacuum-sealed rats. Individually bagged, they'd been positioned in alternate directions so that each set of heads was separated by the long, naked tail of a neighbor.

Too nauseated to speak, I turned away and pulled a long series of paper towels off a dispenser.

She flung the door closed. "Right next to the Lean Cuisines and frozen spinach."

Together, we cleaned up the mess. Claire's microwave clock showed that the time was nearing eleven.

"We only have a half hour," I said.

She nodded. "What are we looking for?"

"I'm not sure. Mainly I want to get a sense of her. But I'd also like to know if she had a history with Platt."

"Anything so far?"

I shook my head. "Let's look upstairs."

Four bedrooms opened off the second floor hall. Jeannie took the master suite and I turned the other direction and stepped into a gloomy room that obviously belonged to one of Claire's boys. Navy blue walls sucked all the light from the space, but his twin bed was neatly made and even his desk was orderly. Again, I noticed that a computer was missing.

The room's centerpiece was what I estimated to be a two-hundred gallon aquarium tank set up to accommodate a fat brown snake. Coiled and still, it lay pressed into a corner of the glass and didn't acknowledge me. A copy of *Your New Burmese Python* rested open, pages down, on the enclosure's mesh lid and I was relieved to at least have an explanation for the frozen rats.

Larger and brighter, the room next door belonged to the other son. Framed prints of airborne skateboarders, some in black-and-white, others in color, hung on the walls. I went from one to another and didn't realize until the fourth image that the same boy was in all of them. A shelf with a dozen or so skateboarding trophies was mounted above a custom desk, fashioned to fit one corner of the room. Once again, there was no computer, but all the ancillary accessories were in place.

Jeannie's voice startled me. "What do you think?"

I turned. She'd posed in the doorway holding a red silk evening gown on a hanger in front of her.

"Unless that dress has a card attached that says 'Love, Wendell' I'm not impressed."

She frowned. "But—"

"The woman that dress belongs to is in jail right now, alone and miserable and missing her kids. Do you think she'd like to know you're fondling her clothes?"

She skulked away.

Twenty minutes later, she found me again, this time in a guest room. Its only point of interest was an enormous bookcase on which Claire kept more photo albums. I was sitting on the bed, flipping through a book of wedding pictures when Jeannie came in with a small wooden box and plopped down beside me.

"Found this in the back of her closet. Bunch of letters inside." She leaned into me for a view of the album in my lap. "That her hubby?"

I tapped a man in an olive green suit and lamb chop side-burns. "Her first, I think. These are old."

Jeannie cocked her head. "You hear that?"

I listened, shook my head.

"Thought I heard a car," she said.

Then, there was the unmistakable sound of car doors thumping closed.

"Someone's here," I said. Jeannie put the box on the floor and I slid the wedding album back into its spot. Below, the back door flung open so fast it hit the wall. Loud, asymmetrical footfalls sounded in the kitchen. We headed for the stairs.

Jeannie followed me down the steps and a pair of sweaty, hurried boys spun around the corner and stopped, staring.

"Hi," I said.

"Who are you?" The younger one's shaggy bangs prevented me from looking him fully in the eyes, but I could see enough to know these were Claire's sons.

"Friends of your mom," Jeannie said, apparently having reached the same conclusion. "She sent us to pick up a few things."

"Have you seen her?" The older one seemed disbelieving.

Unsure how much they knew of their mom's situation, I lied and said no.

I walked the rest of the way down the stairs and peered around the corner to the kitchen, where they'd left the back door open. "Who drove you here?"

The older one shrugged. "A friend. We're getting stuff too." He thumped up the steps, followed by his brother, and we waited in the foyer, listening to them open and close closet doors and talk in hushed tones.

Jeannie pointed at her Tag Heuer. "Gym time."

A gust of wind caught the back door and blew it hard against the wall. "These guys are supposed to be at their grandmother's," I told Jeannie in a low voice. "I want to meet the 'friend.'"

I left her in the foyer and went to the back porch, pulling the door shut behind me. The sky had grown overcast since I'd arrived. Thick air and a heavy breeze suggested a storm was coming.

A Lexus idled in the drive, windows down. Rock music played inside, but it wasn't objectionably loud. Two teens waited in the front seat, unaware I was watching. The driver perched a hand on the steering wheel, a cigarette between his fingers. His friend wasn't smoking but casually flicked a lighter.

"We haven't met." I leaned down on the driver's side, low enough to see both boys. "Can I get your names?"

Too late, I realized I didn't even know Claire's sons' names. The kids in the Lexus watched me impassively.

"Jeff," said the driver. He made no effort to hide his cigarette.

"Chase," said the other.

"What's your plan for today?"

"Skate park," Chase said. "Xbox later."

Then Jeff asked, "Is Kevin around? Thursday he said he'd be around."

"I'm not here to talk about him." I had no idea who Kevin was. "I'm here to talk about *this*." I reached through the window and plucked the cigarette from Jeff's fingers. "You know better."

Claire's boys barreled from the kitchen, now toting backpacks. Jeannie followed them to the car.

I stopped the older one. "Why are your computers missing?"

"Grandma's getting us new ones." He pulled open the back door and slid inside. His brother followed suit.

"Does your mom use her machine much?"

He shrugged. "Nah. We always have to help her. Or her boyfriend will, if he's around."

"Have fun at the skate park," I said.

The older one nodded. Jeff put the car in reverse.

"Remember what I said about the cancer sticks," I told him.

He nodded, a gesture I knew was only meant to placate. We watched them head for the road and Jeannie sidled up next to me.

"New computers for all of them?" she asked.

I shook my head. "I think the machines were taken with the search warrant. Sounds like the kids weren't here when Claire was served and that Grandma's covering up for her. I'm glad about that."

"Why'd they take the computers? Doesn't sound like Claire uses them much."

A rain drop fell on my arm, then cheek. "I'd like to know that too."

Chapter Eight

Jeannie and I stuck to our half-hearted surveillance plan and left, knowing there'd be time to finish searching the house later. We'd driven separately, so I took a few minutes to find the neighborhood skate park Chase had mentioned. The boys were there like they'd said, practicing jumps and tricks. Claire's younger son sat with another park visitor, a strapping blond guy about my age, and seemed to be indicating something of interest on the underside of his skateboard. Satisfied they were staying out of trouble, at least for the moment, I cruised past on my way to the club.

I wanted to meet Diana's daughter, the waxer. Jeannie wanted to touch up her roots and schmooze with Houston's elite. I found a parking spot about a block away from Tone Zone and grabbed an umbrella out of the back seat of my car.

"You look better this time." At the gym's door, Jeannie stole another glance at my sleeveless blouse and dress slacks. "But I wish you'd have borrowed an outfit from Claire. I can't believe you passed up a chance to finally wear some *labels.*"

I ignored her and held the door. She squeezed passed me and flashed her membership card at the desk attendant in an entitled sort of way. I stayed behind, half inside, half out, and shook water from my umbrella before stowing it in an ornate wrought iron rack.

"Meet you in the lounge later." She splintered off toward the salon.

I followed signs to the waxing parlor. Two private rooms opened off a dimly lit waiting area, vacant except for me. Serene candles glowed on each of four cherry end tables. I eased into a microfiber loveseat and inspected the label on the nearest candle, which was Island Guava.

A Dallas-cheerleaders-type girl in tight white jeans and a low-cut, midriff-bearing top emerged to greet me. Even her glittery, strappy high-heels were sexy.

"Emily?" Her exaggerated, glossy smile revealed suspiciously glorious teeth. "I'm Megan." She held out a dainty, manicured hand and I took it. She couldn't have been out of college.

I tried hard not to stare. "Aren't you the cutest thing."

I kept noticing more. Her smooth tan extended so low into her cleavage that I had to look away. She'd parted her highlighted brunette hair with a stylish zig-zag, and several shades of silver eye shadow set off deep brown eyes. Megan was unequivocally striking, like her mother.

"Follow me." She headed toward the room from which she'd appeared. Inside, a salon table was positioned centrally. It was fitted with a satin sheet in a rich shade of brown that seemed to reinforce a slight aroma of cinnamon in the room. A series of what appeared to be crockpots full of various colors of wax waited nearby. I didn't like the looks of them at all.

Megan consulted a clipboard near her wax pots and slipped on a pair of latex gloves. "Looks like we're doing your bikini line."

I'd have been less shocked if she'd said we'd be shaving my head.

She presented a terry-cloth skirt with a slit cut to the waist. "Want a smock?"

I tried not to laugh. When Jeannie mentioned waxing, I'd assumed she'd meant my legs.

I exhaled. "Funny story."

She smiled. "First time?"

I nodded. "Yes. And no. I mean—"

She giggled.

"My friend set this up," I said. "And there's no way in hell I'm getting a bikini wax."

"Thoughtful friend."

"You have no idea. Can you do my legs instead?"

"Only if they're really grown out."

"That's gross."

"We could do your brows, lip, feet, arms, underarms...but there again, only if it's already grown out."

"I guess that leaves my arms. People really wax their arms?"

She nodded. "They'll feel so smooth. You'll love it." Perhaps reading my skepticism, she added. "Don't worry, you'll be fine."

She industriously set out a series of wooden sticks that looked like giant tongue depressors, then pulled two chairs forward to either side of the waxing table. I took a seat and placed my first arm across the silky fabric. Megan made small talk while she smoothed a warm layer of freakishly purple wax along my forearm.

"Does this place have personal trainers?" I asked. Paybacks were fair, after all.

Megan's enthusiastic smile returned. "We have *great* trainers. You should choose one based on your goals." She pressed the wax into my skin and I felt her pluck along its edges. The plucking was agony. "What do you want to work on?"

"I need a drill sergeant type," I said. "Someone to really kick my ass."

Riiiip.

"Whoa!"

"Natalie," she said.

"What?"

"Get on Natalie's calendar."

I took a calming breath and Megan applied a new layer of wax. "Some call her a sadist, but she gets results." She pressed the fresh layer of wax into my skin, then plucked its edge. I hoped Jeannie and Natalie would be very happy together.

"How long have—"

Riiiip.

I collected my thoughts. "How long have you worked here?"

She turned, threw the wax strip away, and came back with a freshly dipped applicator stick, twirling the wax around and around, waiting for it to cool enough to apply. I had the routine down now. Press. Pluck. Pain. Repeat.

"We opened in January and I started then, on account of my mom," she said. "She's the manager."

This was news to me, another of Claire's baffling omissions. As manager, I figured, Diana could certainly access membership files. She could also determine the pattern of Claire's visits. I thought about the anonymous locker-note that led Claire to the murder scene. Diana could easily learn Claire's locker number.

Megan was still talking. "Before this place opened, I was a few blocks away at Beautiful Impressions. Less money. Nicer clients." She caught herself. "Present company excluded, of course."

"If you had it to do again, would you choose the people or the money?"

She looked embarrassed. "The money."

"What'd your mom do before the club opened?"

Megan planted a hand on her slender hip. "Have you *seen* my mom?"

"Maybe," I said. "Names and faces aren't my strong suit." It was only a half-lie.

Megan went back to pressing wax into my shocked and abused skin. "Before I was born she was a big time runway model. New York, London, Paris. That's how she met my dad." She started plucking the edges of the hardened wax.

"Travelling?"

She shook her head. *Riiiip.*

"Aging. My dad's a cosmetic surgeon."

Like Claire, Megan's mother had been a patient-turned-lover of Chris King. I didn't know anything about medical licenses but was pretty sure sleeping with patients was against the rules.

"An aging model married to a cosmetic surgeon," I said. "Handy."

She twirled soft wax around another applicator stick. "When she got too old to model, she switched to agenting. I met a lot of famous people in L.A. because of her." She dropped a few names I pretended to recognize.

"Are you a model too?"

Her smile told me I wasn't the first to ask. "I'm going to be a teacher," she said. "Waxing helps pay the tuition."

I imagined Annette reporting to a teacher who looked like Megan and the thought made me bristle. Then I checked myself. Tone Zone rejected me on appearance alone. Had that taught me nothing? It was also strange that Megan's loaded parents weren't paying her tuition, but I couldn't think of a polite way to ask about that.

She ran a finger lightly over her work and turned my arm slightly to inspect it. "This looks pretty good."

"It didn't hurt as much as I thought it would," I said. "But I'm still not a fan."

I withdrew the assaulted arm and replaced it with the other. Megan gently returned the original arm to the table.

"Not done yet." She produced a pair of tweezers.

"You're kidding."

"Afraid not."

Chapter Nine

Megan left to prepare my bill. Even though the waxing room was windowless, I knew from a persistent, overhead hiss that it was raining harder. I dressed, grabbed my purse, and stepped into the waiting area. Megan, at a discreetly positioned cash register, wasn't alone.

Poised on the loveseat, wearing a fetching sundress, was her mother. Diana cradled a cell phone and pressed buttons with the tip of a long fingernail. Her picturesque hands made dialing look ethereal. She glanced at me, smiled politely, and raised the phone to her ear.

"Your total's eighty," Megan said.

So wax pain came in two forms: physical and fiscal.

I set my bag on the counter and dug for my billfold.

"That's my mom," she said.

I feigned surprise.

"We're having lunch."

In my purse, my cell phone's display was blinking. I'd silenced it for the appointment and had missed two calls. While Meghan ran my credit card, I checked the phone's log. Betsy Fletcher had called first. That was disappointing because it meant I'd missed a chance to talk to Annette. The next call had been from Richard, but since I still felt edgy about the Mick Young situation, missing that one was a relief.

Diana spoke up behind me. "Aren't you the new gal here? The one thinking of doing some work?"

I turned, stunned that my cover story had spread through the club so fast. Diana dropped her own phone into an enormous paisley tote and Megan handed back my card.

"I'm sure it was you," Diana said. "At the funeral."

"You were at the funeral?" Megan asked, clearly surprised.

I nodded and tried to piece things together.

"Natalie said you were a new patient of Wendell's. Said you might give Chris a call." I didn't like her casual mention of a dead man or her pushy way of getting in my business. She stood, smoothed her skirt, and joined us at the counter. "That's my husband."

Megan introduced us and I suffered through a one-sided handshake, high on my list of pet peeves. Diana's limp, disinterested grip suggested I should be flattered to touch her.

I turned to Megan. "Natalie, the personal trainer?"

"Yep."

Not only would Jeannie endure a blistering ass-kicking, she'd get it with Smoothie Nag's bitchy smile.

I signed my slip. Megan put it in her register and locked it. Then she slid a placard onto the counter that said "Back at 1:30."

Her mother reached elbow-deep into her vast bag and came up with a business card, which she pressed into my hand. "I'll tell Chris you might call."

They sashayed away, Diana's posture impeccable.

"Stay dry," I said to their backs, but neither seemed to hear.

"Waxing is a mind over matter thing," Jeannie said. "If you don't mind, it don't matter." She twisted the lid off of a can of Ragu and dumped it into a sauce pan on my tiny gas range. "After a while, it doesn't hurt as much."

"It was totally inappropriate for you to sign me up for a bikini wax." Beside her, I sliced cucumbers and carrots for our salads. Outside, the rain persisted, and now there was thunder too. "Are you completely impervious to social boundaries?"

"It was an exercise in foresight." She angled an open pasta box over a pot of boiling water and slid the spaghetti noodles into the bubbles, where she arranged them somewhat symmetrically. "You and Cowboy could hit the sheets any day now. I knew if I told you ahead of time, you'd never go."

"I got my arms done instead."

"Yeah, that'll turn him on," she muttered.

"I'm ignoring that."

She rinsed out the sauce bottle. "Facials are next. Tomorrow at nine."

"I signed you up for something too."

She clapped. "Yay!"

"Got lucky. There was a cancellation so you get to go *today*."

"A spa double-header. I love it!"

"I hired a trainer."

The lights flickered, but Jeannie didn't seem to notice. Her smile faded. "That doesn't sound relaxing."

I smirked. "Mind over matter."

"Fine," she said. "Turnabout's fair play."

I ripped a few leaves of romaine, sliced a yellow bell pepper, and heaped the veggies into our bowls. "If you drop me at Claire's on your way to the club, I'll probably be finished searching by the time your workout ends. We could do something fun afterward."

"The Galleria?"

I shot her a look. "Do I look like I want a hundred-dollar blouse?"

"Humor me." She pulled two plates from my cupboard and slid them onto the kitchen table. My phone rang, and with no hesitation, Jeannie answered.

"It's Richard." She held the phone out toward me. I reached for it and she snatched it back. "Hey," she said to him suddenly, "What if we split Tone Zone's membership fees fifty-fifty?"

I heard his unequivocal "no" from several feet away and gestured for the phone. Nothing good ever came of a debate between a cheapskate and a spendthrift.

Jeannie shoved it into my hand with a pissy expression I knew was meant for him. "Your boss is cheap."

It was true. He was. But he'd reimburse her the same way he would have reimbursed me had my membership request been approved. He was messing with her. I let it continue because it amused me.

When I finally had Richard on the line, he went straight to the point. "Platt tried to talk to the police a week ago."

I didn't ask how he knew this. Richard was tied to law enforcement like Jeannie was tied to dress shops.

"Platt's home owners' association hires an officer to patrol their streets every Friday and Saturday night," he said. "I asked enough questions and finally got in touch with the guy who was out there last weekend."

"But the murder was Thursday."

Jeannie gave me a sideways look and stirred the pasta.

"I wanted to cover all the bases," Richard said. "Find out if any unusual traffic had been going through the neighborhood, any suspicious activity."

Of course, I thought. Once a cop, always a cop.

"This officer knew Platt from the neighborhood. Last Saturday, he pulled up alongside him while Platt was out for a walk. They got to chatting. At one point Platt said he'd like to get a policeman's opinion about something. About that time, a complaint came in so the officer cut the conversation short. He told Platt to follow-up with a call to the department."

"Let me guess," I said. "He never called."

"Right. So I asked this guy, 'Did Platt say *anything* to suggest what was troubling him?' And the guy says, 'He thought somebody was being swindled out of a lot of money.'"

"Whoa," I said. "That could be huge."

"I think so too," he said. "Maybe blackmail."

"Or fraud." I felt Jeannie's eyes on me and looked up. She poured the spaghetti into a colander waiting in the sink. "If Diana killed Platt," I said, "The scandal he uncovered probably involved her or her husband."

"He might have told someone else what was going on. You follow up with his neighbors," he said. "I'll try his family."

"Sure," I said. "I have a path to Chris King too."

"Good. What is it?"

I told him about Diana's bizarre recruitment. "She thinks I want a nose job and says her husband's the man to do it. I could wiggle into a conversation about Platt while having a rhinoplasty consultation with King."

Richard was quiet.

"What's wrong?" I asked.

"Nothing," he said. "I'm wondering how long it'll take to get an appointment. Might be faster to approach him personally."

I considered that. It did seem unlikely King's office would squeeze in a sudden consultation for an elective procedure.

"But I don't have a credible reason to approach him personally."

Jeannie brought the colander to the table and used her bare hand to move a pile of spaghetti onto each of our plates.

"You're right," he said. "Go for the appointment."

Talking about Chris King reminded me of our earlier conversation regarding life insurance policies on business partners. I scribbled "insurance" at the bottom of my grocery list, which had been shoved to the farthest edge of the kitchen table.

"I'll let you know what his neighbors say."

We said goodbye and I pulled the phone away from my ear as Richard suddenly spoke again. It was too late. My finger was already on the End button and I'd disconnected.

Jeannie came over, sauce pan in hand, and spooned Old World flavors over our pasta. She craned her neck to read my reminder note. "Insurance?"

I stood, brought the shredded Parmesan from the fridge. "I want to find out about life insurance for business partners."

My phone rang and this time she passed it to me. Richard again.

"Listen, Emily," he said, uncertainly. "I should have told you we were working for Brighton and Young."

The mention of it fired me up again, but I appreciated his effort toward making amends. Despite our irresolute professional relationship, I didn't want to lose him as a friend.

"You should have taken your wife's advice." I heard more rebuke in my tone than intended. "But I understand why you didn't."

"I'm taking her advice now."

"You don't deserve her."

"No argument. So are we okay?"

"Don't do it again."

We started to hang up. This time I made the last minute addition. "That wasn't all about you. My anger toward Mick Young, I mean."

"I know." He hesitated. "It might help to talk to somebody."

Across the table, Jeannie began eating without me. She was one of my "somebodies." Jeannie stayed up late with me and paid exorbitant long distance bills so I could self-analyze and cry. She even sent text messages to check on me, her long-distance substitute for wasting time at the office together like we used to before I'd moved to Texas for Annette.

She caught me watching her chew. "What?"

"Like a professional counselor," Richard was saying. "If you don't let some of this go—"

"I hear you, but I need to get there in my own time." The truth was, I'd been seeing a therapist since March.

"Understood," he said. "We're here for you."

"Thanks for the call."

We hung up and Jeannie opened her mouth to say something, but I held up a hand to hold her off. "Sorry," I said. "I have to call Annette first."

When separated from my baby, even for hours, I functioned in a state of mid-level anxiety I knew wasn't healthy. It stemmed from an ever-present fear of losing her again and peaked with certain emotional triggers.

"Hi, baby," I said, after Betsy put her on the phone. "You having fun?"

"I rode a horse today. His name was Leo." Her voice sounded so tiny on the phone. Delicate, like innocence.

"Leo sounds wonderful. Are you having fun with your grandma and grandpa?"

"Grandpa can move his teeth around in his mouth."

I laughed.

"He makes them look funny."

"Give him plenty of hugs while you're there. Grandma too."

"She has a lot of fingernail polish and she shares."

"I share too." It still felt like a contest. The Fletchers in one corner, me in the other. "I'll get a new color for you when you come home. What do you think? Pink or red?"

She thought a moment. "Sparkly magenta."

"Sparkly magenta it is."

"Can I go outside now?"

"Sure, sweetheart. Have fun. I love you."

"Love you too. Bye, Emily." She hung up.

My name pierced like a barb. I wondered if I'd ever be Mom.

Chapter Ten

That evening, I curled up on Claire's sofa, unable to tune out the wind and rain, and shamelessly waded through her private papers. It wasn't my work ethic that had me skipping dinner, losing track of time, but rather my growing obsession with a woman who seemed equal parts sweet and sour. A human yin-yan. For three days, I'd flip-flopped between believing and doubting her.

Jeannie was at Tone Zone working out with Natalie, an arrangement I hoped would supremely frustrate them both. She'd dropped me off at Claire's and would be back soon enough, but waiting alone in a huge house during a monsoon was grossly unsettling. The lights had already flickered twice, but at least I'd found something.

Two term life insurance policies, each for a million bucks, had been misfiled between Claire's parents' living wills. I wasn't surprised that Daniel had listed Claire as his sole beneficiary, but I found it curious that Claire hadn't listed him at all. Her sons would equally share the million dollar payout if their mother died. The policy said their names were Joshua and Logan. Their birthdates put them at fourteen and twelve.

A separate folder, marked Medical, which I'd skipped earlier because I'd expected it to contain boring things like dentist's bills, turned out to have three years' worth of invoices from a therapist. The most recent was dated only two weeks ago.

I paged through financial records. The 401k assets and mutual fund portfolios were all in Daniel's name. I flipped through account statements and did some mental addition. The couple had almost $900,000 tucked away, and my mind swam with questions about what a divorce would mean for Claire and her boys financially.

I returned the paperwork to its folders and headed upstairs for the guest room, where Jeannie had left the box she'd found stashed in the master closet. The upstairs hallway was dark now, all natural light having been snuffed by the storm. I turned at the top of the stairs and passed the boys' rooms, flinching a little at the thought of Logan's enormous snake behind Door Number One.

The box was where Jeannie had left it. Inside, I found letters, cards, e-mails…all manner of random correspondence, spanning decades, written by various people. Soon I better understood, at least in part, why Claire was in counseling.

Dear Claire, one postcard dated 1999 said, *I was not aware that we shared so many anger issues. I am not ignoring you nor your issues with me, but I'm not up to this right now, and so much of what you wrote about is very old. The hiking here is excellent and we've even seen some moose. Not quite as big as the one shown on the reverse. Try to enjoy what's left of summer. Mom*

A different note, written on a sheet of loose leaf, concluded with: *We said we'd do this as long as we both wanted to. I try to want it. But I don't anymore. It's time for me to move on. You know I'll always be here for the boys, right? Tell them I'll always be here for them. —Ruben*

That one had been scribbled eight years ago in tiny little block-looking letters that had been hastily pressed into the page.

Dear Mom, the next one said, written in crayon on green construction paper, *I hat you. your Mean and I wish I had Tanners famule.*

Then, an e-mail: *God I want you. All day long I see your skin, remember your taste. Your lingering perfume gets me hard and I'm crazy when I can't have you. Can you make it up here this weekend? (She's gone until Monday.) Daniel*

For reasons I didn't understand, or maybe ones I understood a little too well, it seemed to me that Claire held on tightly to heartbreak. I read everything in her little cedar box—a rejection from UC Berkeley, two divorce decrees, a prayer card from her grandfather's funeral. Each item was years, if not decades, old. So when I unfolded a note dated only a month ago, my heart raced.

Beside me, my phone rang inside my purse and I ignored it.

I know it's hard for you to trust, baby, but listen to me. There is no one else. Only you. This has been the summer of my life and I want to move this forward. But we don't need my house to do that. When I finish the sculpture, you'll come over anytime you want. I'll give you a key. It's not another woman. It's unfinished art. My job. I love you, Claire. No man deserves you but I'll never stop trying. Kevin

I tapped the paper in my hand, thinking everything over, but too many disjointed ideas flooded me. I pulled a notebook and pen from my bag and scribbled.

53-year-old mother of two
Headed for divorce #3
Loaded, at least for now
Independent boys, maybe troubled
Rift with mom
Fears ex will take kids
Habitual adulterer
Lonely
Wants better

I stared at my list and felt like I'd moved the case forward, though I wasn't sure how. My phone rang again. I reached into my bag and groped for the button to silence it. Whatever was gelling in my head had to set before I could switch gears.

Over and over I read the list, until finally I saw it. *Lonely. Wants better.* Not facts, only hunches. My intuition was finally kicking in.

I thought back to my time in the jail with her. She'd seemed to fear Ruben more than a conviction. It didn't make sense that a woman would spend years in therapy unsaddling old hurts and then do something stupid, like murder a guy, and risk losing her kids right before breaking free from the latest in a series of damaging relationships.

I neatly stacked the notes and letters back into the box and headed toward the master bedroom, wondering, not for the first time, who had it in for both Claire and Dr. Platt. As I crossed the upstairs hall, a door thumped closed downstairs. Then there were beeps. Someone was keying in the alarm code.

I didn't know if it'd be better to wait out of sight until whoever it was left, or to go downstairs and...what? Introduce myself? Whoever was downstairs knew the alarm code, so at least I wasn't dealing with a thief or worse. I descended. At the last step, I remembered the box and set it quietly on the floor.

Rounding the corner at the foyer entrance, I discovered a rain-soaked man standing in Claire's kitchen, wiping water from his drenched hair and fishing for something underneath his dripping poncho. When he saw me, he freed his hand and straightened, almost brightened.

"Well, hi." He smiled good-naturedly, plainly less troubled by my presence than I was by his.

I stayed in the foyer, one hand on the banister, unsure what to say. Truly, the man was utterly soaked. Through the window behind him, I noticed the storm had worsened, a change I'd missed while absorbed in Claire's private letters.

I tried not to sound nervous. "Who are you?"

He shook his wet head in the way of a drenched dog, only more adorably, and ran his fingers through sharply cut blond hair. Then he pulled the poncho over his head and hung it on the doorknob. A pool of water collected at his feet. For an instant, something about him seemed familiar.

"Kevin Burke," he said. "Want a beer?"

I was relieved when he stepped out of view and I heard the refrigerator open. I needed a minute to collect myself, erase whatever evidence of shock might be on my face. I edged as far as the kitchen entrance and stopped. He produced two bottles of Heineken and set them on the granite countertop, then opened the pantry door, stepped on a lever to open the garbage can lid, and spit out gum.

It occurred to me that Claire could be living with this guy. "Do you live here? Am I in your house?"

"It's Claire's house," he said simply.

"Yes, I know it's her house but I thought maybe…" I shook my head. There was no tactful ending.

He grinned. "I still don't know who you are."

I cleared my throat. Told to the wrong person, a lie could be dangerous. "Emily Locke. A new acquaintance of Claire's."

He nodded, but didn't answer.

My instinct was to ask why he was there, but his extreme level of comfort and familiarity with the place put me on alert. If anything, I should probably have been justifying myself to him. But the circumstances were too delicate. I didn't know which of Claire's friends knew what about her recent tangle with the law.

He offered me a beer, but I shook my head.

"Coke then?"

Soft drinks weren't my thing, but I wanted to be cordial. "Sure. Thanks."

He opened the fridge, put the beer back, and came out with a ginger ale. It was the third time in as many months that a local had used the term "Coke" to mean any damn kind of soft drink. This was another peculiarity about Houston life that made me feel like Alice after she'd fallen down the rabbit hole.

I didn't like ginger ale, but opened it anyway.

He leaned backward on the sink and took a swig. I propped myself in the archway leading toward the enormous downstairs hallway and forced a swallow. Too chicken to volunteer why I'd come, but uncomfortable with our silence, I took the age-old cop out. "How long do you give this rain?"

He laughed. "You're kidding."

"What?"

"You live in a cave? Tropical storm just hit between Beaumont and Lake Charles."

"A tropical storm?" I couldn't remember the last time I'd had a chance to read the paper or watch the news.

Kevin took another sip. "*Elena.*" The way he drew out the storm's name made it sound sexy and intriguing, like an unforgettable woman he may have once spent the night with. "Southwest Freeway's flooding. Better stay off the roads tonight." He opened the freezer door. "I'm not staying myself. Just stopped by as a favor to Logan."

Before I registered what he meant, Kevin dropped something hard into the sink. It landed with a loud *thwack* as if he'd tossed in a rock.

"Is that—"

"These guys take a while to thaw. I'll come back when the storm lets up." He paused. "You ever feed a snake?"

I shook my head.

"Amazing the way their jaws stretch." He looked out the window. "I didn't see a car outside. You need a ride somewhere?"

"My ride's coming."

Kevin finished off the rest of his beer and wrangled back into his wet poncho. "Nice meeting you. Stay dry."

I nodded a goodbye and he pulled open the backdoor. The rain was diagonal and loud. Somewhere out of sight, wind chimes were being abused by the gusts, their notes uncharacteristically angry. Kevin closed the door behind him with powerful finality and when the house fell silent in his absence, my unsettled, spooky feeling returned. The lights browned out, and I knew Kevin was right. If I didn't want to get stuck on impassable roads, it was time to go home. I went back upstairs toward my phone, picking up the cedar box on my way. Through the foyer window I watched Kevin's Mustang pull out of the drive.

I checked my phone. The calls I'd ignored had been from Vince and I dialed him right away without bothering to play his messages.

"You okay?" I could hear the concern in his voice.

"Sort of. I'm at the client's house. Jeannie's coming for me."

"Jeannie's with me," he said. "I thought y'all were at that gym so I went over with the truck when I heard about the flooding."

"It only started raining a few hours ago. How can there be flooding?"

"This ain't Ohio, woman. You're at sea level now. Nowhere for water to go."

"So am I stuck here?"

"At least for a while. Guy in front of us has water to his axles. We've been in the car twenty minutes and gone maybe a half-mile. Turn on the TV, you'll see."

I wished I'd been at that snooty gym. Then at least I'd be with Vince and Jeannie instead of stranded in a strange house with a thawing rat.

"I'm jealous," I said.

"Don't be." It was Jeannie now. "You're warm and dry in a swanky house with Versace and Chanel. We're in traffic."

"At least you have each other."

"I'll tell you what I have. A limp. From that lunatic trainer you hired."

"You deserved each other. I'd have taken your place had I known I'd get stuck here."

"Make popcorn or something. Put in a DVD. I know what I'd be doing if I were stuck in that house."

"I'm not trying on her clothes."

"Then try the jewelry."

"No," I said. "This is my job, not a field trip. Put Vince back on." The phone shuffled and I heard murmurs.

"Thank you," I said when he was back on the line. "For trying to help us, and for getting Jeannie out of there."

"Give this a few hours," he said. "We flood fast, but after the rain stops, water recedes sooner than you'd think."

"Guess I'll go mope now."

"Sit tight," he said. "And Emily?"

"What?" I was deep in self-pity now.

"See you soon."

Stupid job. If I had a normal job like everybody else, I'd be in Vince's arms right now. Or at least I'd be in his truck.

We hung up and I loitered in Claire's upstairs hallway, unsure how to pass the time now that I'd searched every nook and cranny and violated her privacy abominably. It had served a valuable purpose, though. A better understanding of our complex, conflicted client had nearly convinced me of her innocence. This freed my mind to address other matters.

For example, revenge was a great motive for Diana to ruin Claire, but so far nothing suggested why she'd kill her husband's business partner to do it.

Then a random, disconcerting thought. Would Logan really send someone out in this storm to feed his snake? He'd been here himself only hours ago.

Chapter Eleven

Vince never came. He couldn't. Downtown Houston was hit hard, the Southwest Freeway under water. Jeannie had urged me to make myself at home, and I knew Claire wouldn't have minded under the circumstances, but I still couldn't bring myself to eat her food, slip into her nightie, or sleep in her bed. So around eleven-thirty, hungry and fully dressed except for my shoes, I collapsed on top of the covers on the bed in her guest room and hoped for a break in the weather.

At some point, I fell asleep and dreamed in a strange way I often did—where real-life noises, like a car engine and a door closing, got incorporated into my dream. Eventually, quiet returned and Vince spooned into me, pulling me tight. His warm, strong hand travelled from my hip to my waist, then over my ribs, and finally inched forward, where it cupped my breast. I felt his hot breath and tongue on my neck and, eyes still closed, I rolled over, gathered him in my arms and pulled him close with a leg. But then he spoke, and the voice was all wrong.

My eyes popped open. A stranger had joined me in bed and he *reeke*d of alcohol.

I thrust a knee into his crotch. He curled into himself and I fisted a wad of his hair and used it jam his head even further toward his chest. He reached up to free his hair and I grabbed his hand and wrenched it behind his back, moving myself over him so that I could drive his shoulder as far out of alignment as possible. He groaned but didn't put up the fight I'd expected.

"I thought you were Claire." There was a subtle slur.

"Who are you?" I pushed his unnaturally bent arm further up his back. He grunted but didn't struggle. My purse, with pepper spray inside, was a few feet away on the dresser. I let go of his arm and lunged for it. A bedside lamp switched on.

In the new light, I watched a middle-aged man with still-toned pecs and abs but a pasty complexion and swollen left jaw rub and stretch his shoulder. He regarded me with what I interpreted as drunken amusement. Naked except for boxers, he propped himself on an elbow.

His eyes twinkled, not in the kindly Santa Claus way. "A saucy one, you are."

"How'd you get in here? Who are you?"

He sat up. "I used my key."

Hell, I thought, is there anyone in town who *doesn't* have a key to this house? And the security code?

I felt around for the pepper spray inside my bag while I bumbled into my shoes.

"Don't tell me you got a piece in there, honey."

"I'm leaving," I said, heading for the door. "If you know what's good for you, stay in that bed."

"I'll stay in this bed because I'm plain-ass tired, not because my wife's latest romp tells me what to do."

In the doorway, I stopped and flipped on the overhead lights. "Daniel?" It made sense he'd sleep in the guest room.

"I didn't know she was into girls now."

"Where have you been since Thursday?"

"None of your damn business."

"The police want to talk to you."

He leered at me, dropping his gaze to my legs and then letting it crawl back up. "They probably wanna talk to you too, sugar."

"I'm not a hooker."

He shrugged.

"They thought you might be dead. And that Claire did it."

He managed something between a laugh and a snort. "She's crazy enough." He flipped off the bedside light, sprawled across the bed, and closed his eyes. "Turn out the lights."

"Don't you care where she is?"

"No."

"You don't wonder why a stranger's in your house?"

"No."

"At least tell me where you've been."

"If I do, will you leave?"

"Sure."

"Vegas."

I turned out the light. "Your wife's in jail."

"About time."

I left through the kitchen, forgetting until the door closed behind me that I had no car. Rain had let up but the driveway was partly submerged and I accidentally sloshed into a puddle and waterlogged my shoes. Claire's security lights got me to the end of the drive and then the neighborhood street lights took over from there. The block was stone silent, porch lights the only sign of life.

My cell phone said it was quarter past four, but what startled me more was seeing the date, July thirteenth. In my haste to get away from Daniel, I'd forgotten it was my birthday.

Joy.

Still fighting my stupid new nails, I successfully dialed my apartment on the second try but Jeannie didn't answer. I figured she was sleeping hard and tried again, but there was still no answer.

Next I tried her cell with the same result. Then I tried my apartment one more time.

Maybe they'd stayed at Vince's.

"Emily?" he said, heavy sleep in his voice. "You okay?"

"Fine," I said, "But my Goldilocks gig is up. Papa Bear's back."

"The husband?"

"Yeah. A real charmer."

Vince exhaled, and I imagined him pushing back covers, sitting up. No shirt. An image so sexy it was cruel. "Where are you?"

"Walking south on Larchmont."

"In *this?*"

"In what?"

"I swear, woman, you're a handful. Try not to get blown away before I get there."

I didn't know what that meant but was glad he was coming. A few blocks later I rounded the corner, continuing on the route I knew he'd use. Under street lamps, I saw that low-lying areas were submerged, and below me, the rapid *whoosh* of water pulsing through the neighborhood's drainage system reminded me how much water had already receded.

The temperature had dropped to probably the mid-eighties and the air was so thick and damp I thought I felt the smallest of rain drops on my face and bare arms. The unmistakable scent of steaming blacktop hung in the air as I passed sleeping houses and dormant cars. I didn't hear a single motor anywhere. Nobody wanted to be out on a morning like this.

Thoughts and counter-thoughts came at machine-gun pace, and I knew that only a long, hard run would organize them. But it would have to wait until I got home and could change. Nothing good ever came from running in mules.

Instead I planned my day. Top priority was a visit to Platt's neighbors. With any luck, someone would know what had bothered him enough to prompt his question to the police. Then there was the nine o'clock facial at Tone Zone that seemed not only frivolous but pointless, since breaking into Diana's inner circle was obviously impossible. I made a mental note to cancel the appointment. When the hour was decent, I'd call Richard. His police buddies would want to know that Daniel still had a pulse.

Then I reconsidered. *If I'm awake, Richard can be awake too.*

But Linda answered, gracious even in slumber, and I wanted to kick myself for rousing her. A big, fat drop landed on my head. If it hadn't been cool to the touch, I'd have sworn it was bird poop.

"Hold on, honey," she said. "I'll put him on."

Another huge drop hit me, then another.

"What's up, kiddo?" Richard said. I pictured him sitting up in bed too, checking his watch and rubbing a stubbly cheek. My shirtless Vince image had been way better.

"Claire didn't off her husband," I said.

"How do you know?"

"I just got out of bed with him." The wind picked up and I ducked my head. "Tell your police buddies he's at his house if they want to question him."

"You didn't say you were going to their house."

"I don't say a lot of things. See what you can find on a guy named Kevin Burke. This is one messed up marriage."

"We sort of got that from the neighbors."

"Right, but there's more. The financial accounts are Daniel's. She gets a million dollars in life insurance if he dies and probably also inherits all the stocks."

"Again, no surprise."

"But if *she* dies, the insurance pays out to her kids."

"Okay."

"They're in the middle of a divorce. What happens when they split?"

"It's is a community-property state. Unless there's a prenup, she'll get half of those portfolios and everything else."

"Say he wants to keep his share and hers too. There's not much incentive to kill her. It's a lot of risk and effort and he wouldn't get any insurance."

"No, but he'd keep his investments."

"Sure. But maybe he keeps them anyway. Say he squirrels the money away while she's all tied up in jail and can't do anything to stop him. He could hide it off-shore or something."

"You think Daniel framed Claire to give himself time to hide their money?"

"The murder weapon came out of their toolbox. Easy for Daniel to get. Harder for Diana."

"There's a problem, of course."

"A huge one." Bigger than my immediate problem—saturated clouds now freely dumping rain that pelted me like marbles.

"Why would Daniel want Platt dead?" Richard asked. Our connection was breaking.

I shook my head, frustrated. "Why would Diana?"

"We have to assume—" he dropped out, then came back "—ties into what Platt tried to—" then dropped out "—someone was getting swindled."

I thought the spotty connection had more to do with a wet phone than with signal strength.

"Call you later." I hung up, unsure if he'd heard.

It was a half-hour before oncoming headlights bounced in the distance. The rain had settled into a steady, persistent tempo and having no place to take shelter, I ignored my soaked clothes and ruined shoes and continued walking the route I knew Vince would take. I squinted toward the approaching vehicle, hoping to make out Vince's pick-up, but water only streamed down my forehead and pooled in my eyes. The truck passed me before I recognized it, spraying water as it went, and I pulled my phone out of my water-logged bag but the damn thing was on the fritz.

I watched Vince disappear down the boulevard behind me. At one point his brake lights flared and I held out hope for a U-turn, but no luck. The lights dimmed, grew even smaller. The only motorist out at four-thirty in the morning continued his diligent search for a stupid woman stomping and cursing blocks behind him.

Chapter Twelve

"Thank goodness you're here," Jeannie shouted from my bedroom. "I can't move!"

Vince had rescued me on his second pass down the boulevard and wrapped me in a blanket he kept in his truck for his dog to lay on. With it still draped over my shoulders like a cape, I flipped on my living room lights and we wound around the sofa, through my short hallway, and found Jeannie lying flat on her back in the shape of an X on top of my rumpled comforter. She'd left my nightstand lamp on and had *Cosmo* draped over her chest. For once, she'd selected modest sleepwear—thank God.

"Your fan blades are dusty," she said, staring overhead.

The comment, made in front of Vince, ratcheted up my already-high irritation.

"What do you mean you can't move?" he said.

Jeannie pulled her eyes off the fan and turned her head as if it were the only mobile part of her. "Hi, Cowboy." She sighed in a familiar, self-pitying way. Without energy she added, "This is all *your* fault, Em. It was that trainer from hell."

I dropped my blanket-cape and yanked the pillow from under her head. Her big blond curls rebounded off my Serta. "Why didn't you answer the phone? I thought somebody broke in here and slashed your throat."

"I told you. *I can't move.*"

"Bullshit." I clutched her ankle and pulled it over the edge of the bed. She winced.

"Uh, Emily—" Vince edged in, but I ignored him and tugged again.

"Get up," I said. "It can't be that bad."

Jeannie shrieked. "My *back*!"

Vince pulled me off her and whispered. "I think she really is hurt, darlin'."

"She's faking." I said it loud enough for her to hear. "She didn't want to interrupt her beauty sleep to get up and answer the phone."

Jeannie glared at me. "You'll be sorry for that if I end up paralyzed." She closed her eyes, her side of the conversation over.

"Too much estrogen in here," Vince said. "I'll make breakfast."

He disappeared around the corner and I stomped to the bathroom and peeled myself out of soaking wet clothes I didn't care if I ever saw again. Then I wrapped myself in a towel and scuttled back for the last word.

I leaned close to Jeannie's ear.

"Faker," I whispered.

Then I bolted for the bathroom before she could answer.

"Amazing what a shower and dry clothes does for you," Vince said when I joined him at the breakfast table. "Hope you never come after *me* like that."

I bit into a piece of jelly-smeared toast. "You wouldn't ignore my calls."

He smiled.

Because Jeannie's a good actress and Vince is a softie, he'd delivered breakfast to her in bed before I could stop him. It was just as well. I was too annoyed for more theatrics. Jeannie could make a paper cut seem like a skin graft. I didn't understand how a crybaby like her had endured so many nips, tucks, lipos, and lifts.

Under the table, my bare foot was in Vince's lap and he massaged it with his free hand.

"I'm going to talk to Platt's neighbors today," I said. "And Jeannie made spa appointments for us that I'd rather skip."

"Keep the appointment. It's a chance to relax and you might learn something at the club."

"Maybe." I nodded toward my bedroom. "Doesn't look like Queen Diva will be stepping out anytime soon."

He stood, put his dishes in the sink, and kissed the top of my head. "I've got a long day."

I followed him to the living room, where he gathered up the now-folded dog blanket I'd borrowed. "Thanks for rescuing me."

He slipped his arms around my waist and buried his face in my neck. "Don't make a habit of it."

I turned and kissed him. "I probably will."

He palmed his black Stetson off my cluttered end table and winked. "I know."

The sun came up as I left I-10 to turn onto Heights Boulevard at 6:25. It was a majestic road with a lush, wide median full of huge shade trees and a twisty gravel walking trail. The temperature was down and so were my car windows. I barreled through puddles and listened to the violent spray hit my fenders.

It was too early to knock on doors but I at least wanted to get a feel for Platt's neighborhood. The best way to do that was on foot, so I'd come dressed to run.

I found and passed his address, not wanting to park in front. A block west, on the corner of Heights and 7th, I pulled into a small grass lot that adjoined the most extravagant playground I'd ever seen. On the spot, I resolved to bring Annette as soon as she returned.

At a slow jog, I backtracked to Platt's street and noticed the homes. Each was as likely to be a grand, restored Victorian as it was to be a well-maintained cottage.

Platt's wooden siding was the color of weak chocolate milk. His front door and windows were accented with cream and burgundy, and the skillful blend of colors impressed and bugged me the same way it had at Claire's.

A wrought-iron fence at the sidewalk, coupled with wooden privacy fences in the side yards, gave the home a false air of impenetrability. Under different circumstances, I might have adored that little cottage, but an irrational distaste for it washed over me. I didn't like when things weren't what they seemed.

"Starting or finishing?" It was an approaching runner. A ninja, judging by her eerily silent stride.

I fell in step beside her. "Starting."

Her breathing was hard. She'd been at it a while. "You live on this street?"

"My sister lives a few blocks down," I lied.

"I saw you checking out that house."

"She told me what happened."

"My daughter..." She took a breath. "...and I were coming home from soccer. Five police cars."

"Never good."

"I slowed down to ask a cop about it," she said. "I'm nosey that way."

"Wasn't your little girl scared?"

"She was playing her Nintendo. Anyway, the guy said there'd be a 'death investigation.' But we didn't find out until the next day that it was a murder."

We passed the first imperfect house I'd seen in the neighborhood—a bungalow with garbage bags on the porch and a random, upside-down clawfoot bathtub in the side yard.

"Did you know the guy?" I asked. Somewhere, bacon was frying.

"My housekeeper did."

I wanted to stop and shake her. "You had the same housekeeper?"

At the next cross street, she veered left without warning. I made a late correction and followed.

"No, Monica cleaned the house next to his. But she said the guy was real nice—" She held a hand out, as if to confide something. "—Not like the nut she works for."

"Everybody has a kooky neighbor," I said. "Mine swears there's a ghost in her shower." That was actually true. Florence, bless her heart, had quirks.

Ninja Runner chuckled and then stopped abruptly. She nodded to a cottage, this one quaint and clean. "This is me."

I stopped too, already breathing hard. "I like it."

A lady-bug flag that said "Welcome, friends" waved over her landscaping bed.

"We like it too," she said. "*Now.* It was built in thirty-four."

"Fixer upper?"

The smile she gave me said *You have no idea.* She raised the latch on her gate. "Have fun with your sister."

I waved goodbye and went back to the running. As I circled the block and criss-crossed the boulevard, my thoughts drifted to Annette as they so often did. She'd be in a cozy bed somewhere in Wichita right now, dreaming of horseback rides at her faux-grandparents' hobby farm. I regretted letting her leave for so many days. The Fletchers were an unrelenting imposition on our delicate relationship and, right or wrong, I viewed each day she spent with the people she *thought* were her parents as a setback to her future with me. But to Annette, I knew *I* was the imposition—on her life with them.

Frustrated, I ran faster and breathed harder. I imagined I was strong. I'd have to be. The only fair way to mother Annette was to let go when every instinct screamed to hold on tight.

Chapter Thirteen

I showered at Tone Zone and made myself presentable for my very first facial, which, like everything else at the club, sounded inviting but was overpriced. Asked to choose between treatments derived from desert plants, marine elements, or sunflower seeds, I'd reclined for forty-five minutes and had my face washed with a series of cleansers made from "real crushed pearls" and come away with a hundred and twenty dollar invoice that I was fairly certain Richard wasn't going to reimburse. The crowning jewel was being advised by the esthetician—whose youthful face was frozen in an unnaturally innocuous stare—that Botox would be my best friend in five years.

Happy Birthday.

In the locker room, I gave Richard the run-down on my cell phone while gathering my things. "This entire subculture is nuts. Women here do this *all* the time. They call it 'maintenance.'" I was alone; I'd looked under shower curtains and bathroom doors to be sure. "I almost didn't come this morning, and now I wish I hadn't. But I do have some good news."

"At least one of us does." He sounded far away and his words were discontinuous. I worried that the earlier storm had ruined my phone.

Tone Zone's locker area offered upholstered love seats and lounge chairs, a step up from the shiny metal benches I used at the Y. I dropped into a Victorian high back and crossed my feet on its lush ottoman. "The Westside Cosmetic Surgery Center had a cancellation," I said. "I'm seeing Chris King at two."

"To find out what it'll take to fix your schnoz?"

"Shut up."

"Be careful," Richard said. "If he's a bad guy, you don't need to be on his radar."

"I don't?"

He ignored the joke. "When will you go back to the Heights?"

"Straight from the appointment. How's it going with Platt's family?"

"It's not." Even the poor sound quality couldn't hide that he sounded pissed. I didn't ask for the story.

"You dig anything up on Kevin Burke?"

"No."

"Well, what am I paying you for?"

"It's next on my list," he said, not amused. "And I've been thinking about your Daniel angle. It doesn't make sense. If he were hiding assets, it'd come out in the divorce. Claire's attorney would uncover it during the discovery process. A big chunk of change turns up missing, someone'll ask."

Beauty treatments were confusing, but I knew even less about divorces. Richard was probably right, but my suspicion lingered. "If he's responsible for this, surely he's smart enough to find a way around a paper trail. You're thinking like Joe Public. Think like a sophisticated criminal. They get away with things we can't imagine."

"Daniel had no reason to want Platt dead."

"Neither did Diana."

"No reasons that we know about, anyway."

"True."

I thought he sighed but it might have been a yawn.

"How about Jeannie?" he asked. "She your partner again today?"

"No. We were supposed to come here together but she threw her back out. For all I know, she's watching soaps and eating all my ice cream. I'm going home for a sandwich and a nice, long

Internet surf before my nose job consultation. I want to learn more about how insurance works between business partners."

"I'll check out Burke."

We said goodbye and I snapped my phone closed and dropped it into my bag, wedged in the chair beside me. When I stood to leave, I wasn't alone.

Kendra, the one normal person I'd met since working on Claire's case, stepped out from a partition that divided the changing area from the sinks. The disappointment on her face said I should spare any weak excuses I was considering.

I did a fast mental rewind, trying to gauge how much she might have overheard.

"Janitor's closet," she said. "I was re-stocking. What are you really doing here at the club?"

I checked my watch. So much for spending my pre-King hours surfing the Net.

"Come with me." I flung my gym bag's strap over my shoulder. "Let's have lunch."

"You joined the club to spy on Diana." Kendra's tone implied she thought I was an idiot. She lifted a bite of salad onto her fork.

"She spends a lot of time here," I said. "And the note that sent our client to the murder scene was left for her here, in her locker."

"Do you have the note? I might know the handwriting."

I shook my head.

"Did you see it?"

"No."

"So there might not even *be* a note. Maybe the right person's already in jail."

I didn't tell her I'd once shared similar thoughts.

We picked at our salads. The Bistro, one of two healthful eatery nooks nested inside the club, had been Kendra's idea. I rolled a cherry tomato to the side of my plate and stabbed a crouton. Kendra took a sip of her bizarre aloe-seaweed drink.

She lowered her voice and leaned in. "Diana would never kill someone. She's a great lady."

"She's weird if you ask me. Why do you like her?"

"She turned my life around."

I leaned back in my chair, floored. "Don't tell me she recruited you to some kind of new fangled church or something?"

"She got me this job."

I relaxed a little. "So you're loyal, not born-again."

She smiled, but only a little. It was genuine, though. "Seriously. I couldn't afford a membership here without my employee discount. And being a member of the club has opened so many doors. I do odd jobs for some of our members, everything from personal errands to babysitting to clerical stuff. Fat checks, easy work."

"And you ascribe this good fortune to Diana?"

"Who else would hire an inexperienced girl at a fancy place like this?"

"Why'd she take you?"

"I'm friends with her daughter."

"The waxer."

She nodded. "You know Megan?"

"We've met."

A tiny Asian waitress, who could have been twelve or thirty for all I could tell, deposited a marinated Portobello mushroom in front of Kendra and a spinach quesadilla in front of me.

Kendra began slicing her mushroom and I did the same with the quesadilla. Anywhere else, I'd have picked it up and eaten it like a pizza wedge. But we were seated near a ceiling-mounted security camera and I imagined that somewhere in the vast building, in addition to what I was wearing, my table manners were being monitored and discussed.

I pointed toward the camera. "Are those things all over the club?"

She turned to see what I was indicating. "Sure."

I returned to my entrée, probably pressing my knife a little too hard into the dish.

"Why'd you ask that?" She sipped her seaweed juice and watched me over the rim.

"Where's the footage archived?"

Kendra squinted at me. For the first time, I noticed expertly blended eye make-up. I felt a little betrayed by that.

Her eyes widened again. "Oh no. You are *not*."

"I have to, Kendra. It's my job to get to the bottom of this."

"What if you get caught?"

"I won't. I'll have inside help."

"Who?"

"You."

She set down her utensils and straightened. I'd overstepped.

"I told you how much I need this job," she said. "I won't risk it."

"But you *like* me." It was another attempt at levity and, like all others that day, it flopped.

"I like Diana more."

There we go, I thought. *Cover blown.*

I tried again. "Instead of looking at it as helping me, maybe you could look at it as helping Diana. If she had nothing to do with Dr. Platt's death, then whoever really left that note will be somewhere on Thursday's tapes. Diana will be cleared."

"She's already cleared," Kendra said. "Nobody else thinks she's done anything wrong. There's no way she killed Dr. Platt. They were *friends*. And even if she did—which is ridiculous—why would she pin it on a club member? That's a stretch."

"Her husband's a big time cheater. He slept with the woman arrested for Platt's murder. They had a long term affair and Diana knew about it."

Kendra opened her mouth to say something and, presumably thinking better of it, closed it again.

"I don't know why Diana would kill her friend," I said, "But if she's guilty, it's easy to imagine why she'd hang it on our client. The point is, if there was a note, and if I find out who left it, these questions might disappear."

Her gaze fell to the tabletop. To my half-eaten salad, actually. "There are no tapes," she said. "The security recordings are digital. They get saved to a computer."

"Even better," I said. "I'll copy the files. Where's the machine?" She looked at me again. "In Diana's office. She's the manager."

We agreed I'd come back later with a thumb drive. Fearing she'd have second thoughts, I steered the conversation toward another topic of great interest to me—her exquisitely strange drink. When the bill came, I picked up the tab. Kendra's twenty dollar mushroom would be worth every penny if I ended up scoring Thursday's security footage.

Chapter Fourteen

It was clear what kind of women got Chris King's attention. Flashbacks of Diana and Claire danced in my mind and I knew my fake nose job consultation would require serious prep work if I was going to make any sort of impression. I skipped up the steps to my apartment, where Jeannie waited with cosmetics and accessories like a zealous stage mom.

"I printed a bunch of stuff." She pointed to the tiny laundry room off my kitchen, the only place in the apartment where I could spare room for a printer.

I dropped my keys on an end table. "Tell me about it while you work. We don't have much time."

She directed me to the kitchenette, where I sat in a chair and waited. She hobbled a few steps behind, her posture stiff.

"It needs to be comprehensive." I ignored her pain, which I knew was exaggerated. "Face, hair, clothes. You have an hour."

Jeannie lifted a hot pink sundress, still on its hanger, from the back of the chair across from me. "I'd have rather seen you wear something of Claire's," she said, "but this'll do."

"Whose is it?"

She held it close, stroked it. "Mine. *Armani*."

"Why would you pack that?"

"I bought it yesterday at the Galleria. You should be ashamed of the frumpy shit in your closet."

I reached for the dress.

She pulled it back. "This won't come down to how you look, you know. He'll see right through that."

Behind her, our breakfast plates were stacked in the dish drainer and the coffee pot had been cleaned. I decided against telling Jeannie that I valued her domestic help more than her advice.

"Go in there with the attitude of the woman you're pretending to be," she said. "It's the whole package."

I knew she was right. Exfoliated skin and new acrylics could only take a woman so far. "I'll channel my inner actress."

"Good girl. Now go wash your face."

I did what she said and rejoined her at the table, where she laid out an array of high dollar cosmetics, none mine. She removed the top from a bottle of foundation and began blotting it into my face with a sponge. It smelled floral, but went on cold and sticky.

"They did a nice job on your skin," she said.

I thought of the crushed pearls. "Cost more than a week of groceries."

She pressed and dabbed and I felt like a kid getting made up for Halloween. "Look up," she said, and I obeyed. "When you introduce yourself to the doc, be confident. Flirt. Stroke his ego."

I started to protest, but she admonished me to be still.

"Give him a reason to want to impress you," she continued. "Trust me. I know his type." She grinned. "I love his type."

"You don't even know him."

"Educated guess."

"I wish you could go instead."

"Me too, sweetie." She added final touches below my jaw. "But *my* nose doesn't need any work." She clucked her tongue and pulled the sponge away.

I cut my eyes to her but we were so close that it strained me to stare very long.

A thick layer of powder came next. "You're gonna take this in your bag, Em, and put it on before you get out of the car. No shine on your face, hear me?"

She sounded like me when I talked to Annette. *Don't forget your backpack. Are you sure you brushed your teeth?*

Lipliner, eyeliner, brow filler. Eye-shadow. Mascara. Lipstick. Gloss.

She stepped back and evaluated. "Where's your Chi?"

I looked at her. "My…natural energy of the universe?"

She put a hand on her hip. "Your flat iron."

Getting only my blank stare in response, she reassessed. "Then an up-do. Got bobby pins?"

On and on it went, Jeannie with her good-smelling hair products and hair twirling and bobby-pinning. Me, immobilized in the chair, fretting over the time.

"Anyway," she said, working on a new section of my hair, "The articles I printed talk about what happens when a business partner dies."

I spun to face her. "What does happen?"

She smacked the back of my head. "Hold still."

"When you go into business with somebody," she said, "You can sign a buy-sell agreement and get life insurance on your partner. Then if he dies, you can buy out his share using the insurance."

"What's the agreement do?"

"It sounds like a prenup for business partners. Something to nail down who can buy an owner's interest and what price they'll pay."

"Are doctors like regular business partners or is a medical practice different?"

She shrugged. "Not sure it matters. Killing a guy to buy up his share of a practice is a stretch. You see that, right?"

I dropped my head into my hands, frustrated. She thumped the base of my skull with a hard flick. "Sit up."

"Until I figure out who wanted Platt dead," I said. "Everything's a stretch." I tapped a shiny fake nail on my watch face.

Jeannie shellacked my hair with a bottle of Paul Mitchell and told me to put on the dress. I squeezed into it and she pulled the zipper up in back.

"Your legs look *awesome*," she said, when I turned around for her inspection. The hem of her dress was alarmingly high on my thighs. "But the neckline sags. We have to push up your boobs."

I didn't own bra pads, which Jeannie said was worse than not having a Chi iron. She fashioned a set by cutting and balling up an old pair of my pantyhose and telling me how to stuff it under my breasts inside my bra cups. When I finally got a look at myself in the mirror, I was pleasantly shocked.

Jeannie passed me the thin stack of articles she'd printed and followed me to the door, where her parting action was to spritz me with Giorgio Beverly Hills. I pulled the door shut behind me, feeling as elegant as her perfume, and descended the steps. At the bottom, I emerged from the building's shadow into the sun and when its warmth washed over me, the transition felt metaphoric.

I did vain, stupid things during my drive to the surgery center. I tilted the rear-view mirror at me so I could admire my sexy lips. Sometimes I glanced at the faint reflection in the driver's side window for another look at my too-cute hair. Once I lowered the sun visor so I could see the way my fingernails looked as they played over the steering wheel.

I drove a little faster than usual, not because I was late, but because glamour was exciting, even in a Taurus.

When I pulled into the surgery center, I re-applied facial powder as instructed and stepped from the car, approving my reflection in the window one last time before taking long, confident strides toward the building. Jeannie had swept my hair up in a way that looked sharp and classy in the contour of my shadow. I watched my silhouette cross the pavement and marveled at how empowering the new style felt compared to my usual ponytail.

By the time Dr. King met me in an exam room twenty-five minutes later, I was so full of myself I used his first name.

"Good to meet you, Chris."

He shook my hand with almost no eye contact and reached for my patient folder. After a brief glimpse inside, he said, "Tell me your reasons for considering rhinoplasty."

Then he reached behind him for a wheeled-stool and pulled it forward without ever looking at it. He rolled forward, studying my face without really seeing me, and as he drew nearer, my Giorgio Beverly Hills mixed with something equally divine on his end.

"I'd like to smooth the bridge." I ran a finger lightly over my nose. "And maybe bring the tip down a little bit."

He propped my chin on his hand and turned my head, considering it from the front, then sides. "Your overall facial structure is proportional," he said. "Pretty chin, nice cheekbones."

"Thank you," I said. "Dr. Platt thought so too." I turned my eyes away and gave what I hoped was a convincing sad smile.

King flipped backward in my chart. "You saw Dr. Platt?" he asked. "It's not in your folder."

I waved off the question. "Informally. We were to meet here for our first visit, but then…you know."

"Mm," he said, more to himself than me. "We certainly miss him." He scribbled something in my chart, then looked up abruptly. "The concerns you express can be addressed with minor reshaping. It would be a closed procedure." He lifted a plastic model from the countertop. "We'd make incisions within the nose and separate the skin from the bone and cartilage here. Once that's done, tissue can be removed or reshaped as required. We can correct the asymmetry too."

"Asymmetry?"

"The way your columnella—" more pointing to the model "—is offset to the left there."

I tried not to take offense.

"The procedure will take about an hour or two," he continued. "Will this be your first surgery?" He flipped around in my chart some more and paused on my medical history form.

"Yes."

I watched him study my file and wondered how to bring things around to his business arrangement.

"What happens now?" I tried. "Do you have twice as many patients? Will you get another partner?"

King clicked his pen and dropped it into his pocket. "It'll be an adjustment. But things always work out somehow, don't they?"

He'd answered my question with a question. I recognized this as one of Richard's tricks.

"Let's do your photos," King said. "Our computer imaging package will approximate your new look. You'll have an opportunity to review various possible outcomes and let me know which most closely captures what you'd like to achieve. I can't guarantee the final result will look like the picture, but we get very close."

He stood and opened the door. I remembered Jeannie: *Give him a reason to impress you.*

"I know how computer imaging works." I passed him in the doorway. "You're my third consult."

He escorted me down the hall.

"I want the right surgeon," I said. "Someone to make me feel as comfortable as Dr. Platt did. Diana insisted I meet you."

"Ah." A new bright tone came to his voice. "My wife is matchmaking."

"She recruited me at Tone Zone."

"She lives for that place," he said. "Hell, she lives *at* that place."

"Girl's gotta do what a girl's gotta do." I smoothed the twist Jeannie had pinned in my hair. "We're not twenty anymore."

"You're lovely, both of you," he said. "And I know you work very hard at it."

Unsure whether that last bit was a compliment, I didn't answer.

He peeled to the right and we passed Platt's office, identified by a chiseled name plate mounted on the door. Open cardboard boxes waited on his desk and I wondered who among Platt's circle would come to claim his things today. Dr. King gestured to a crowded little room with a backdrop and diminutive flash umbrella against the far wall. He flipped on the lights and I went inside and sat in the empty chair where I would pose for my Before shots.

He deposited my folder on the counter. "Lucy will take care of you."

I crossed my legs as suggestively as I could. "The other doctors took my pictures personally."

"I'm a better surgeon than photographer. We'll talk again when she's finished."

He left the room, evidently less impressed with me than I was. And when Lucy finally came, she was no help either. I asked what would happen to the practice now that Dr. Platt had passed. She said, "They-never-tell-us-anything-look-to-your-right-please" and raised the camera. She snapped pictures of my asymmetrical nose and left me alone in the room. I viewed her abandonment as an opportunity.

Two doors down, I slipped into Platt's office and closed the door to barely a crack. I peered into the half-packed boxes on his desk and found books and picture frames, two coffee mugs and a sweater. He used one of those desktop calendars that cover the full writing surface of a desk. I moved the boxes aside and ripped off the top page, July, without reading it. I folded the giant sheet over and over until it was small enough to shove in my bag. Then I replaced the boxes and tried his desk drawers, all locked.

A quick look around the room suggested nothing else of interest, only wall-mounted diplomas and overflowing stacks of medical journals. When I returned to the photography room, Dr. King was waiting, reading a message on his iPhone.

"Ladies room," I apologized, and dropped back into the chair. "Are my images uploaded?"

Chapter Fifteen

Kendra found me loitering in the lounge, flipping through a celebrity gossip rag.

"You snoop in style." Her eyes took in Jeannie's dress, which I was growing to like.

"I feel radioactive." It was the first time in my life I'd worn hot pink. "I made a salon appointment for later, in case anyone wonders why I'm here twice in the same day."

She nodded. "How will this work?"

"I need time in Diana's office." A pair of women in tennis skirts passed, smoothies in hand. "How much time depends on the file sizes."

"The best chance is during her staff tag-up," Kendra said. "It lasts fifteen, twenty minutes."

"When's the meeting?"

"Whenever Diana says."

I checked my watch, not that it mattered. "Put my number in your phone, okay? Call me when it starts."

"I'll text you. It's quieter."

"Fine."

She pulled out her phone and stopped. "Give me a few seconds, then follow me. Don't make it obvious."

Before I could ask, she turned and walked away. I gave her a nice head start before following her through the twisty-turny hallways to a strangely shaped nook between a ladies room and a storage closet. Kendra was waiting beside some drinking fountains, leaning against a fire alarm box.

"No security cameras here," she said. "Tell me your number now."

I thought her precautions were a bit extreme for sharing a phone number, but I gave it to her without commentary and she punched it into her cell.

"All of us can't be at the meeting, obviously. People still have to man the floor. So if you get caught—"

I rested a hand on her shoulder. "I won't throw you under the bus."

She forced a smile, lips tight. "You'll need this." She pressed a key into my hand.

"Thanks."

I turned to leave but she touched my wrist. When I looked back, her bold, brown eyes were intense. "Diana didn't do anything wrong."

"Maybe not." I turned the key over in my hand. "But somebody here did."

◇◇◇

Situated on the building's second floor, Diana's office opened off of an elevated, rubberized running track that encircled a colony of Pilates machines. A poster on her door advertised the July special: two free chemical peels with the purchase of permanent make-up.

Unwilling to draw attention to myself by circling the track in a tight dress and strappy heels, I found a nearby bench and pretended to read the latest issue of *Houston Woman* while waiting for Kendra's all-clear text message.

I checked my phone compulsively. During one idle pass through its menus, I saw I'd missed several calls. They'd been logged throughout the afternoon, but the callers weren't listed. Immediately, I thought of Annette. Then before I could investigate further, a message from Kendra arrived: "Go."

At least I was still receiving texts.

Her key, warm from its time in my hand, felt like a secret weapon. I carried it purposefully toward Diana's office, unlocked the door as if I had every right to, and closed myself inside. Like everything else at the club, the office was plush to the point of being overdone. I stepped across thick, well-cushioned carpet to a chair behind her desk, dropped into it, and wiggled her mouse to wake up the dark computer monitor.

Diana kept a spiral notebook and a file caddy on the corner of her desk, right next to a glorious amethyst geode the size of a basketball. I wanted a look at her papers but forced myself to stay focused. I had no idea where I'd find the camera files on her hard drive or how long they'd take to copy and I wouldn't leave without at least having those. Her screen came to life.

I scanned the Programs folder for software applications that sounded remotely relevant. After a few duds, I found the right package and figured out how to get to last week's files. I decided to copy both Wednesday's and Thursday's footage, just in case. When I clicked on the first one, the screen divided into quadrants with views from various cameras around the club playing in each corner. Tabs at the bottom of the screen let me switch to even more camera views and I was instantly drawn into the activity playing out before me. *Copy now, watch later, Emily. Don't be stupid.*

I plugged my thumb drive into Diana's computer, which she kept under her desk. While the files copied, I pilfered through the papers on her desk. Diana's appointment calendar was as empty as mine and I thought she might be the sort who remembered all her engagements without writing them down. Or maybe she tracked them digitally with one of those fancy phones that does every damn thing. I bristled, annoyed because my own impaired phone had probably been permanently damaged in the morning's downpour.

Diana's desk drawers didn't give up anything juicy until I came to the last one. There I discovered a blue folder with a collection of neatly arranged newspaper clippings inside. Filed in reverse chronological order, the most recent article, a week old, was on top: *Houston's Tone Zone to Open Second Facility.*

Last month, it had been: *Local Health Club Donates $5,000 to United Way*

I flipped through the stack.

April: *Tone Zone Fundraiser Offers 5K/10K Challenge to Area Runners*

March: *Fitness Club Donates Rodeo Scholarship Funds*

January: *Women's Health Club to Open Doors This Month*

August: *Investors Announce Plans for Ladies Gym*

With a steady hand, Diana had meticulously highlighted specific quotations and as I studied them, the complexity of Claire's case skyrocketed. Five investors shared ownership in the club, but neon yellow said Diana only cared what one of them had to say. The quotes she'd highlighted were all ascribed to Wendell Platt, MD.

I chewed on a fake thumb nail and stared at his name.

Plenty of folks had multiple business interests, especially rich people. But, at the surgery center Platt worked with Chris King and at Tone Zone, he worked with King's wife. The arrangement had Triangle written all over it.

I slipped the newspaper articles back into their folder and returned them to the drawer. The files finished copying and I was about to eject the thumb drive when Diana's doorknob twisted.

Almost reflexively, I grabbed the telephone handset and raised it to my ear. Natalie burst inside and, upon seeing me, stopped. I held up an apologetic finger and continued talking to nobody about a car that wasn't broken.

"But yesterday you said I'd have it today," I said. "Am I at least getting a loaner?"

I shook my head at Natalie. She gave nothing back.

After a suitable pause, I muttered insincere thanks and hung up with a huff I hoped wasn't too much.

"Cell's on the fritz," I said. It wasn't a total lie.

"How'd you get in here?"

I shrugged. "Door was open. Seemed as good a place as any to get the bad news."

She regarded me for a moment. "You're not dressed to work-out."

I leaned down, as if to scratch my ankle, and pulled my thumb drive from the computer's USB port. Since I'd taken the drive without the usual "safely remove device" ritual, a familiar error message appeared on the screen and I made a conscious effort not to look at it.

"Hair appointment." Foresight was working for me now. "Thought I'd try a new look."

Natalie couldn't see the screen, but Diana would wonder about the message when she returned. There was no way to close the error box without being seen so I left it there and stood.

Natalie swiped a spiral notebook from the file caddy on Diana's desk, returned to the door, and twisted the little lock in the knob. "After you."

She stepped aside so I could leave first.

Outside on the rubberized track, she closed the door behind us and push-pulled it twice to check that it was locked. She left me behind as she headed downstairs, apparently scurrying back to Diana's meeting. I watched her calf muscles flex as she descended the first few steps. My phone chimed.

It was another text message from Kendra: GET OUT NOW. I flipped the phone shut, pissed.

Chapter Sixteen

Driving to the Heights, I thought about Thursday's security files buried in my purse beside me. A big clue waited somewhere between my sugarless gum and lipstick, but first I owed Richard a report from Platt's neighbors.

My thoughts flitted between three things—how best to approach those interviews, what I'd learn from the security files later, and the faint chemical smell wafting around my head.

My crutch in all things cosmetic—Jeannie—hadn't been there for my impromptu hair make-over, so I'd left all decisions to my stylist, a spiky-headed blond who I wanted to believe had cheekbone implants because she was inhumanly gorgeous. She brought my length up six inches, cut in some sassy layers, and punched up my natural auburn color to a bolder, lustier shade of red. I liked it and wondered what Annette would think.

In front of Platt's bungalow, I unfolded the July page from his office calendar and spread it over my steering wheel, letting the car idle so I could keep the A/C running. His calendar margins were scribbled with phone numbers, some with doodles and others with characters traced over and over until they were thick and dark. A few numbers had names beside them, but not most, leaving me to wonder if maybe this was the place the doctor jotted phone numbers when he retrieved his voice mail.

Through the windshield, I watched a gaunt neighbor water her hydrangea bushes without leaving the front porch. The attachment on her hose sprinkled water in a wide cone that reminded me of my grandmother's old watering can. I turned off my ignition, stepped from the car, and passed a mailbox painted to resemble the Texas flag. Inside its star, "L. Herald" was written in silver glitter glue.

Approaching her, I took care to obey the "Please Stay Off the Grass" signs. When I turned up her front walk, she removed her hand from the nozzle trigger and the flow dwindled to a pathetic trickle.

"Not interested," she said. "No solicitors." Behind her, a posted sign over the doorbell said as much.

"No worries, I'm not selling anything. But I wonder if you'd talk to me about your neighbor, Dr. Platt."

"You a reporter?" She looked me over, spending particular time on my naked legs. "Don't look like a cop."

I tried to put her at ease with a smile, but it had no effect.

"Dr. Platt's family hired me to look into a few things. It seems that shortly before he died, something was troubling him, but we don't know what that was. Do you have any idea?"

She planted her free hand on what would have been a hip had she not been a bean pole. "No."

Her tone, somewhere between insulted and surprised, made me think she was hurt that Platt hadn't confided in her.

She squeezed the trigger on her hose again and immediately a conical spray enveloped the plants. A lawn ornament near her steps caught my eye, a miniature outhouse fashioned to look like a medieval castle.

I decided not to ask.

"How many years have you been neighbors?" I raised a hand to my brow to block the sun.

She moved to the next bush. "Eight."

"Were you friends?"

"Sometimes he helped move my ladder."

My head cocked sideways involuntarily. I forced it back to neutral.

"Tell you what," I said, groping in my bag. "I'll write down my number, and if you think of something that might help us figure out what was troubling Dr. Platt, I sure would appreciate a call."

I carried a slip of paper to her and she took it without looking at me. Holding it at arm's length, she squinted at the print. I turned to leave.

To my back she said, "I used to have a car named Emily. Nineteen seventy-seven Ford LTD II."

Touching. The Ninja Runner had mentioned Platt's kooky neighbor. I wished I could give her a big loud Amen to that.

At the end of the walkway, I turned toward Platt's other next-door neighbor and as I crossed the property line, the old woman shouted after me, "She was the last V8 I ever owned!"

Two doors over, a stately three-story Victorian overshadowed Platt's smaller home. When I rang the bell, a figure moved behind the door's ornate beveled glass, but no one answered. For a moment I doubted what I'd seen. Then interior shadows shifted again and I realized I was being ignored.

I rang again.

On the other side of the door, a figure was nearer now, but still not answering. Jeannie, in the same situation, would have pressed her hand to the glass and gaped inside to see exactly what was going on. I couldn't make myself do it.

A white aura grew larger on the other side of the decorative panes and the knob jangled. Finally, someone cracked the door open about three inches.

I saw a white undershirt, stretched over an impressive paunch, and an eyeball. That was it.

The eyeball, overcast with an unruly brow, scrutinized. Judging by the ruddy complexion and deep lines surrounding it, I guessed its owner to be in his late sixties.

"You're p-pretty." He spoke with a pronounced slowness. "But you're n-not allowed in." His eye was glassy and a little too red in the corners, like maybe he had a cold. Behind him, Patti Page's "The Tennessee Waltz" ended and immediately began again. "My name is William Henry S-Saunders the third."

"Emily Locke."

"The third?"

"No, the first."

He regarded me a moment, then shut the door. The deadbolt thumped.

I tapped on the pane. "William?"

On the other side, his blurry white undershirt rocked back and forth, back and forth.

"Please open the door, William. I won't come inside."

My phone squeaked out a hurt noise, some vague semblance of a ring, and I fished it out and checked the Caller ID, which had only garbled characters.

I flipped it open, rapped on the door again.

"William?" and into the phone, "Hello?"

It was Vince.

I pressed nearer to the door. "My father was a third, William."

"A third what?" Vince sounded amused. "Who's William?"

On the other side of the glass, the rocking stopped.

"I'm trying to coax an interview from William Henry Saunders the third. What's up?"

"You sound stressed."

William opened the door—the same three inches as before—and his single visible eye scowled at my phone.

I flipped it closed. Vince would understand.

"Thanks for coming back," I said.

"What was his n-name?" He hesitated at the beginning of each word, framing it on his lips before his reluctant voice followed.

"Joseph Alan Hennessey the third." Three-fifths true.

"Did he watch f-football?"

I nodded.

"What team?" He pushed "team" out with effort.

Dad had been a lifelong Browns fan. "Oilers."

"Their last game—" it was a struggle for him to get out "last" "—was December 22, 1996. I didn't go." He raised a finger, concentrating. "M-mother's birthday."

"William," I said, "Did you know Dr. Platt, the man who lived next door?" I pointed toward the empty home.

William blinked. "*He* was not a th-third."

"Ever talk to him much?"

William shook his head. "Mr. B. wouldn't like that." His eye scanned the sidewalk behind me. "He w-wouldn't like you either. Strangers aren't safe."

"Who's Mr. B.?"

"He t-takes care of me."

"Is he here? Can I talk to him?"

He studied me. "No."

I wasn't sure which question he'd answered.

"I'm going to write down my phone number for Mr. B., William. Would you give it to him?" I fumbled in my purse again for a pen and paper.

"No."

I looked up from my bag.

"Why not?"

"I'll g-get in trouble for talking to you." He shifted his weight and a Ford Mustang horse logo flashed on the left side of his chest and then disappeared again. I doubted William could drive.

I printed my contact information on a notepad. "Then I'll leave this in the mailbox instead. He can find it later. How's that?" I ripped the sheet from its miniature spiral binding. Another question came to mind.

"Did Dr. Platt have a dog?"

"No. Dogs are loud and they sh-shed and make m-messes in your yard." He paused. "Joseph Alan H-Hennessey the third liked the Houston Oilers."

I smiled. "It was nice to meet you, William. Thank you for talking to me."

He closed the door with no goodbye and turned the dead bolt. I descended the steps, careful of my footing in the unsteady high heels. At the end of the walk, I slipped my note into the mailbox, where I hoped Mr. B. would find it.

A smoky barbecue aroma somewhere on the block gave me dinner ideas. I opened my phone, hoping to catch Vince, but my display was dead.

◇◇◇

The first office supply store I visited didn't have the software package required to open Diana's surveillance files. The second had the right package, plus cookies and punch near the register—a bonus. I passed on the offer to apply for an in-store credit card, but helped myself to a cookie anyway. I even grabbed a couple for Jeannie before paying and going home.

The sun had set an hour ago but summer heat and humidity pushed down hard on me anyway. I swung my apartment door open, cookies in hand.

"Got something here for—"

The cool blast of A/C was divine. But instead of finding Jeannie, I was met by six gray-haired African American women drinking cocktails in my living room. At once, their faces brightened and they rushed toward me, spraying wild colors of silly string.

"Happy Birthday!"

"Surprise!"

It was surprising, indeed. I didn't know a single one of them.

People I hadn't noticed at first, but thankfully recognized, started streaming from my kitchen with wide, goofy smiles. Richard and Linda. Florence, my neighbor. Jeannie. When Annette came barreling around the corner, arms extended, even the sight of Nick and Betsy Fletcher trailing behind her couldn't bring me down.

She leaped into my arms, "Happy Birthday, Emily! We have cake!"

I hugged her close and picked her up. She wrapped her legs tightly around me in a full body kid hug.

"You're home early." I kissed her cheek. She smelled like high-dollar perfume.

"It was a trick," she said. "We were always coming home today so we could be at your party but we told you we weren't coming home until Friday. The cake is chocolate."

I glanced at Betsy, who'd followed her from the kitchen, and mouthed my thanks.

"You smell nice," I said, trying not to sneeze.

"I know! Aunt Jeannie has the *best stuff.* And I *like* your new hair."

With an open palm, she stroked the side of my head as one would pat down a horse. "And your dress," she added. "I *love* pink."

It couldn't have been more than a few hours and she was already talking like Jeannie.

I kissed her again, and she squirmed out of my arms and raced back to the kitchen, where she tugged on Jeannie's sleeve. I nodded to let Jeannie know I'd make my way back there shortly.

My neighbor Florence pushed some kind of apricot brandy drink into my hand. "Hope you don't mind," she said, nodding to the unfamiliar ladies gathered in my living room. "I brought the girls."

She introduced me to her senior citizen Bunko group who, it seemed to me, had already enjoyed a few brandies.

Florence leaned toward me, somewhat conspiratorially. "My friend's been quiet lately."

She was speaking of the ghost that allegedly haunted her shower. This topic always made me uncomfortable. Not believing in ghosts, I couldn't go along with her. Yet I adored her too much to outwardly say I thought she was loopy.

"Maybe he's gone for good."

She took back the brandy she'd given me and raised it to her crimson lips. "Here's to that."

I made my way to the kitchen where Jeannie was kneeling on the floor, penciling in Annette's eyebrows.

"Jeannie." I thumped her on the head. "She's five years old."

"Can't start too early."

"Aunt Jeannie's giving me *definition.*" Annette was careful not to move.

I knelt on the tile beside my friend. "You did all this for me?"

She cut her eyes at me and then returned them to the task at hand. "Yes. And you called me a faker."

The doorbell rang.

I stood to see who it was and Florence opened the door for Vince. He stepped in, removed his cowboy hat, and smiled at me across the narrow living room. The Bunko crowd looked him over and one grinned her approval at me. From behind his back, Vince produced a single red rose and began the short journey around the coffee table to bring it to me, but Annette—eyebrows slightly reminiscent of Mr. Spock—swooped in for the interception.

She took the flower and hugged his leg, then squeezed past me again on her way back to the kitchen, presumably looking for a vase.

Vince squinted at me, confused. "What happened on your head?"

"On my head?"

"Your hair."

"Yeah, I get it. But *on my head*?" He laughed in his infectious, sexy way and I couldn't take offense. "You don't like it?"

His only response was to wink at me. "Great dress."

"Jeannie's Armani."

Vince gave it another look. "You should wear dresses more often." He scooped me into a delicious hug and slipped a second rose into my hand. "I'm getting better at juggling two women."

The faint scent of sawdust lingered on him and I knew he'd left an important job to come to the party. I raised my head and kissed him lightly, thinking that Jeannie was right. It'd been four months since we'd met and I knew he was a keeper. Still, there was Annette to consider. Even less time had passed since I'd met her.

The doorbell rang again and I turned my head in time to see Florence reluctantly admit a very prim and sour-looking Diana King.

Chapter Seventeen

"Why were you in my office?" Diana glared at me across the room. She made no effort to be discreet. "Who let you in?"

The living room quieted.

I stole a quick glance at Jeannie but the oh-shit look on her face told me she'd be no help.

"Needed a phone." I shrugged. "That's all."

She stepped nearer. The heels on her stilettos disappeared into my shag carpet. Florence stayed at the open door, apparently unwilling to close Diana inside.

"That's *not* all," Diana said. "We both know it." The scent of her Danielle Steele perfume enveloped the space around us. It reminded me of Platt's funeral.

I wanted to get her out of there before Annette caught on that something was wrong. "Let's go outside."

Vince touched the small of my back as I stepped toward the door. His simple gesture fortified me.

I followed Diana outside to the landing, curious how much she knew. She was talking before I closed the door.

"You got into my office with a key. Where'd you get it? What were you doing?"

"Where I got it isn't important." I kept my voice level and matter-of-fact, placed a hand casually on the banister railing to give the illusion I was calm.

"The hell it isn't. I'm calling the police."

"To tell them what?"

"That you broke into my office."

"I didn't. I used a key. You just said so."

"A key that you *stole*."

"You gave me that key."

"*What?*"

I shrugged. "Your word against mine. I don't have it anymore. If you want, I'll pay to change the lock."

She looked at me impassively. The key wasn't what was bothering her.

"I went into your office to copy security footage from last Thursday." Maybe frankness would neutralize her. "What can you tell me about those files?"

She blinked and shook her head in visible disbelief. "What would I…Wait a minute." Her expression hardened. "Why Thursday? Who do you work for?"

"Do you know something about Wendell Platt's murder that the police don't?"

"You work for that tramp." She spoke in the defeated way of the exhausted. "That makes me sick."

She turned for the stairs.

"You think she did it then?"

Diana stopped, looked me in the eye. "Of course."

"She thinks it was you."

Diana scoffed. "She'd say anything. She's a liar and a whore." Her tone, calm and smooth, seemed ill-suited to the conversation but consistent with everything else about her. It was ninety-five degrees and, even in a linen dress and with hair loose around her shoulders, Diana's face wasn't even shimmering.

"Did your husband gain anything business-wise when Platt died?"

"I'm not having this conversation." She walked down the stairs, her stride as soft as her voice.

"Or did you?" I said to her back. "Was he a tyrant to work for? Not the nice guy everyone painted him to be?"

She didn't look back, just directed her answer into the thick, sticky night air. "I adored Wendell and so did Chris. That woman will burn in hell."

"Why are you sure it was her?"

She stopped and looked up at me. "The fingerprints, the murder weapon, the e-mails…Frankly, I can't see where there's room for doubt."

"How much do you know about those e-mails?" I asked this as if I had an inkling what she was talking about.

"Enough to know she was off her rocker. An obsessed has-been, pining for a man who'd never give her the time of day."

I chewed on that a moment. "Assume you're wrong about Ms. Gaston and that she's wrong about you. Who else might have had a score to settle?"

I'd have felt a whole lot better about the exchange if I'd had a chance to look at Thursday's videos first. As things stood, Platt's killer might have been standing on my front steps at that very moment, plotting how to break into my apartment later and kill me with a screwdriver.

Diana surprised me.

"Don't come back to the club." She muttered this from what seemed like a far off place in her mind, as if too distracted to put forth much effort. Then she pulled her keys from her purse and walked to her Mercedes in the distracted way of a person who's tuned out her surroundings.

I returned to find Florence and her friends trying to teach Annette the Bunny Hop, though all she wanted to do was spin in circles. Someone had slipped a sequined doo-rag onto her head and applied a crooked line of orange lipstick over her tiny mouth. She looked like a twirling gypsy midget.

I joined Betsy on the loveseat. "Thanks for bringing the dancing queen."

We watched Annette copy Florence's moves. She stomped and swayed off-beat and clapped so eagerly her hands missed once.

"She'll sleep great tonight," Betsy said. I felt her turn to look at me, but pretended not to notice, keeping my eyes on Annette instead.

"What was that about before?" she said a moment later. "With the woman at the door?"

"Just work."

"What are you working on?"

"Richard took a new case. He's helping a defense lawyer try to clear a client."

"Of what?"

I glanced at her, weary. "Homicide. I'd rather not talk about it. It's draining." *Plus, it's none of your business.*

She shifted her weight on the cushion next to me and everything about the motion made me uncomfortable. I feared she was as determined to press the issue as I was determined to drop it.

She started in again. "Please don't take this the wrong way…"

To be polite, I looked at her and forced a tolerant smile, or what I hoped would pass for one. I tried to seem genuinely interested in whatever was coming, but really I wanted her to leave. I wanted everyone to leave. Then I could watch the security footage and try to piece together Diana's role in the whole mess.

"Do you think this is an appropriate line of work?" Betsy wanted to know. "With Annette in the mix, I mean. Seems dangerous."

She had Annette's interests at heart. I knew that. Still, I was so totally jealous of this woman—this imposter my daughter had grown up loving as *Mom*—that anything she said felt like a thinly veiled judgment or criticism.

"It's not in the cards forever," I said, a bit terse. "Right now it pays the bills and the flexibility's a must."

"We know that," she said kindly, and I grew edgy with the knowledge that she was speaking for both herself and Nick now. "It's commendable that you'd sacrifice your career to make more time for Annette."

I didn't consider my hiatus from a career in chemistry to be a sacrifice, but I wouldn't share that with Betsy. She waved for Nick to join us from his post at my kitchen counter. He was using a plastic "spork" to pile blueberry cobbler onto his plate, a chore that required multiple scoops. When he finally finished, he came over.

"Tell her about Steve," Betsy said.

Nick grinned. "The perfect job for you, Emily. Dow Oil and Gas. Buddy of mine has an open position. He'll consider the part-time arrangement too." He used the edge of his spork to try to cut through the cobbler's crust, but it wasn't working. "I'll put you in touch."

I watched his ineffective sawing and wondered what was wrong with me. Nick and Betsy were only trying to help. They were nice people. Too nice.

Maybe that's why they irritated me.

No, I thought. It's not because they're nice. It's because Annette loves them better.

From the front of the room, she squealed. "Mommy, watch me spin!"

Betsy and I both looked. The proud little grin that I loved so much wasn't directed at me.

Richard caught my eye and I knew he wanted to talk about Diana's visit. Before he could bring it up in front of Betsy, I excused myself saying I was thirsty. We met in the dining room— unfortunately only a few steps away from the couch—and I nodded discreetly in Betsy's direction. Richard got it.

"You know anything about e-mails between Claire and Platt?" I asked in a low voice.

Richard, crunching an ice cube from his drink, only shook his head. After swallowing, he asked what I was talking about.

"Diana said that Claire sent a bunch of stalker-like e-mails to Platt. I'm not sure what to make of that. Claire said they'd never met."

"How does Diana know about the e-mails?"

"Suppose Platt told her? It sounds like they were friends." I thought about the missing computers at Claire's house. "Or maybe the police found the e-mails at Platt's house."

"I'd know if that were the case."

My face twisted in doubt I couldn't hide. "We'd like to think so. But you're not a cop anymore. They can't tell you *everything*."

I watched him mentally weigh that.

"All the computers at Claire's house were gone," I said. "If there was evidence she'd been e-mailing Platt, the police would have taken those with a search warrant."

He knew I was right. "I'll see what I can find out."

"Listen, Richard." I looked at my watch. "In about fifteen minutes I'd like you to leave. Make a big production out of it. Tell Linda to do the same thing. Hopefully everybody else will follow you out. I want to clear this place out and look at Thursday's footage from the club."

He looked at his own watch and then stole a glance at the make-shift bar in my kitchen. "No problem."

Annette, fully jazzed on sugar, bee lined between us and Richard stepped back. She ran in the direction of her room and he crunched another ice cube.

"She staying here tonight?" he asked.

I hoped she would. I'd loaned her room to Jeannie for the week, but the nice thing about kids was that they all loved sleeping in forts. Any piece of furniture could be converted.

"We'll see." I glanced at Betsy, still in the same place on my sofa.

Richard picked up on it. "She's *your* kid. Betsy's permission isn't required." When I didn't answer, he made an obscene point of making eye contact with me. "Your kid," he said again.

I hated when Richard got fatherly with me.

"I already told them they could have the week with her. But it was easier to share when I thought they'd be out of town."

Annette barreled from the hallway with one of my cast-off handbags, the crocheted one I knew had checkers and marbles inside. She moved so fast it seemed she'd been launched.

"On second thought," he said, "She's wired. Let her spend the night with them."

I smiled—not at the thought of Nick and Betsy wrangling a hyperactive five-year-old, though that did sound funny—but because I knew she'd crash hard any minute now. Getting her to sleep would be no problem, and I felt a little surge of progress because I'd learned this about her.

"I'll figure something out," I said. "You just worry about your grand exit."

Chapter Eighteen

Despite his best efforts, Richard didn't come through for me, but his wife Linda cleared my small apartment in a matter of twenty minutes. The Bunko crowd was delighted when she offered up the leftover soft drinks and booze. They filled their arms with bottles and cans and shuttled drinks across the landing to Florence's place. I especially liked that Linda managed to rid my kitchen of leftover cake and chips—she knew I didn't like that stuff around. Florence and her tipsy friends moved the party next door and that left us with just the Fletchers.

Feigning interest in Annette's newly-decorated princess bedroom, Linda disappeared with her into the hallway, and when they returned Annette was in her pj's, dragging Georgina the Giraffe at her side.

"Give everybody a hug and kiss goodnight," Linda was saying. "Then go crawl into your beautiful royal bed."

I could have kissed her.

"Just for tonight," I assured Betsy. "She can spend some time with Jeannie while she's in town, and then I'll drop her off tomorrow so you can finish your week together."

This seemed to satisfy her, or else she pretended it did, and Annette said her goodbyes. Nick and Betsy left, and Richard and Linda dutifully followed.

I shut the door behind them and leaned backward on its frame, my hand still on the knob. "That woman is my hero."

We dimmed the lights and settled Annette onto the couch, figuring it was easier to set her up there than to resituate Jeannie, who'd already made herself at home in the princess room. Since Annette was all but asleep, I didn't trouble myself to make a fort.

Behind me, Jeannie cleared a spot for my laptop at the kitchen table. While she booted the machine and opened the software package I'd bought, I lingered on the couch and stroked my baby's hair, happy in the moment's simplicity.

Then Jeannie came around the far end of the sofa, pulled her glittery pink phone from her purse, and plugged it into the charger she'd situated near my TV.

"I think my phone is toast," I said. "It sounds awful and the Caller ID is hosed."

"Still under warranty?"

I nodded.

"Where is it?"

I pointed in the general direction of my purse and she took it upon herself to fish it out, turn it off, and remove the battery. She looked inside.

"Not anymore," she said. "This little sticker is red. It changed from white when the phone got wet. Water damage voids most warranties. Got insurance?" She answered her own question before I drew a breath. "Of course you don't. You're cheap."

"How do you know all this? Been sleeping with a Verizon guy?"

She smiled. "Sprint. I dropped mine in a hot tub and he hooked me up. You can bleach those stickers white again, you know."

"I'm not going to bleach a sticker."

"You can do what Tina did." She took my phone to the kitchen and started opening cabinets. "Put it in uncooked rice. That soaks out all the moisture."

"Pantry," I said. "And that sounds ridiculous." Secretly, I hoped it would work. I didn't want to pay for a new phone.

She found a mixing bowl, dropped in my phone and battery, and poured rice over them. "Worked for Tina."

She brought the bowl to me in the living room and set it on the coffee table in front of me as if were a cracker tray and I were her guest. Then she returned to the kitchen table and hoisted a CD on one finger, her acrylic tip prominently displayed through the hole in its center. "Want me to put this in?" She waggled the disc back and forth.

I turned and nodded, growing drowsy with the powerful urge to scoop up Annette and fall asleep with her. Behind me, Jeannie's nails clacked on the keyboard and the rhythm was strangely hypnotizing.

"Whoa," she said, a moment later. "Rebecca Sleitzer is preggers!"

I turned again, annoyed. She was reading my e-mail.

"What the hell are you doing? Who reads somebody else's mail?"

She looked up, startled, but not finding much anger in my face, she relaxed. "Not my fault. I opened a browser and the default page is your webmail. *Apparently,*" she tisk-tisked, "you leave yourself logged in."

I glared at her. "That doesn't mean 'Read this.'"

She shrugged. "Aren't you glad your friend's pregnant?"

"Is the install finished?"

She minimized the browser and I stood up and joined her at the table. I watched the last steps of the installation and, too weary for the user's manual, clicked on new icons and fumbled through pull-down menus until the files from my thumb drive were successfully loaded. So far I'd located feeds from thirty-one cameras—everything from the parking lot to the indoor pool.

"The place opens at five and Claire found the note around lunchtime...Or, the note could also have been left the day before. I grabbed those files too."

Jeannie yawned. "That's a lot of hours to watch. Do we have to do it all tonight?"

"Don't *have* to," I said, feeling a little badly. This was her vacation, after all. "But I'm itching to see who's on here. You should go to bed. I'll fill you in tomorrow."

She wasn't one to argue for the sake of being polite. Instead, she slipped out of her slingbacks, rolled her ankles, and flexed her toes. "Don't stay up too late."

She walked toward the hall, shoes dangling by straps that were hooked over a finger. Before she shut herself into the bathroom, I stopped her. "Hey."

She leaned back out.

"Thanks for my party."

She gave a thumbs-up and closed the door. Water started running, and I turned my attention to the computer. It didn't take long to get the hang of how the new program worked. The camera feeds were motion-based, so if a period of time passed in which nothing moved, the camera for that zone didn't tape. That made it easier to zoom through all the views, although by about eight o'clock the gym was so busy that somebody was doing something in every nook and cranny.

I started with the camera that overlooked the entrance to the locker room. Women I didn't know came and went at regular intervals. Most had preened for the gym the same way I would for a fancy night out. Even more astonishing, they somehow managed to beautify themselves even *more* after their work-outs. They'd return to the locker room, tired and disheveled, and then emerge again even more crisp and lovely than when they'd arrived. I only recognized Kendra, who'd been working Thursday morning. On multiple occasions, Diana strode through the corridor in her pressed linen dresses—a sunflower print on Wednesday and a violet number on Thursday—but she never went inside, which both comforted and vexed me. By all appearances, Kendra was right and Diana had nothing to do with any note that might have been left in Claire's locker. But, she'd been the easiest explanation for how it could have been left. Now I was left to wonder who among all those other ladies might have done it. If Daniel were involved, he would have to have given the note to one of them.

Then another thought. Perhaps he gave it to somebody at the reception desk, with a message to pass it to Claire. I dismissed it. A desk attendant would have given it to her when she checked in, not dropped it in her locker.

I clicked my fake nails on the table and thought. For lack of a better idea, I ran Wednesday and Thursday's camera coverage of the desk. More trophy wives and debutantes in fitted clothes and high heels. I remembered many of the faces, and outfits, from the locker room camera's view. A startling number of members visited twice a day—early in the morning and again in the evening. When I had more time on my hands, I vowed to come back and figure out what they did there. The petty side of me believed most came for facials and pedicures, not for hard, sweaty work like we Plain Janes did at our affordable local YMCAs.

At any rate, forty-five minutes later I'd gone to a whole lot of trouble for nothing. The footage was a bust and I was worn out. I closed the program.

My webmail application, still open in the background, displayed a new e-mail from an address I didn't recognize.

Stupidly, I opened it. A microsecond later I knew I'd probably invited a virus onto my machine. What I found instead was potentially worse.

Somebody named FastCruzn had left me a one-liner: *Go back to chemistry.*

I might have ignored it, chucked it up a spam message, if not for the very personal reference to the career I'd recently given up.

I stared at it, sufficiently freaked out. How could some crazy person possibly single me out in cyberspace? Immediately, I Googled "find someone's e-mail address" and learned that for $14.95 I could get a list of e-mail addresses, social network results, and current address and phone number listings not only for fourteen Emily Lockes, but for anybody else I damn well pleased.

I closed the laptop and checked that the door to my apartment was locked. Annette, even at five, still felt small in my arms as I lifted her off the couch and moved her to my room. I placed her gently on the bed, no longer willing to sleep apart from her, and changed into my pajamas and brushed my teeth. Then I snuggled in close with her under my comforter, listened to her slow, soft breathing, and fell asleep stroking her smooth, tiny arm with the pad of my thumb. She smelled like frosting.

Chapter Nineteen

"I have so much to say to you, I don't know where to begin."

My tone, two parts irritation and one part flat-out mad, didn't seem to faze Claire. She stared through our dividing pane, phone to her ear, appearing wild-eyed for a moment. The impression passed, and I realized I'd witnessed a transient after-effect of Dr. King's handiwork. When she moved her eyes a certain way, they widened unnaturally. At least his surgeries had left her natural-looking most of the time—not fantastically stretched and rearranged like the celebrities in the news rags. I pulled my eyes away and scavenged in my purse until I found my little notebook.

"More lists?" A slight lilt carried in her voice. I thought she was making fun of me.

I flipped to the page I wanted but didn't look up. "If you won't cooperate for yourself, at least do it for your boys. The games you play will ruin your sons."

Squeezing a nasty jail phone between my shoulder and ear further eroded my mood.

"Games?" Her voice was muffled and far-off, the result of the phone slipping out of place in the crook of my neck. I made a mental note to bring Clorox Wipes to any future jail interviews.

I found the paper I wanted, looked up again. "Tell me about the e-mails you sent to Platt."

She drew her head back, in the way of a person who's heard something strange. "I didn't know him. There were no e-mails."

"Diana King said you e-mailed him a lot. That has to be the reason for the search warrant to take your computers."

She only shook her head. I thought of the bizarre e-mail I'd received the night before and a new question materialized. Computers and search warrants were one thing. Getting a subpoena for e-mail accounts and text messages could take a while.

"It's only a matter of time before they look through your entire e-mail history…sent mail, deleted items. You name it. Anything in there that raises an eyebrow could become a real problem."

Claire ran her thumbnail between her teeth, studying me. I waited to see if she'd talk.

"I don't suppose you've ever been in jail." She swallowed visibly. "There's no modesty here. I have no expectation of privacy anymore. All I care about is getting back out, to my kids. I use Yahoo for my e-mail. My oldest, Josh, set it up. You want to know who I've been e-mailing?" She shrugged. "Log in and see for yourself. The address is ClaireGaston1@yahoo.com. Password's 'new woman,' no caps, no space."

Her candor floored me. I couldn't imagine freely sharing personal information like that—not only the log-in details, but all the messages I was sure to find in her account. I managed a weak thank-you and pressed forward.

"Last night I was at your house when the storm came through," I said. "The roads were impassable and I ended up sleeping there. In the middle of the night, Daniel came home."

"Did you tell him about me?"

I remembered Daniel's pleasure upon learning Claire was in jail. The last thing I wanted was to trigger another outburst.

"He knows the situation," I said. "The police will likely question him today if they haven't already."

"Did he say where he's been?"

"Las Vegas."

She nodded. "He's done that before. Gotten mad and left for a while."

"At least he's alive," I said. "We don't have to deal with the suspicious disappearance of your husband on top of everything else." I glanced at my list, more for something to do than because I needed it. "There were some files in your study. Life insurance policies, retirement portfolios."

I hesitated, hoping she'd take it from there, but she only waited.

"Are there any financial accounts not documented in your filing cabinet? Maybe something you're tracking strictly on-line?"

"I don't understand."

"Almost all the assets I found are listed in Daniel's name. I was hoping you'd tell me that you bank separately and that your portfolios are somewhere else."

"No," she said. "He handles all that."

"Is it possible then that *he* set you up? Maybe he wanted to move money around or hide it somehow before the divorce... to keep you from getting your half."

Her mouth twisted into a tentative frown, a silent Maybe.

"He's greedy and mad," she finally said, "But not that smart. He wouldn't have the first idea about hiding assets."

"Maybe not personally," I said. "But he could get help if he were so inclined. Think he's capable of it?"

"Probably."

"Your being here could give him time to organize a scheme like that."

I watched her mull over my suggestion. That anyone other than Diana might be responsible for her circumstances was clearly difficult for her consider. Still, I could tell she was trying to keep an open mind.

"But Daniel didn't know Dr. Platt. Daniel's no Boy Scout, and I could see him scheming for money, but I really don't think he'd murder for it. Killing an innocent man to get me out of the picture seems a stretch, even for him. "

"As far as we can tell, Diana had no reason to kill Platt either." I remembered my talk with her the night before, and how she'd seemed wounded by his death. "It's something we'll keep working on," I concluded vaguely.

Claire moved the handset to her other ear and smoothed some wayward hair out of the way. Even in a government issued jumpsuit, she was graceful. I consulted my list again, this time because I'd lost my train of thought.

"I found the box in your closet," I said carefully. "I read all the letters. Who is Kevin?"

Her eyes flashed. "That's over."

"Fine, but he wrote you last month so it's still important that I understand who he is."

"You know the type." She flicked her wrist casually, as if swatting a gnat. "Handsome as the devil and just as devious."

Mercifully, I had no experience with the type, but I gave a knowing and sympathetic nod anyway. I remembered Kevin, soaked in Claire's kitchen, and could at least attest to the handsome part. "He seemed very taken with you judging by the letter I read."

Her lips curved into a tired, exasperated smile. "I'm pretty sure he had a wife."

So what? You had a husband.

"You miss him?"

She raised her eyes to look at me. "I miss my *kids*."

"I'll get to them in a sec," I said. "Help me understand the deal with this guy."

Her eyes searched the space above my head like she might find words there. "Things between us clicked. You ever have that with a guy? Where it just *clicked?*"

I nodded.

"But something was off. He paid for everything with cash, even though his wallet was full of credit cards. Never invited me to his place, always stayed at mine. Wouldn't bring me around his friends. Sometimes left his cell off. The whole thing reeked of Wife." She paused for a moment, somber. "I saved that note you found because, for a little while, I thought he was different. Special."

"I met him yesterday. He came to your house when I was there."

"Why? Did he hear about what happened?" A muscle in her hand twitched as her grip on the phone tightened.

This inexplicably worried me. "You still carrying a torch for this guy?"

"No," she said with confidence I didn't believe. "I just told you that."

With effort, I resisted the urge to press further. "He said he was there to feed Logan's snake."

"He wants to keep up his relationship with my boys," she said. "His way of hanging onto me. I should put a stop to that but I feel guilty having another man come in and out of their lives so abruptly."

"I met them yesterday too," I said, more brightly. "They came earlier, before the storm." I was unsure how much to tell her, not wanting to worry her about the teens and cigarettes in the car. "Joshua said they were picking up a few things."

"How'd they look? Did they ask about me?"

"I wasn't sure how much they knew so I said I was on an errand for you. They looked good. They miss you." I started to say more, to question their choice of friends, but thought better of it. She had enough to think about. Nothing good would come of bringing that up now. Besides, my visitation time was limited, and I was running out of it.

I took out Claire's miniature refrigerator calendar with all its encrypted initials and asked her to walk me through their meanings. With the phone wedged between my ear and shoulder again, I held the little calendar to the glass with my left hand, and took notes with my right. We started with May.

"M is Marcus and K is Kevin," she said. "I had a little overlap between those two, if you know what I mean. Show me June."

"Who's Marcus?" I flipped the page.

She waved the name off. "A fling I hardly knew. Harmless." She squinted at her notes for June. "J is my massage therapist, Judy. K is Kevin again, and P is Pat."

"Male or female?"

"Female. Why?"

"Not sure. Who's Pat?"

"Friend from the club. We have drinks sometimes. Let's see July."

I turned the page again. July was sparsely populated because we were only in its second week. Claire tapped the dividing glass with her nail as she named each person.

"Pat and Judy again, and KT is Kathy Taylor—her divorce was final in April and she's been a good listener. These people are all friends, Emily. Don't waste your time."

I tapped my pen on the counter, thinking. Then I flipped to a new page in my notebook. "I'd like to make a list. Tell me the names of all the people who can get into your house."

She looked as if I'd asked for the square root of six thousand.

"Start with family."

She exhaled. "This might be hard."

"How so?"

"Four of us live there. We all know a lot of people."

"Right, but we're only talking about the ones who have access to the home."

She gave the confounded stare again. I set down my pen. "Talk to me."

"I don't know all the people. There's my mother, of course, and the maid. Our neighbor has had the key before, but only when we've been away. It's the copy I use as the hide-a-key now."

I jotted some notes.

"Josh and Logan go without saying," she said, "but I assume they haven't shared keys with anybody. They each have a copy but I can't imagine why they'd have duplicates made. I'm not sure they'd even know how to go about it."

"How about Daniel?" I said. "Has he shared copies?"

"I've been disconnected from Daniel for a long time. I have no idea what he does." As if worried the answer were unsuitable, she added, "When our marriage died, we stopped asking questions."

I drew a breath, wanting to follow up, but I knew that challenging her judgment would solve nothing.

"You're saying that besides your family, housekeeper, and parents, it can't be said with certainty how many individuals might have access to the home because Daniel is a wild card."

"Right." Her voice, softer now, was all regret.

I started collecting my things. "Thanks for your honesty, and for letting me go through your stuff. Later I'll check out your e-mail, try to get to the bottom of that."

She forced a smile. "When this is over you'll probably write an exposé."

"I'll start with the rats in your freezer."

She dropped her head into her free hand, embarrassed.

"Hang in there," I said. "We're doing everything we can."

She raised her eyes again, glistening now, and I knew she wouldn't speak. I nodded and hung up. As I turned to leave she started to break down. I'd breached so many of her personal boundaries already, but this was a privacy I could afford to let her keep. So I left the little visitation chamber without looking back.

Chapter Twenty

The day was so insanely hot that wavy translucent forms radiated upward from the blacktop around me, playing tricks on my eyes. There was no mistaking the envelope wedged underneath my driver's side wiper blade, though. It bore my name in thick, blue marker and was not only sealed, but taped shut.

I scanned the jail's quiet lot, mostly occupied with county vehicles and police cars, and didn't see anyone suspicious. In an adjoining field several hundred yards off, an unsupervised trustee in an orange jumpsuit like Claire's was cutting the grass on a riding mower—no fences. He made me nervous as hell.

I pulled the envelope from my windshield and opened it. Inside I found a key fastened to a cheap metal ring with a paper tag attached. It took me a minute to recognize the address printed on the label. Other than the key, the envelope was empty.

Who would have left me a key to Platt's bungalow, and why here?

I unlocked my car and leaned in to start the ignition, but I waited, one foot propped in the door frame before climbing inside. Better to let the super-heated interior come down a few hundred degrees first. Meanwhile, I studied the unfamiliar handwriting on the key's label. Maybe this was a trick, some kind of ruse to get me inside Platt's house the same way Claire had been lured there. But then what? Would someone be waiting inside? I thought about last night's strange e-mail and didn't like the idea of following a mysterious lead to an empty house. It wasn't a protected crime scene anymore but might become one again if I didn't watch out.

When the temperature inside the Taurus was tolerable, I headed across town to meet Jeannie and Annette for an early lunch at a family-style buffet that Annette favored. My phone squawked its sick noises again—someone wanted to talk to me, but the water-damaged display provided no clue about who that person was. Obviously, Jeannie's rice treatment had been a bust.

It turned out to be Richard. "What was in the envelope?"

"How'd you—"

"Did you know you were being followed?"

I tried to catch up. "You had me followed?"

"Not you." He chuckled. "Diana. I have a guy on her, remember? And he said Diana spent this morning watching an apartment. When he gave me the address of that apartment— yours—I knew something good was coming."

"That's creepy." I wanted to tell him about the e-mail, but I could tell he wasn't finished.

"When he told me Diana followed a redhead to the county jail, I got worried she might confront you again."

"She didn't."

"I know. She left a note on your windshield and drove away. What'd it say?"

"I'll show it to you later," I said. "Right now I'm in some heavy traffic here and I need to hang up."

The white lies came easily. I needed to think about whether to tell Richard about the key.

◇◇◇

"Why keep it under wraps?" Jeannie smoothed honey butter over a home-style dinner roll and passed it to Annette. "This is big news. Richard would want to know."

"He'd never let me use it."

"Why the hell not?" She glanced at Annette, an afterthought, and made an apologetic face at me for swearing. Then she dumped a package of sweetener into her iced tea and stirred it with a finger.

Annette was too busy peeling off pieces of richly buttered bread to notice Jeannie's linguistic slip. She folded a bite of the roll onto her tiny tongue and chewed, oblivious.

"If Richard breaks the law he could lose his license. He might be fined or sanctioned," I said. "Or even go to jail. I'm not telling him about the key."

"I'm confused. How would he be breaking the law?"

"Entering a house without consent."

"Consent's impossible," Jeannie said. "The owner's dead."

"*Somebody's* the custodian of that property now. Without that person's permission, going inside is breaking and entering. Even with a key."

"No it's not."

Yes, it is, I wanted to say, but with Jeannie there was no point in arguing, so I sipped my ice water instead.

"You planning to go alone then?" she asked. "That doesn't seem very smart."

"Not sure."

"I'll go with you," she said. "For insurance." Then she snapped her fingers, remembering. "Damn. It's usually in my handbag but stupid airport security…I feel naked without it."

"You feel naked without airport security?"

"No. Without my Ladysmith."

Annette perked up. "What's a Ladysmith, Aunt Jeannie?"

"It's…kind of like a super soaker, kid. Only instead of getting a person wet, it stops him cold." She stabbed a piece of chicken fried steak onto her fork. Then to me, she added, "Nine millimeter."

"I want a nine millimeter!" In her excitement, Annette said this loud enough to draw a look from the next table.

I glared at Jeannie. "I don't like guns. Even when they're toys."

Annette's enthusiasm dampened and I caught Jeannie giving her a look I didn't fully understand—the kind that suggested the conversation wasn't over.

"No guns, water or otherwise," I said to them both, by way of clarifying. I was glad she'd had to leave her weapon behind in Ohio, otherwise it would likely be getting passed around the dinner table now.

"Hey," Annette said, the final bite of dinner roll having disappeared into her mouth. "Now can I go to the dessert bar?"

Her plate was still full of veggies and chicken. Jeannie looked at me expectantly, clearly bursting to spoil my daughter. I reminded myself that she wasn't in town that often and that everything was okay in moderation. They pushed their chairs back the instant I gave the nod, and Annette led the way to a tall stack of clean plastic plates. I watched them ogle a spread of cobblers, pies, cookies, and cakes and then I looked away, fearing the impending sugar buzz.

Annette came back with two cookies and a heaping bowl of vanilla ice cream with a side dish of Gummi Bears. She dumped the bears into the ice cream and stirred tirelessly until it melted into some kind of smoothie. "See what I'm doing?" she asked Jeannie. "Like this."

And Jeannie, who'd brought an identical compliment of goodies on her own tray, first copied Annette, then sampled the frozen treat, and finally pronounced my daughter a culinary genius.

"Think you two can manage without me for a few more hours?" I asked. "I have a little more work to do."

Jeannie squinted at me, her suspicion obvious.

"Don't worry," I said. "I won't go alone. I'll take Vince."

"He's funny." Annette set down her spoon. She pulled her lower eyelids down and pushed the tip of her nose up as far as it would go. "He showed me how to do this." She looked back and forth so that her eyeballs went to the extreme left and right sides of their sockets. As I took in the capillaries and stared up her nostrils, it seemed everyone I knew was conspiring against me where raising this child was concerned.

"Don't do that," I said. "Your face might get stuck that way."

Annette laughed. "My dad says that too."

He never had a chance to.

"Only that's when I flip my eyelids inside out like this." She started to demonstrate, but I tapped her arm.

"Not now, sweetheart. People are eating."

She picked up her spoon again, suddenly self-aware, and returned to her ice cream.

"Sure, Em." Jeannie used the edge of her spoon to isolate a trio of Gummi Bears. "We've got it all under control. Say, does Vince have a…super soaker?"

Annette giggled.

"No."

"Shame. He's almost perfect."

I laid some bills on the table and got up to prepare a To Go box for Vince. Pulling that cowboy off an important job would be tough, but my few experiences with him had indicated that all things were possible with the right combination of "fixins."

Chapter Twenty-one

"This is trouble if I ever saw it." Vince pulled a handkerchief from the back pocket of his jeans and wiped sweat from his face. He stared through my open window to the Styrofoam box sitting on the passenger seat next to me. "What are you doin' to me, woman?"

I squinted up at him. The midday sun beat down on both of us, but whereas his Stetson shielded his eyes from the glare, I took it straight on the retinas. "You busy?"

I knew he was.

"We're gonna finish framing this today." Behind him, another cookie-cutter house in the latest master planned community had begun to take form. I didn't like the uniformity of the floor plans or the way new neighborhoods were laid out in barren fields with seedling trees. The homes on this street, each in different stages of assembly, all looked drearily homogenous and devoid of personality.

He leaned closer to my window and, even though he was dripping sweat, I hoped for a kiss. "Do I smell green beans?"

I cut my eyes toward the box. "Maybe."

"Well now we're talking. Let's have 'em."

"Here's the thing." I popped the top on the Styrofoam and let him take inventory. Sirloin, green beans, mashed potatoes with dark gravy, two rolls, and...

"Gummi Bears?"

"From Annette."

He smiled. Lord, I loved that smile.

"But I need a favor. Can you get away for an hour? Eat in the car?"

He reached into the car and grabbed a few green beans, then turned without explanation back to the house-in-progress and walked away. He tossed his head back to chuck the beans into his mouth, and veered toward two men in hard hats who were examining a blue print at one corner of the lot. It was always a treat to watch Vince walk away, especially in worn, dusty old jeans.

I rolled up my window to keep the air conditioning. A moment later, he returned and climbed in the passenger side. I gave him my sweetest, you-are-so-good-to-me face. He made the same face right back at me, his version more sarcastic than sincere.

"You're making fun of me."

"Just a little." He winked, grabbed the seatbelt without looking. As soon as its buckle clicked into place, he took the plastic silverware from my console and tapped the lid on a sweaty thirty-two ounce Coke in the cup holder. "This mine too? I'm afraid to ask where we're going."

He started to eat and I filled him in.

"So you're not taking Richard because he wouldn't go inside?"

"Right."

"But you think Diana might be Platt's killer?"

"Maybe."

"And you know for sure she's the one who left you this key."

"Yes."

"So it might be a trick."

"Correct."

"And my part in all this is what?" He laughed. "Protection?"

"That's not reassuring."

"You said it's breaking and entering even with a key."

"Yes, because I don't have permission to use it."

"So if we get caught we'll get in trouble?"

"Yeah."

"Trouble. I knew it as soon as I saw the food."

"You don't have to search with me. Just help me make sure the house is empty first. Please?"

I took his silence as an unspoken yes. For several miles, he sat quietly and ate, working his way, one at a time, through each divided section of the Styrofoam box. First the meat, then the potatoes and beans. When he was on the first roll, he stopped and turned suddenly toward me.

"Hey," he said. "What if you find something in there?"

"That's the idea."

"No. I mean, if you find something, you'll have to tell Richard where it came from."

"Depends."

"When you say where it came from, you'll have to explain how you got in the house."

"Sometimes it's better not to tell him stuff."

"Sometimes it is." He tapped his chest, indicating a scar I knew was underneath his damp, gritty work shirt. A few months ago, he'd taken a bullet, arguably the result of another time I'd withheld information from Richard.

I didn't answer him but my eyes must have given me away. He stroked the hand I'd been resting on the gear shift. "You know that's not what I meant. I meant that I don't want it to happen to you."

I opened my hand, palm up, and he intertwined his fingers with mine. I loved his purposeful, deliberate grip. We didn't let go until I pulled into Platt's driveway.

"Here goes nothing." I turned off the car. We walked up Platt's carefully painted front steps and let ourselves inside, assuming the use of our key would assuage the worries of any curious onlookers.

The house reeked.

Its air conditioning had been turned off, leaving the place stuffy and grotesquely hot. I didn't know in which room Platt had been killed, but I hoped the sickening odor of violence I smelled wouldn't worsen as we got deeper into the house.

"No one's hiding here," I said. "Too foul." I closed the front door.

Vince casually peeked into a coat closet on our left anyway. He flung the door open wide to show me its contents—sports jackets on hangers, wing tips neatly paired below.

Platt's furnishings were decades old but, like the cottage itself, impeccably maintained. The stoic feel of hardwood floors was softened somewhat by a large oriental area rug he'd chosen for the front room. Opened letters waited on the oiled surface of a walnut coffee table and I skimmed the envelopes, all utility bills.

A sofa and chairs lined the perimeter of the expansive rug, the sofa facing the front door and the chairs angled in near the corners. The chairs, I thought, hadn't been used much but the sofa cushions had wear marks in their centers. Throw pillows crowded the left end of the couch, one wedged between the armrest and seat. A smallish flat screen TV had been mounted on the opposite wall. I imagined Platt winding down on the sofa after a long day and wondered if his had been a lonely life or one of intentional solitude.

An ornamental mirror and two nondescript paintings decorated the walls, but I found no portraits, which struck me as a little sad. Then, on an end table, I spotted a framed 8x10 wedding picture of Platt and his late wife, who'd been mentioned at his memorial service. The photograph added the only real personality to his otherwise utilitarian living room.

Ahead of me, Vince roamed toward the kitchen and dining areas, two narrow, connected rooms running left to right across the back of the house. I noticed the back door Claire had used a week ago when this whole affair had started, and tried to picture her hesitantly pushing the door open, calling for a dog that didn't exist. Black fingerprint dust remained along the doorframe and knob, probably forgotten among the more obvious cleaning priorities.

Vince opened the pantry and found only canned vegetables and the usual staple foods.

"Come on." I headed for the hall.

The little bungalow had only two bedrooms and a single bath. I looked under the bed in the first room while Vince stuck with checking the closet. As expected, nobody was there.

Across the hall, a smaller room facing the street served as a simple, no-frills home office. The centerpiece, a plain wooden desk, faced the only window and, although a keyboard and mouse pad had been left, his computer was absent.

On the other side of the glass, my old Taurus baked outside in the drive. I was glad I'd remembered to leave its windows down.

Platt's bookcases held more papers than books and his walls were bare except for a deep beige coat of paint. When I noticed the dark smear stain on the floor planks, I stopped, feeling strangely more determined.

Platt hadn't left legions of friends and loved ones behind to rally for the truth about his murder. Everyone assumed his killer had already been caught. I'd come to the investigation aiming to clear an innocent mother, wanting foremost to reunite her with her kids. Standing where Platt had died strengthened my resolve. Not only did Claire's boys deserve their mom, Platt deserved justice.

Being near his personal things moved me. Walking his floors, seeing his wingtips, I knew a simple man had lived here. Near as I could tell, he'd kept to himself any time he wasn't out helping people.

"Bathroom's clear too," Vince said, stepping into the room. I hadn't noticed he'd left. "What now?"

I turned to him, sickened by the lingering smell of washed-up blood and sorrowful for a man I'd never met. "I have to figure out who did this to him."

He stole a glance at his watch. "Eighteen minutes. I'll take the bedroom."

I watched him turn and leave. In three strides, he was in the room across the hall.

I started with the desk. Its top drawer was for pens, pencils, and sticky pads. The middle was for a stapler, tape dispenser, and spare computer mouse with a cord so tightly wound around itself that it was disturbing. And the bottom contained extra printer paper. At my own desk, all these items would have been crammed into a single drawer.

His closet was equally neat. Instead of jackets and shoes like we'd found in the foyer, this one was filled with the components of a model train set. A plywood base rested on-end against the closet's wall. The shelves were stacked end-to-end with small, meticulously arranged boxes containing individual rail cars. Segments of track, capable of snapping together in interchangeable patterns, were nestled in an opaque Rubbermaid tub at the foot of the plywood base. And that was it. There were no rolls of wrapping paper jammed in the closet's darkest corner, no forgotten knock-around shoes, and no board games. There wasn't even a winter coat for Houston's fluke cold days. Just trains.

Apparently, Dr. Platt didn't believe in Miscellaneous. Even the papers on his bookcases were categorized: back issues of professional journals, Xeroxed articles, manuscripts in-progress, and sheet music for an instrument I hadn't yet determined.

As I was about to give up on the room, I caught sight of his phone. It was a standard cordless model made to stand upright in its base while charging. The display said READY and its prominent capital letters got me thinking. I lifted the handset and pressed the Caller ID button with my thumb. Forty calls were in the log. I helped myself to a pen out of Platt's top drawer, a sheet of paper from his third, and got busy writing down names and numbers. When a repeat entry appeared, I kept track by adding checkmarks.

"Found something here," Vince called from the bedroom.

I noted the final entries from the log, folded my list, and tucked it into the back pocket of my shorts. Across the hall, Vince waited in a reading chair that occupied the far corner. A manila folder was open on his lap.

"You're going to want to take these." He indicated the stack of papers inside the folder. "There's no time to read them here."

I didn't like the idea of removing property, but Vince was right. We'd run out of time.

Then I noticed something on the end table next to Vince's chair. "I know that geode." It was impossible to miss.

He turned. Prominently displayed on the nightstand between Platt's bed and armchair was an enormous amethyst identical to the one I'd seen at the club.

"The other half's in Diana's office."

Vince pulled open the drawer in the same end table. It was empty.

"This is where I found the folder. It's full of letters from Diana."

My shock must have been visible.

"Old letters," He added, quickly. "From back in the eighties."

I couldn't wait to see them. Probably sensing as much, Vince snapped the folder closed and stood to leave. "Later," he said. "I have to get back to the site."

We backtracked through the short hall and were nearly through the kitchen when I noticed a neglected fish bowl in Platt's recessed window sill. Olive algae adhered to the sides of the little bowl and a red Betta fish hovered in the murky water, probably afraid to move and stir up any funk. I imagined the poor guy hadn't eaten for days. I crossed to the window and lifted the bowl, figuring there was no sense losing two lives in that house.

My car was obnoxiously hot despite its open windows. I settled behind the wheel and passed the bowl to Vince. Ahead, William Saunders' automatic garage door lowered. I didn't figure William had a driver's license, so that meant his caregiver Mr. B. was probably home and that I'd missed him again. Mentally, I started to prioritize a growing list of people to call and ideas to follow-up, but my focus was lost when my phone squawked to indicate a new voicemail. This was a surprise because the phone hadn't rung.

The message from Richard was so distracting that for a moment I stopped blaming him for ruining my phone.

"We should talk," he'd said. "Diana King is named in Platt's will."

Chapter Twenty-two

I didn't feel like returning Richard's call.

I dropped Vince off, killed the radio and drove away in silence. The chatter in my head was overwhelming again, demanding that further input of any kind be stopped—whether that was the Top Forty on my radio or Richard's theories about Claire's case. *All rooms full,* my brain said. *Try again later.*

Bothered, edgy, and physically tense, I wondered what was wrong with me.

On autopilot, I turned toward the YMCA and, when I realized my mistake, I figured my subconscious was trying to tell me something and decided, for once, to listen to it.

It was almost two o'clock, way too hot for an outdoor run, but I did have a swimsuit, cap, and goggles in my trunk. The mindless repetition of dozens of laps would free me to think. Exercise, I knew, would bring me out of my worsening mood.

The pool turned out to be packed. In the shallow end, kids tossed diving sticks or clung to kickboards. Four lane ropes had been removed to make room for a water aerobics class—all stocky grandmothers, near as I could tell. Two lanes remained, both occupied, but I knew the etiquette for sharing. I lowered myself into a lane, disappointed to find the water temperature almost as warm as a bath.

I stretched my latex cap around my head and pushed my ponytail underneath it. My goggles, scratched since the day Annette had commandeered them as space-explorer lenses, were tinted and water tight. Wasting no time, I pressed them over my eyes and submerged. My feet got a strong push off the wall, and I headed out for Lap One, which I'd decided would be devoted to Platt's fish.

Nobody had questioned my walking into the gym with a fish. I didn't want him to boil in the car, so I'd carried him inside and put him in my locker, along with my purse and clothes. Fish, I figured, would be neither claustrophobic nor afraid of the dark so he shouldn't mind. There'd be time to clean the bowl before Jeannie and Annette got home from their movie. I hoped the surprise pet would earn some points.

My breathing found its rhythm and I began to reach longer on my stroke than usual, really working on stretching out my back muscles each time. I gave myself over to the buoyancy of the pool and let my head relax. The muscles in my neck relaxed too. It was quiet in the water. Except for bubbles when I exhaled, the pool was silent. I started to form a list.

Webmail. Later that day I'd explore Claire's e-mail history. If possible, I'd do it without Jeannie reading over my shoulder proffering her wild theories.

Old letters from Diana. Diana and Platt may have been lovers thirty years ago or as recently as last week. Did it matter either way?

Platt's will. She'd been named in his will, so maybe it did matter. If Platt had left her a large sum, and if she'd known beforehand, maybe she killed him for the money.

His Caller ID log. Making cold calls to a bunch of strangers didn't excite me—I was fairly sure I'd botch it—but unless I wanted to bring Richard into the mix, this job would fall to me. The prospect would be less frightening if I could assume all the people on the list already knew he'd died. What worried me was ringing up those who had no idea.

Mr. B. Even as my tension surrendered to the work-out and mental clarity made its slow return, I knew I should have gone back to Mr. B's house instead of coming to the pool. He'd been home this afternoon and I'd passed up a perfect opportunity to approach him. There was no guarantee he'd have anything useful to offer, but I berated myself for not following through. Mr. B was a lingering stone I meant to turn.

My spooky e-mail. Learning someone's e-mail address was neither difficult nor expensive, but last night's e-mail put me on high alert anyway. If someone from last spring's ordeal were involved in this case, no matter how remotely, through an association with Mick Young, it was possible I was dealing not with a single menacing criminal but with a network of them. I wanted to believe I was being paranoid, but if I'd learned anything from working with Richard, it was not to underestimate paranoia. I lost count of my laps thinking about that e-mail.

Then two girls ducked under the lane ropes to cross the pool and my rhythm was broken. I stood and moved to the wall, watching them, and took a moment to catch my breath. My own little girl would be their size in a couple years. With a strange mixture of shame and regret, I realized she was also on my list.

Annette. I pushed off the wall and resumed. The world fell silent again except for my breathing. The *world*, I remembered, was twenty-five thousand miles in circumference. I pictured my daughter and me on the Earth, only a few feet apart. Rather than close our gap by walking toward each other, it seemed we'd head opposite directions and meet thousands of miles later, clear on the other side of the planet. Loving her, I feared, would always mean taking the long way.

My apartment smacked of acetone and I knew Jeannie had given Annette a full-service manicure, pedicure, or both. I was relieved to find her note: *At movies. Back for dinner.* It meant I still had a few hours to deal with Diana's old letters, Claire's e-mail, and Platt's call list.

I took care of the nasty fish bowl first so Annette would come home to a cheerful pet. Then I set it next to me at the kitchen table, among used-up cotton balls and assorted nail polish bottles, and booted up my laptop. Logging into another woman's e-mail account felt vile.

I typed "Wendell Platt" into the search box and nothing came up. That didn't necessarily mean anything though, because everyone seemed to use some form of alias these days. With millions of people using these free accounts, any given name was likely already taken. I tried variations but nothing hit.

For good measure, I scrolled through her Sent and Deleted folders and read an exhaustive series of messages, but nothing to or from Platt. I checked her Contacts list and it was equally useless. If she'd ever e-mailed him, the messages had been purged. It'd take a subpoena to pull them off Yahoo's servers.

I weighed Diana's statement that Claire had been pining after Platt, haranguing him with e-mails. She'd either tried to mislead me or she hadn't. I was more bothered by the possibility she'd told the truth. Claire denied ever having written Platt, a claim her e-mail history supported, and I believed her. If Diana believed otherwise, her information had come from *somewhere* and the only sources I could think of were Platt or someone in the HPD. So either I was a fool or someone was spreading rumors.

Taking that a step further, it didn't make sense that Platt would tell Diana about e-mail messages that didn't exist. The only reason to do that would be to garner sympathy or jealousy and Platt seemed too mature for either. That left someone involved with the investigation. If a detective had leaked this information, I could hardly draw a conclusion. I'd heard of officers holding information back from the public, but I didn't think they ever leaked false details. That was a question for Richard.

I dismissed the remaining possibility, that Claire had known Platt after all and did, in fact, e-mail him. By all indications, she was an adept liar, but my operating assumption was that she wasn't lying to *me*. It didn't fit that a guilty person would offer full run of her house and free access to her e-mail account. Most *innocent* people wouldn't do that.

Then it occurred to me that she might have multiple e-mail accounts. Perhaps she'd offered up access to one that was clean. The house, too, could have been volunteered for my search if she knew that nothing inside would be linked to the crime.

I studied the Betta and envied his grace. The Claire-Diana-Chris love triangle, squirrelly history between Diana and Platt, and unsettling e-mail from the night before squelched my second-guessing. No, no, and *no*, I told myself. Claire was not lying. Something fishy was going on, and not just in the bowl beside my keyboard.

I moved on to Diana's letters, struck by the difference in how Claire and Platt stored their special papers. Claire had stashed hers in an elaborate curio box lined with purple velvet, probably an antique. Platt had opted for a twenty-one-cent office folder.

Reclined on my sofa, legs stretched, I made my way through Diana's old notes.

September 19, 1981

¡Hola, Wendell!

Today I saw El Palacio Real, The Royal Palace, and it was indescribable. There are 2,800 rooms!

Afterward I stopped for lunch. I understand so little of the menus here. The waiter said I could have "un hamburguesa con potatos" and I thought it was weird that the Spanish put potatoes on their hamburgers but, since I want to give new foods a try, I said okay. When the meal came, it was a burger and fries.

It would have been so much funnier with you. I think about you every day, always moving backward in time seven hours from whatever I'm doing. When the burger and fries came, your alarm clock was about to go off. Last night, when I walked the bustling streets, I knew your workday was only halfway over. At midnight when I turned in, I imagined you at your little stove, fixing dinner. Probably something out of a can. Baked beans?

Please write soon. I miss you.

Love,
Diana

September 21, 1981

Hi Wendell,

Today was our last day of fun before we start gearing up for the show. We spent it in Toledo, about fifty miles from Madrid. I went inside my first cathedral. There were spires and carvings in the stone, and there was a beautiful tower clock. No pictures were allowed inside. I thought of you and how you always said that "No Flash Photography" rules are scams to make people buy stuff in gift shops. Maybe so. I got you a little something, so the scam worked.

Heard from my father. Fall semester's underway and he still worries I'll never go back to school and make something of myself. Would love to phone and talk to you about it...I resist only because I promised. Tomorrow morning we'll catch a train to Barcelona. Pasarela Gaudí kicks off the day after tomorrow. Models could tell my dad that being in this show proves I've made something of myself, but I don't suppose he'd value their opinions. What could a bunch of pretty young girls who've never been to college possibly know?

Will try to write from Barcelona, but my days are about to get really tight. Back in the U.S. in just over a week. Can't wait to see you.

Love,
Diana

Similar letters came that year from Milan, Paris, and London. It wasn't clear from her notes how long Diana had been jet-setting the globe in the name of high fashion, but she was certainly committed to make the most of her travels, often describing the landscape and buildings in great detail. In 1981 she'd have been in her early twenties and I was impressed such a young woman would expend as much effort as she had to absorb every morsel of the world that she visited. I tried to imagine her then—energetic and hopeful, more worldly than most women twice her age. Platt, only a few years older, had probably been in medical school during Diana's burgeoning modeling career. There was no indication how or when they'd met, but it was probably a safe assumption that any man who knew Diana back then never forgot her.

June 24, 1983

The Space Shuttle Challenger landed out here in California today. You used to give me so much grief about my travel. Well, how about that Sally Ride? Two and a half million miles in six days. My hero!

Same stuff here…still living out of suitcases and racking up frequent flyer miles. If you're ever in L.A. look us up. Hope you and Melissa are well.

Best,
Diana

The lines had been scrawled on a postcard with progressively-shrinking characters until she'd run out of room. Her closing sentences wound across the bottom of the card and up the right side until they blended with his address. I stared at the phrases "look us up" and "you and Melissa" and wished I had information that would bridge 1981 to 1983. The last item in the stack was a Christmas card. Two black bears in sweaters hauled a decorated tree into their den.

December 14, 1985

Fair warning, I'm moving back to town after New Year's, this time as a divorced woman. Save your speeches, I've heard them all from my father.

I read about the new practice, can't say I was surprised. No one deserves it more than you. When I get back to Texas I hope we'll catch up. Plus I want a nose job and could use your opinion.

Happy Holidays,
Diana

Maybe it was the fresh sting of divorce, but the tone of the card sounded more like the Diana of today. The mid-eighties were possibly when Diana's nature deteriorated from exuberant to prissy. I thought this was a shame.

What did it mean that Platt had saved these notes? Had she sent more that he hadn't kept, or was this it? Plenty of folks kept boxes upon boxes of worthless, forgotten crap in their attics or basements. Ask them what was in any given box and they never knew without opening it.

But this wasn't the case with Platt. His home was Spartan and crisp, organized to a fault. He didn't accidentally keep anything, and that worried me. For thirty years and through a marriage, he'd saved Diana's letters—maybe hidden them—and then had kept them in a safe spot, reserved only for them, until the end. Why?

I stacked them neatly and returned them to their folder, then pulled his phone log list from my purse. I skipped what appeared to be business calls—those from places like Baylor College of Medicine, a local music store, Tone Zone, and Purple Heart. Of course, the Tone Zone calls might have been Diana calling, but if that were so, then calling that number back wouldn't get me anywhere anyway. That left a list of sixteen personal calls.

I needed to figure out an excuse to use when I called these people. Some might not even know Platt was dead. Contacting them, probing for their history with him, would require delicacy and tact—scripts that, for me anyway, required a few drafts.

I went to my kitchen junk drawer. Platt would have frowned at the Chap Stick, luggage tags, burned out night lights, freebie magnets, expired coupons, and spare guitar strings I shoved aside before finding a notepad and pen.

One problem was settling on a verb. *Passed* or *passed away* were softer than *died, was murdered,* or *was killed.* Yet, it was important to be direct. I was looking into a homicide—*That's good,* I thought, *Write that down*—and I didn't figure homicide investigators sugar coated things. Homicide, though? I'd scale it down and simply say I was looking into a "death." I corrected it on my paper.

A work-sponsored course in Effective Communication had once reinforced what intuition told us anyway, that bad news should be preceded by a tip-off. *I have something difficult to tell you... We need to talk... I think you should sit down...*

I scribbled a list of openers and summarily rejected each one. They seemed more appropriate for bailing out on a blind date than for breaking news like this.

When it was as good as I could make it, I placed the first call. An answering machine picked up and I panicked, my thoughtful preamble now all for nothing.

"My name's Emily Locke," I said, struggling for a graceful transition to the next sentence. "I'd like to speak to you about Wendell Platt." I hoped this individual knew enough of the circumstances to respond. "If you could call me back..." I fumbled through my phone number and hung up, frustrated. It hadn't occurred to me to prepare a separate spiel in case of answering machines.

As I was dialing the next number, the doorbell rang.

I replaced the phone in its stand and surveyed the room to make sure everything case-related was tidied up. I slipped my list of phone numbers into the folder with Diana's old letters and crossed the room. The last thing I needed was a string of questions from Florence about my week's adventures in "private detecting."

It was Richard, though. "You're not answering your phone."

His short-sleeved button-up and crisp Dockers did nothing to disguise his malaise. Like everyone else who spent any amount of time outside, Richard's weary posture and flushed complexion underscored one truth: July beat down Texans indiscriminately, whether natives like him or transplants like me. I ushered him into my foyer, not to be polite but to keep my A/C inside.

"My phone hasn't worked right since I got stuck in yesterday's monsoon," I said. "That's work-related damage. You want to reach me? Replace my phone."

Without invitation, he made for the kitchen, pulled open my refrigerator, and extracted two bottles of Sparkletts, apparently both for him. The first went down in two passes. He sat at my kitchen table in the same chair I'd used while searching Claire's mail. I leaned on the arm of my sofa, facing him.

"I'm not kidding," I said. "I'm buying a new one today, as soon as you leave, and you're going to pay me back."

"Platt's Uncle Carl talked to me today." He spoke as if he hadn't heard me. "Guy's almost ninety." Richard twisted the cap off the second bottle and took a sip, this time slowly. I didn't know what to make of the sudden change of topic, but I figured there'd be time to deal with the phone later. "Says Platt and Diana King go way back."

"Thirty years, actually."

He looked at me in a mocking, suspicious way. Unsure if he was impressed or skeptical, I didn't elaborate.

"Sounds like Diana's up for a fair chunk of his assets, namely his share of that fancy health club." He tipped the water bottle toward me as if making a big point. It was an important point—I knew that—but I kept my reaction neutral.

"Who gets his share of the surgery center?"

"The uncle. King's already angling to buy it."

"What are those businesses worth? His shares in them, I mean."

Richard stared at me. "Come on, I couldn't ask *that*."

"Seems a little early to be reading a will."

"It is. This is all based on Carl's earlier talks with his nephew. It'll be a while before folks get around to the will."

"Then it's not confirmed."

He cocked his head by way of agreement. "But it's on good authority. Why do you suppose he didn't leave the gym assets to his uncle too?"

I shrugged. "Sometimes it's hard to know why folks leave things to the people they do. Who gets the house?"

"The remainder of his estate goes to the American Cancer Society."

"Wow." I imagined the remaining assets. "Some donation."

"It was ovarian cancer that took his wife Melissa."

I thought about Platt's house—its simple furnishings, sparse decorations—and felt disappointed that no family or close friends would be coming for those things. Maybe the jarring absence of personal artifacts like jewelry and photographs could be explained by the premature death of his wife. Losing Jack and Annette had taught me that recovery is sometimes easier without reminders in full view. Maybe Platt had known that too and emptied his cottage of painful memories, sending Melissa's things home with her friends and loved ones years ago.

"Strange, don't you think, that he left so much to Diana?" Richard tapped his open palm on my tabletop. His wedding ring clanked each time. "With the club doing as well as it is, that was probably a hefty bequest. Maybe it was enough motive for Diana to push him out of the picture."

"If that's your rationale, you should start looking at Uncle Carl too."

He scoffed. "He's ninety!"

"Just because a woman's named in a will doesn't make her the Grim Reaper."

"She hated Claire and stood to gain a lot if Platt died. It makes sense."

"Not to me."

He didn't answer right away, opting instead to shift his weight backward in the casual manner of a one who's finished a satisfying meal. He stretched one arm to the side so that its elbow rested on the back of an adjacent chair. "You know something."

"I think so."

"What did that note say? The one she left on your windshield this morning."

"The note's a problem." A question was forming on his face, so I kept going. "Actually, that's only true for you. Or it could be. So here's the deal. We can't talk about it. Don't ask me about the note anymore."

He'd rehydrated and cooled off enough. Richard was an ex-police detective, an even-keel, logical thinking sort of guy. His clarity and focus on an average day beat mine by a long shot even when I was at my best—which I was not. My thinking was muddied. I weighed the day's newest discoveries against the necessity of misleading Richard about how I'd made them. Meanwhile, he sat patiently and watched me, so cool and sharp that he might as well have been reaching into the folds of my brain tissue with bare, steady fingers to hand-pick the very facts I was trying to keep private.

"I don't like when you look at me that way."

"You feel guilty about something."

"Shut up."

I must have been an easier mark than the criminals he'd once interrogated because he made no effort to conceal his huge, smug grin.

"I'll tell you what I know *if* you don't ask how I found out," I said.

His moment of levity came to a quick end. "You didn't do something illegal?"

"That was a question," I said. "Those aren't allowed. Just listen."

Chapter Twenty-three

Richard was never a very good sport when I went subversive on him.

He had decades of law enforcement experience, extensive training, and masterful foresight for the way evidence would play out in court. But for all his skills, Richard remained impervious to what I thought was the most important piece of any investigation—people.

"You're telling me Platt was in love with Diana."

"They were in love with each *other*. At least at one time." I hesitated, remembering the strange evolution of her letters. "I think."

"You think." It was more muttered than spoken.

I couldn't tell him about the letters or the matching halves of the enormous amethyst geode. There was no way to summarize what little I knew of their history without explaining how I'd found out about it. I couldn't describe Platt's otherwise barren domicile and express the significance of his having saved something—*anything*—of hers. The fact that Diana had kept her own key to his bungalow, and given it to me, spoke volumes. But I couldn't tell Richard that either.

"You're going to have to trust me," I said. "Something was going on between those two that transcended time and multiple marriages. Maybe love, maybe friendship. Possibly both. But whatever it was, Diana King's not his killer. She was special to him."

"Yes," he said. "So he left her his share of a very profitable business. This doesn't mean he meant anything to *her*, though."

"He did. I'm sure of it."

"How?" A brief, forced exhalation communicated his worsening impatience. "Right. You can't tell me."

"Look, Richard. I'm not trying to be a problem. The opposite, actually. You just have to trust me." There was that word again. "Listen to what I'm telling you. It wasn't Diana."

Absently, he flicked the tabletop in front of him, slowly at first, then faster, and eventually only in spurts. I slid from my sofa's arm rest down into a proper seat on its cushion and hugged a throw pillow while I watched him brood. It was during times like these that I thought his salt and pepper hair most suited him. When he was thoughtful, he looked impossibly distinguished. At that moment, I knew he was mentally reorganizing. The most helpful thing I could do was sit still and wait.

A few moments later he stood and moved to the love seat across from me. He dropped into it, all signs pointing to exhaustion, crossed an ankle over a knee, and spread his arms wide over the cushions on both sides—body language he'd once said indicated an open mind.

"So what do you think?" He finally said. "Where does that leave us?"

I shook my head. "Daniel?"

He shrugged. "Or Claire?"

Ugh. I did not want to go down Claire Road again.

"What?" he said. "What's that look?"

Claire and all her paradoxical personality quirks would quickly and totally deplete my energy if I allowed more second-guessing. I'd convinced myself of her innocence. At some point, a person must simply commit and stop looking back.

"Let's look at it this way," I said. "Mick Young's paying us to help him defend her. For purposes of our work on his case, let's assume she's off the table."

He nodded. "We're short on leads."

"Hey, I forgot something." I pushed myself off the couch and returned to the laptop. "Claire's e-mail account."

I brought Richard up to speed and told him what I'd failed to find in her e-mail folders. The machine had booted and I'd launched my browser when the front door swung open and slammed into the wall behind it.

"We're home!" Annette paraded into the living room carrying a leftover bag of movie popcorn. "Want some? Hi, Richard."

Jeannie kicked the door closed behind her. "It's so hot out there that Satan's looking for shade." Her hands were full of shopping bags and empty Slushy cups. She brushed past Richard and me on her way to the kitchen. "Hi, Bossman. What are you kids up to?"

He took a handful of popcorn from Annette's bag. "I hope you kept your friend on a short leash." He winked at her.

Annette giggled. "She's not a dog."

He chuckled and returned to my laptop.

She brought me the popcorn next but instead of reaching inside I took the whole bag. "I'm starving," I said. "Thanks." Then I kissed her cheek.

"Wow!" she said. "A fish! Is it ours?"

She spun to face me, pigtails bouncing. I hadn't thought she could muster more energy, but everything from her huge eyes to her jumpy, skittish movements said we'd reached a new level of hyper. Overcome with excitement, she could not stand still and I *loved* it.

"Not ours," I said. "Yours."

"Can he live in my room?"

"He can live anywhere you want."

"Yes!" She pronounced this with a hiss, like a teenager who's scored the car keys. Carefully, she lifted the little bowl, and right before she slipped out of view, I grabbed her arm and pulled her back. Water sloshed out of the bowl.

"Am I in trouble?"

I smiled at her. "No. What's this?" I stroked the base of her ear. Fake sapphires, new since this morning, glimmered in her delicate little lobes.

Annette's grin was enormous. "Do you like them? It didn't hurt much. I got candy for being really still. Aunt Jeannie bought me other, fancier earrings but I have to leave these in for six weeks so the holes won't close. They're blue because I'm September."

Richard turned in his chair. "Hey, Emily, what's—"

"Not now." I shot him a look.

I pulled Annette in close, more carefully this time out of consideration for the fish. "They look really pretty and you were very brave. I'm proud of you." I hugged her.

She let go of me first, her normal thing. "I'm going to put the fish away and then go look in your jewelry box. I'll share my earrings with you if you share yours with me." She was around the corner in the hallway before she'd finished talking.

"Emily," Richard said. "Who's—"

"I'm going to have to explain that to Betsy and Nick," I said. Jeannie and I had discussed the earring milestone earlier. Annette had been asking for weeks and Jeannie was looking for a bonding event. Still, I couldn't help but worry about how the surrogate family would respond.

"You don't have to explain jack to anybody," Jeannie said. "You're her mother." She shook her head, annoyed. Richard didn't finish what he'd started to say, but I knew he wouldn't wait long to try again.

Jeannie continued. "You have more important things to think about than Betsy Fletcher." Without waiting for a reply, she slipped off her shoes and padded around the corner to go play with Annette.

"She's right." Richard said. "Who's FastCruzn?"

"Huh?" I dropped into the chair next to him and checked my watch. It'd be nice if he left before household conversation turned to dinner ideas. I didn't want shop talk to extend into mealtime.

"This e-mail from FastCruzn in your Inbox. The subject line says 'No favors for Claire.'"

I took the mouse from him. My browser had opened to my webmail account as usual but, unlike Jeannie, Richard had been too decent to read my messages without asking first. "Is this somebody helping with the case?"

"No."

I clicked to open the message, another one-liner: *I know where you were today.*

We stared at the screen. I wondered how to explain.

"Where *were* you today?" Richard asked. "Who's FastCruzn?"

When I didn't pull my eyes off the screen right away he snapped his fingers in front of it.

"I don't know who that is," I finally said. "I got an e-mail like that yesterday too. It said to go back to chemistry."

He looked appalled. I knew he was worried about whoever had sent the notes, but a quick study of his eyes told me that the person he was most disgusted with was me. "You didn't say anything."

"I wasn't keeping it a secret," I said. "There's been so much going on today that—"

"That you're not telling me."

"That I forgot to bring it up."

"Somebody threatened you and you forgot to bring it up."

Annette returned to show us the collection of rings and bracelets she'd used to adorn her tiny hands. Jeannie trailed behind wearing what looked to be every necklace I owned. She reminded me of Mr. T.

Richard stood to leave and looked pointedly at Annette, who was busy admiring her new accessories, before returning his gaze to me. It was the kind of stare that bored into me and he was clearly holding back for her benefit.

"No more poking around without me," he said. "That worked for a while, but now all bets are off."

I nodded.

He walked to the door. "I'll call you tonight. This isn't the time to be coy. I need to know exactly what happened today."

I disagreed, but to avoid having that discussion in front of my daughter I simply waved goodbye and let silence misrepresent my intentions.

He caught the door behind him before it closed. "This is against my better judgment," he said. "I'm meeting with Mick Young tomorrow at nine."

"What's against your better judgment? Meeting with that slime ball or telling me you're doing it?"

He didn't answer, simply raised his eyebrows to communicate the obvious question.

"Yeah," I said. "I'll be there." Before he could voice more protests, I shut the door.

◇◇◇

"I had to tell her." I took a final swipe at my lips with a new wine-colored gloss Jeannie had brought me the night before. I checked myself in a compact mirror and then dropped it back into my purse. "There's this antiseptic cleanser she has to put on the piercings three times each day. I had to tell Betsy about that."

Richard shook his head. "She give you grief?"

"No. I think she was just thankful to get Annette for the rest of the week." I screwed the lid back on my lip gloss and put that away too. "In fact, she was even more excited for Annette than I was. No wonder Annette likes her better."

"That's not fair," he said, a little distracted. He checked his watch, compared it to the one hanging on the wall behind Mick Young's receptionist. I smoothed my hair for what might have been the tenth time.

"What's with you?" Richard said.

I wished I knew. I wasn't aiming to look attractive so much as put-together and professional. The only other time Young had seen me was at his previous trial and I'd been a mess throughout. "He's late."

Richard stretched his legs, careful not to knock over his briefcase, and crossed one ankle over the other. He'd chosen dress slacks and a long sleeved button-up—a masochistic choice in the summer—and finished the look with a plum-colored tie. The ensemble worked, but it bothered me that Richard had put forth extra effort.

For my part, it was worse. In a fitted pantsuit and dress shoes, with full make-up and neatly arranged hair, I felt like a candidate waiting to interview for the worst job ever. Fact was, the job was already mine and I didn't expect Young to be very happy to find that out.

He opened the door and waved for us to join him in his office, no discernible surprise on his face upon seeing me there. The men shook hands. I nodded and took a seat. Young studied me a little longer than was comfortable.

"Something's different," he said. "Change your hair?"

"Yeah," I said. "That, plus not having been recently stabbed and shot at by your psychopath client like last time we saw each other."

"Emily." Richard's voice was low and sharp.

Young let it go and dropped into the chair on the other side of his desk. Richard joined me on the visitors' side. It wasn't even nine thirty and Young already looked like he'd worked a full day. Probably in his early forties, he had a slender, athletic build and a deep tan. I figured he spent his fat lawyer salary on watercrafts and beach excursions. Like Richard, he'd dressed crisply. His designer spectacle frames and nice clothes were attractive enough, but he needed a trim.

A nearly invisible scar from his top lip to the outside of his nose surprised me. I hadn't noticed it at the trial. In my recent dealings with Claire, Diana, and their elitist compatriots at Tone Zone, I'd lost sight of the value of plastic surgery as a reconstructive option.

Young lifted a shiny little pen from his desk and flipped it smoothly through his fingers in the tricky way I'd seen some kids do back in college. "I have news," he said, "But let's hear what you have first."

Richard opened his briefcase, extracted a legal pad, and skimmed the haphazard notes he'd scrawled. "We've been keeping an eye on Diana." He glanced over the top rim of his cheaters. Young nodded. "Nothing out of the ordinary there. She goes to work, runs her errands…" He shrugged. I wondered if he'd mention Diana's visit to my apartment or the envelope she'd left on my car. He didn't. "It looks like Platt left his share of the health club to Diana."

Young tipped his chin, apparently catching Richard's suggestion, and then turned to me. "What do you think about that?"

"I don't think Diana had anything to do with this."

There was a snotty, involuntary edge in my voice and I avoided looking at Richard. He'd have something to say about it later.

Young gave no indication of having noticed. "Ms. Gaston says you've been to see her."

I nodded. "A couple times."

"She's a tough nut to crack."

I inhaled, fought the urge to say too much. "Yep."

Young shifted his weight. "Said you went to her house?"

I nodded.

"Wanted a look at her e-mail folders?"

"Yes," I said. "I heard she'd been in touch with Platt via e-mail. She denied it and offered up her e-mail username and password to placate me."

"And?"

"The account was clean."

With no apparent effort, he flipped the pen across his knuckles again but didn't take his eyes off me. "When I heard you'd been to see her, and why you'd gone, I asked for the same privilege but she refused."

His words hung for a moment. I wondered if he expected me to explain her behavior.

"She's weird like that," I finally said.

The faintest trace of amusement flashed in Young's eyes.

Richard broke in. "Let's not read too much into this." Facing me, he added, "We've been over the possibility that she could have multiple e-mail accounts."

I didn't argue.

Young slid his gaze to Richard. "Do you agree that Diana King isn't a likely factor?"

"Not necessarily," he said. "She's openly hateful toward Claire. And Platt left her a sizable stake in Tone Zone."

"That's not verified," I said.

"It's as good as verified," Richard said, quickly enough to be terse.

I tried to force a professional, impassive expression but I was pretty sure my face had Sour written all over it.

Young spun his pen, studied me. To Richard, he said, "What about Diana's husband? The surgery center?"

Richard shook his head. "King will buy Platt's interest in the practice from the elderly uncle. The buyout price from an estate or from heirs is set by a third party. No chance of King low-balling the old guy."

"Perhaps *low* chance," Young said. "Can't be sure about *no* chance. I know from this practice, for example—" he opened his hands to indicate the room in general—"that there are multiple ways to structure business exit and succession plans, not to mention tax and estate planning." He paused, tapped his pen once on the table for emphasis. "But I'm inclined to agree with you. King's a visible member in the community. Has a large client base at stake. It'd be difficult, if not impossible, for him to acquire Platt's interest in the center for less than its fair market value and not draw attention. And even if he could pull it off…what a risky way to get a discount, no?"

He pulled a sticky pad from his top drawer, wrote something down. Then he looked up at us again, letting his eyes flit from one of us to the other before finally settling on Richard. "Anything to suggest someone we haven't considered?"

Richard tapped his thumb on the arm of his chair. Its thumping, noticeably severe, reminded me that despite middle age, Richard was still a solid guy. He stopped suddenly and surprised me.

"Emily thinks we should have a look at Daniel Gaston."

Young smirked. "Interesting you should bring him up."

Richard's cell rang and he pulled it from his belt holster. "Excuse me." He read the display. "It's about the case." He motioned that he'd be a minute and slipped out the door before I could fully register the awkwardness his absence would leave in the room.

The door clicked shut behind him and Mick Young and I were left alone to stare at each other over the wide expanse of his shiny, intimidating desk.

Young folded his fingers together and rested his chin on top of them, evaluating me. His fancy glasses, I noticed, had been upgraded with the nice, no-glare feature. It occurred to me he probably kept spares all over the place for convenience. I imagined an extra set in his desk at that very moment, another in his Jag, maybe an old pair at the beach house…all framed by Versace or Dior. It irritated the hell out of me that Young paid for his stupid frames, annoying pen, and Presidential, double podium, high-gloss desk with money earned from defending my husband's killers.

"Nobody's looked at me that way since Jimmy Basso," he said.

"Am I supposed to know what you're talking about?"

"Riff-raff we put away years ago when I worked in the D.A.'s office."

"Before you sold out, you mean. When you still worked to put criminals away instead of set them free."

"That's what you think of Ms. Gaston?"

"I'm not talking about Claire and you know it."

He held my gaze a moment, started over. "Anyway. I'd just finished questioning Basso at trial. I took my seat at the plaintiff's table. Basso was excused from the stand, but he didn't move. He was excused again. Same thing. I looked up then. He was staring at me hard. I knew right then, no doubt about it…if we didn't put that guy away he was coming for me."

I crossed my own hands in my lap. They were sweaty and I felt my face growing warmer too. It took everything I had to fake the appearance of being unaffected. "I'm not sure what the point of your story is, but I have no intention of coming after you."

He chuckled. "A relief. Still, you don't care for me much."

"That's right." My voice, quieter now, nearly caught but I forced myself to continue and even managed eye contact. "There are few people I hold in lower regard, actually."

I was surprised at my boldness and complete lack of shame, but despite how it had come out, I hadn't meant the remark as a dig. Rather, now that I could finally confront Young personally, the overwhelming feeling he elicited was not rage or disgust, but supreme disappointment that one human being could so completely fail another. It seemed to me that somebody should point that out.

"Your client," I said, "had my husband murdered and almost got me too. *Twice.* My little girl is five years old and doesn't understand why she suddenly has three parents. Why does she have to live with the strange, new mother now instead of the one she's known since infancy? She's too young to remember her dad and she has no idea what to make of me. You did everything in your power to restore the liberties of the monster that did this to us. That makes me sick."

I was prepared for a scathing response, perhaps a reminder that I worked for him, but Young said nothing. Instead he lifted a tissue box from the corner of his desk and offered it to me even though I wasn't crying. What to make of that? Was he giving me permission to cry or was he insulting me? When I didn't move for the box, he dropped it on his desk, not in its original spot, and it landed with a punctuated thud.

"It's not my job to decide guilt or innocence," he said. "Everyone deserves the best defense I can present. Understand, your specific circumstances were not part of the charges that we—"

I motioned for him to stop talking. "Spare me."

"That's not fair."

"Don't talk to me about fair."

I started to absently read the diplomas and certificates on his wall, wishing Richard would come back.

"While we're on the topic of jobs," he added, "Yours is to collect evidence. Since you have such strong feelings about working for me, quit if you'd rather. Although, I asked for you specifically and would regret seeing you go."

I turned back to him. He wasn't watching me anymore, just scribbling something on the same pad he'd used before.

"Excuse me?"

"When I hired Richard. The work you did last spring was impressive, particularly with no experience. I knew he'd picked you up after your move to Houston." He glanced up from his writing for a moment.

"But that was *against* your client."

"That's not the point. Ms. Gaston's my client now. A strong defense requires apt investigators. If you were accused, wouldn't you want the best defense you could get?"

"I'm not a murderer."

"Again, not the point." He set down his pen again in the same decisive way. "You showed that you were capable in March. Sharp reasoning, observation…maybe intuition. Your skills were a problem for me in that case but I'd like to capitalize on them this time. I hope Richard's paying you enough that you'll stick around despite our differences."

I wanted to scoff at his assumption that my decisions, like his, were motivated by money. Instead I studied him and grew a little uneasy with his flattery. If he were dirty like his recent clients, in cahoots with their collaborators, maybe he was trying to get close to me because he wanted to avenge pals I'd helped send to the state pen.

He switched gears. "You're more confident than Richard about Diana King's lack of involvement."

I took a moment to refocus. "Richard's not convinced because he doesn't know everything. It's not in his best interests, or yours, for me to elaborate."

Young grinned and drummed his knuckles twice on the glossy desk. "A delightfully coy presumption."

"It's your case," I said. "Say the word."

He leaned back into his chair and it squeaked. Richard burst through the door.

"Sorry to be so long." He took his seat again. "Got some interesting news."

"The husband?" Young asked.

Richard's eyebrows shot up and gave away his surprise. "Yeah. How'd you—"

"I got the call right before you arrived. It's why I was late to meet you."

Catching my annoyance before it ballooned, Richard filled me in. "Daniel Gaston was murdered last night."

Chapter Twenty-four

So much for my hunches.

"Murdered?" I said. "What happened?"

"He was shot in an apartment. Rice Village."

"I heard it was in the carport," Young said.

"Whose apartment? Does Claire know?"

Inside his dark frames, Young's eyes narrowed. It was enough to tell me that he hadn't considered how she'd take the news. "I'll tell her."

I feared his delivery might leave something to be desired. "No," I said. "Her mom should probably do it."

He nodded. "Of course."

I wondered how that exchange would go. Upon hearing the news, she'd be equally capable of smug satisfaction or inconsolable grief. "This is nuts."

Young continued to scrutinize. I couldn't tell if he wanted me to shut up or continue.

I didn't care. "Claire says she and Platt didn't know each other, yet crime scene evidence points to her. Diana has a plausible motive to frame Claire *but* she and Platt were close. It doesn't make sense that she'd be involved. In fact, I think Diana's more affected by Platt's death than she's letting on."

Young leaned forward, drew a breath.

"That's all I can say," I added, before he could question me.

I felt Richard's eyes on me but didn't turn. Young, I thought, deserved to know about the strange e-mails I'd received, but

Richard hadn't offered them up so I refrained. It seemed unlikely that the crazy person threatening me would be the same one to provide a key to Platt's house. Presumably, one of those people wanted to stop the investigation and the other wanted to move it along. In my book, this was compelling evidence of Diana's innocence but I couldn't openly share that without compromising Richard's professional ethics. Or Young's, if he had any.

"So Daniel's dead and Diana's off the table," I said. "Frankly, I'm glad Claire's in jail. It proves we're overlooking someone."

"Your generalizations aren't working for me," Richard said. "We can't dismiss Diana that easily. What exactly did you do yesterday? Let's hear it."

Young stood. "Let's not."

He came around to our side of the desk and motioned toward the door. "At least not yet." The wheels were turning, spinning out. Young wanted the full story—they both did—but not at the expense of jeopardizing Claire's defense. "I'd like to regroup later…by phone is fine. Let's see what details shake loose about last night. I'll get in touch with Ms. Gaston's mother. You—" he watched me gather my purse and stand to leave "—keep it on the level. Please."

Richard, already out of his chair, waited for me to be first out the door. I sensed silent admonitions and what-the-hell-were-you-thinkings as I passed through his aftershave aura on my way to the reception area. Behind me, he and Young muttered low enough not to be overheard. But thinking I heard my name, I turned. Neither was looking. Richard was probably working on damage control.

Later, at a pastry shop midway between Young's office and Richard's, I tried to make amends by buying brunch. Richard eschewed the bistro's assortment of gourmet coffees in favor of a large cup of regular black, and instead of a signature crepe or quiche, he took an unadorned bagel with plain cream cheese.

"No cinnamon swirl or blueberry?" I said. "No flavored schmear?"

He cut a glance at me, clearly unwilling to make up.

I felt a little overindulgent with my Hawaiian Kona and baked egg soufflé but not enough to deny myself. The rich aromas were simply too compelling.

We inched through the tray line.

"Nobody likes their job every single day," he finally said.

"I know."

"Plenty of people work for folks they don't like."

"Yep."

"You think I like sitting behind the wheel of my car for six hours watching a house? Rummaging through trash? Combing through old records?"

I hoped this would be a short lecture.

"Fact is, on some level, anybody who works in investigations is capitalizing on another person's misfortune. In this job, sometimes you're going to have to do stuff you don't like."

"Yeah," I said, "I get it."

"Even when it's personal," he said. "I'm sorry that where Young's concerned, the misfortune was yours, but you have to learn to compartmentalize. Otherwise, this job—and I don't just mean this case—will eat you."

I slid my tray to the right and rooted in my purse. "It's not like I don't think about this, Richard. I do."

His career guidance heart-to-hearts, though infrequent, were infallibly uncomfortable. I pulled my billfold from my bag, kept my gaze on the check-out girl, and nodded.

He let the subject drop.

I kept thinking about it though, and remembered Tuesday's talk with Betsy. Self-doubt, in the way it so often does, encapsulated me before I knew what was happening. When it was my turn at the register, I was glad for a reason to push the thoughts aside.

At the register, the tab came to $11.47 and having only a ten, I handed over my Visa. It was swiftly denied.

The checkout girl frowned. "Is there another you'd like to try?"

"What'd it say?" I asked. "Could you try again?" I turned to Richard. "Sometimes those magnetic strips get scratched."

She swiped it a second time. "It says 'Contact card services for billing information,' same as before. Sorry."

Richard reached for his wallet.

"No," I said. "I got it." I took back the defunct Visa, switched to MasterCard.

She ran it and shook her head. "Same thing."

"What the hell?"

Panic set in. I took the second card back and left Richard to pay and deal with the trays. My cell phone was out of my pocket before I reached the nearest empty table.

The Visa representative explained that unusual account activity had resulted in the temporary suspension of my card privileges. Messages had been left on my home and cell phones.

Thinking back, I realized I hadn't checked my answering machine after returning home from dinner with Jeannie and Annette the night before. But my cell phone? The voicemail icon hadn't been on my display.

I listened as she read backwards through over eight hundred dollars in recent charges, mostly at automotive and electronics stores. None were mine. She explained that the most I'd be responsible for was a fifty dollar cap, likely to be waived considering the circumstances. Paperwork would follow in the mail.

We hung up. I dialed into my empty voicemail box and was astonished to find messages waiting. I glared at Richard. "This is all your fault!"

He was chewing. "Mine?"

I pushed the button to get the first of four new messages.

"The voicemails were here but the *phone* is screwed up and didn't tell me they were waiting."

"I thought you were getting a new phone yesterday."

"We went out to dinner. The store closed."

I left out that Jeannie had convinced me to bake my phone in the oven all night at 125°, another apparent failure at cellular resuscitation.

It was the same story each time. Three more credit cards with suspicious activity and one message from Betsy, who wanted to know if it was safe for Annette to swim with newly pierced ears.

I called MasterCard. Six hundred dollars.

Discover. Twelve hundred.

Dick's Sporting Goods. Less than a hundred, so no suspicious activity had been flagged, but even so, the charge wasn't mine.

"Your *sporting goods* card?" I thought Richard was making fun of me so I ignored him.

"Damn," I muttered. Replacement cards with new numbers would come soon. "Do you have any idea how many automatic bill pay accounts I'll have to re-map now? You're so lucky I'm not on the hook for those charges."

He wasn't listening. He was scanning the various cards I'd laid all over the table so I could find the customer service numbers. "You have all your cards here, but they've all been hit."

Unsure if I was expected to draw a conclusion from this, I just nodded, annoyed.

"I could see a single card being hit, like if a waiter copied your number when he took the card away to run it," he said. "But all of them on the same day? And a sporting goods card?" He set down his bagel. "Who could have gotten into your purse?"

"It's with me all the time," I said.

"You mentioned automatic bill pay. Who can use your laptop?"

I shook my head. "I never take it out of the apartment and these accounts are password protected anyway."

"What about your wireless network?"

"It's secure," I said. "Secure network, password protection, locked apartment. My purse is always with me."

He grew more agitated with every assurance. "I'm afraid of what we might be dealing with. A slick, sophisticated thief bothers me way more than a third-rate purse snatcher or a sleazy waiter. Maybe Jeannie left the apartment and forgot to lock the door."

"No way," I said. "She's a city girl."

"Your apartment was empty yesterday while you were out doing your secret errand. Jeannie took Annette to the movies while you were gone. Was anything out of place when you came back?"

"They leave stuff out everywhere, all the time." I remembered the nail polish and cotton balls strewn across the table and the left-over party mess in the kitchen. "It was nothing worse than usual."

He finished his coffee. The paper cup made a sharp hollow sound when it hit the table. "Sorry about your phone." He pulled out his wallet and passed me his small business credit card. "Use this to get a new one."

I stood up, pocketed it, and amassed all our trash on my tray. "If I get stuck with those fifty dollar maximums, you're covering those too."

He pushed back from the table, checked his watch. "What's on your plate today?"

"Besides this?" I walked to the nearest trash can and dumped the tray.

Richard's visit to the apartment the night before had interrupted my work on Platt's Caller ID list. Jeannie, Annette, and I had gone out for dinner afterward, and the evening ended at Betsy and Nick's where we'd dropped Annette off to finish her promised week with them.

"I have some calls to make." I wondered what percentage might land in voicemail boxes. "And tomorrow's Jeannie's last day here. I should take her somewhere fun before she leaves. What about you?"

"Also calls. See if anybody will talk about Daniel." Something in his voice told me he expected bad luck. I was beginning to feel like I'd hit a dead end myself.

When we got back to my apartment, he parked the car. "I'm going to talk to your neighbors." He turned off the ignition.

"About what?"

Four seconds had passed and already the car was heating up. I opened my door and let one leg dangle out.

"To ask whether anybody strange has been by your place."
He opened his own door. I'd had enough company for the day
and didn't like where this was headed.

"No." I scooped up my purse. "I'll ask them myself." I stepped
out, shut the door, and climbed the steps to my apartment
without looking back.

Behind me, a door slammed shut and his motor started.

Maybe Jeannie was right. Assertiveness could be learned.

Chapter Twenty-five

I continued through the list. One after another, each call ended in voicemail. Granted, it was late Thursday morning and folks were probably at work, but part of me suspected that the very tool that had delivered these phone numbers—caller ID—was preventing me from reaching anyone. After all, no one on my list would recognize my name. I was another junk call to them.

On the seventh number, my luck changed.

"You're talking to him." The voice on the other end of the line belonged to Joel McGowan. His accent confirmed that the 732 area code I'd dialed was in New Jersey, and a clip in his tone said he was a no-nonsense kind of guy.

I came straight to the point.

"Mr. McGowan, my name's Emily Locke. I'm calling from Houston, Texas, regarding the death of Wendell Platt. Did you know him?"

The line fell momentarily silent. "Who'd you say you are?"

I repeated my name. "Is this the first you've heard?"

"I just talked to him last week."

"Yeah." Finding a vocal balance between sympathy and professionalism was difficult. "I found a record of that in his Caller ID log. It's how I knew to call you."

I let another moment pass, figuring McGowan was processing the news. "How'd you know each other?"

"School cronies," he said. "Back in the day, we were like brothers. Harder to stay in touch as time went on, but we did what we could. What happened?"

"He was killed." So there'd be no confusion with, say, a five car pile-up, I added, "Murdered." I regretted the word choice but couldn't think of an alternative.

McGowan's breath caught in a tremulous way I wished I hadn't heard. By way of avoidance I pushed forward. "Before he died, he asked a patrolman in his neighborhood about some kind of underhanded money scheme. I'm not sure if it was blackmail, embezzlement, bribery—"

"Elder abuse."

"Excuse me?"

"He thought it might be identity theft, which is why he called me. I specialized in financial crimes. But from what he described, it was elder abuse...a tough crime to prove."

"Are you a detective?"

"Was," he said. "Retired."

"So Dr. Platt called to get your take on a crime involving an elderly person?"

"His neighbor. He was looking for some advice about what to do."

My thoughts flitted between crazy Ms. Herald and eccentric William Henry Saunders the third. "Do you know which neighbor?"

"He said it was an old guy, not quite right in the head. Some lowlife was taking him for everything he had."

"What'd you tell Dr. Platt?"

"I asked him about the situation. Sounded to me like theft would be a real hard thing to prove. It's always this way with the old folks."

"What do you mean?"

"It's easy for crooks to talk them into things. If they write checks or hand cash over to somebody with a smooth story, it's a gift, not a crime."

I thought about Florence, probably sitting in her apartment across my landing right now watching Days of Our Lives. She had a fourteen hundred dollar vacuum cleaner in there, purchased a couple years ago from a good-looking twenty-something who told her he was a back-up lineman for the Texans.

"Anyway," he continued. "Not much I could do from up here except explain all the work that lies ahead. I told him to tell the story to the local police and see if there wasn't something they could do."

I checked my notes. "You had this talk two weeks ago?"

"Sounds about right."

"Dr. Platt say anything about approaching the neighbor?"

"Not that I recall."

"Thanks, Mr. McGowan."

"Call back if there's more I can do."

We ended it there and I sat on my couch with my phone clutched tightly in-hand and stared straight ahead at the wall. It had something to do with Saunders, and we were dealing with a con man. The morning's credit card fiasco dovetailed nicely into this new information. But when Platt got close to exposing whatever scheme was underway, he'd ended up dead. So far I'd only come into scary e-mails and fraudulent charges. Why?

Too weary and lazy to deal with the blazing heat, even for the five steps it would take me to cross my landing, I speed-dialed Florence. It reminded me of years past when I worked across the hall from Jeannie but would e-mail her instead of walking to her desk.

"Hey lady," she said. TV noise squawked in the background. "What's going on?"

"Quick question."

"Shoot."

"Anybody new been around my place lately?"

"Don't think so, no." She hesitated. "I saw the exterminator yesterday. Don't even tell me something's missing."

"Everything's fine," I told her. "Don't worry."

I hadn't checked around yet and I'd never called for an exterminator. Until my talk with McGowan I'd assumed Richard was being paranoid, but if the apartment manager had sent someone to work in my unit, I'd have been notified. It was important not to rattle Florence.

"Richard's being careful about our new case," I said. "He asked me to check that nobody strange has been around."

"Don't think so. Anyway, what kind of bugs? Whatever you got is gonna head over here next."

"Ants."

She made a throaty, disgusted sound. "Long as it ain't roaches."

"The guy they sent over…was he the short cute one with the blond hair? I like that guy. Hard worker."

This was what Richard called a fishing expedition. I'd never met any of the complex's exterminators and wouldn't have remembered them if I had.

"No, honey. This guy was tall—even taller than your friend." Vince. "And he had brown hair and one of those weird beard things on his chin with no mustache."

"A soul patch?"

She laughed. "Whatever you kids call it. Looks stupid." She sighed. "But I guess as long as he kills those ants, don't matter."

"Thanks. And in case Richard's right, if anybody happens to ask about me, say I keep to myself and that you don't know me."

"Got it."

"Stay cool in there."

"You too."

We hung up and I pushed myself off the sofa and started to have a look through my things, beginning with my jewelry box, which most definitely had been pilfered. Jeannie and Annette had played with my necklaces the day before and the box's contents were in disarray. At first I held out hope that nothing would be missing, only misplaced. But as I reorganized and sorted, I discovered, one by one, which of my favorites had been taken. Topping the list were my wedding and engagement rings that I'd only recently stopped wearing. That had been a reluctant decision made mainly out of courtesy for Vince. I thought now that if I'd given myself more time to think about it, maybe listened to my heart a little more closely, they'd still be mine.

I curled up on my bed and pulled a pillow to my chest, not caring what I saw outside when I stared passed the mini-blinds. Tears came, the quiet kind. This time there would be no sniffles, no tight throat or jagged breath. Only the gentle, lingering memory of my husband, skipping down my cheek again, landing silently on his pillow.

Later it puzzled me, the things the burglar left. There was my entire CD collection, plainly labeled and still unpacked—perfectly packaged for convenient theft, yet left untouched in the far corner of my bedroom. A whiskey jug that once belonged to Jack's grandfather was still waiting on the corner of my dresser. Inside was two or three hundred dollars' worth of spare change I'd accumulated, never feeling sufficiently motivated to schlep it to the bank's coin roller machine. My TV had been left behind, but I figured that was because it was archaic. Before moving from Cleveland last spring, I'd finally upgraded to a better road bike. My clean, new Cannondale still leaned against the wall in the laundry room and I stared at its gorgeous frame, thankful but befuddled at the same time. Even Vince's guitar, a 1966 Martin I was disinclined to return, had been spared.

I thought it over. The only explanation I could conjure was space constraints. An impostor exterminator could leave the apartment in plain sight with his pockets stuffed with my jewelry, but he'd be hard pressed to explain a bike or guitar. I doubted he was after my stuff anyway. In light of everything else going on, the jewelry theft seemed more like an opportunistic afterthought. My laptop had even been left behind.

I booted up. No doubt about it, there would be mail.

I was not disappointed.

FastCruzn had been back, and this time he was prolific: *Julius Caesar, John Keats, Andrew Jackson, Ella Fitzgerald, Johann*

*Sebastian Bach, Babe Ruth, Aristotle, Marilyn Monroe, Leo Tolstoy,
John Lennon, Malcolm X, Edgar Allan Poe, and me. But not
Annette Locke unless you leave no choice.*

"What the hell is that supposed to mean?" Jeannie, not allowed
to smoke in my apartment, chewed a stick of Wrigley's like
a zealot. She snapped the gum between thoughts. "All those
people are dead."

"Um, no." Richard made no effort to conceal his annoyance. "It
says 'and me' and whoever wrote that note is obviously not dead."

"You know what I meant. Emily, why'd you even call him?"

"Guys, focus. You're worse than kids."

I was sandwiched between them. Jeannie, on my left, sipped
from an oversized mug of coffee, her third cup. Richard had
brought two waters to the table, one for each of us, but I was
eyeing the joe. Jeannie must have noticed.

"Yes you do," she said. "Need caffeine." She got up and went
to the kitchen for me. I didn't argue.

When she returned, a long sip of coffee provided unexpected
clarity. "I'm going to write back this time."

"What? No." Richard shook his head. "No way."

"Go for it," Jeannie said. "Call the bastard out."

"It's a mind game." Richard spoke louder than usual. "He's
manipulating…goading you."

"He's talking about Annette," I said. "I have to do *something*."

Jeannie took her seat beside me again. "How do you suppose
he got your e-mail address?"

I shrugged, disgusted. "How'd he get my credit card info?"

"That one's easy," Richard said. "Where do you keep your
statements?"

I pointed to a thick vinyl accordion folder at the far end of my
bookcase. Richard stood and retrieved it. He moved to unhook
the little elastic loop that kept the folder closed and then, apparently concerned for my privacy, handed it to me. "Open it."

I used my fake nails as pinchers, gathered the rubber band, and lifted it off.

"Run us through what you have there."

I started at the front. "Up here are copies of some court documents…then receipts from a doctor I've seen a few times." Actually, it was a therapist. I kept that to myself. "Next are print-outs of the credit card statements I mentioned. Insurance forms, a copy of my lease, last year's tax return…general stuff."

"So basically everything a normal person would keep in a filing cabinet."

I shot him a look. "Do you see room for a filing cabinet in here?"

"Your birth date's there, your social security number, all of your credit card account numbers. With that information, a thief can do anything."

"We need to call the police," Jeannie said. "File a report on your missing things."

"I've been thinking about that but, if I report it, the officer will want to talk to Florence and I'd rather not upset her. She thought she was doing me a favor and if she finds out what really happened she'll go berserk. Besides," I looked at Richard, "I really doubt there's any chance of recovering my jewelry at this point."

His expression turned to regret and he shook his head.

"Anyway, Richard," I continued. "You think he came in here to get this credit card information and then took my jewelry as a bonus?"

"Hard to say. The bigger question is how to keep you safe now."

"What you *need* is a Ladysmith." Jeannie moved her fingers into the shape of a gun, pointed at me, and pulled her thumb trigger.

Richard took back my folder and put it away. "I don't think it's safe for you to stay here anymore."

I didn't think so either. Richard probably would have invited me to stay with him and Linda for a while if it wouldn't have meant the additional imposition of having Jeannie under his roof. She'd fray his nerves spectacularly, no doubt. Booking a hotel crossed my mind, but the indefinite nature of the stay was daunting. That could get expensive.

Richard surprised me. "Think you could stay with Vince for a while?"

Jeannie's eyes opened wide, her excitement unmistakable.

Richard continued. "Until we see what's what."

He had no way to know how complicated it was and I sure wasn't going to try to explain. So I nodded vaguely and took another sip of coffee, this time wishing it were wine or maybe hard liquor, anything to dull my worsening anxiety.

Chapter Twenty-six

Paranoid about my own car being spotted, I'd opted for a change in vehicles. Jeannie's rental, an Altima she'd cluttered with an alarming collection of empty Starbucks cups, was our ride back to the Heights. I pulled alongside the curb and the front tire bumped.

"We're curbside four houses down," I told Richard via cell phone. I put the rental in park and left it running, feeling like a guilty, selfish Earth-hater for my unwillingness to part with air conditioning.

"Alright," Richard said. "Let's see who's home."

He hung up and I waited, phone in hand, and watched William Saunders' stately Victorian through the windshield.

"Bet his phone's ringing right now," Jeannie said.

I'd asked Richard to call Saunders so there'd be no chance he'd associate a female voice with the personal visit I hoped would follow. His number was a public listing still in his father's name. I'd asked Richard to block his own number with *67. Our assumption was that Mr. B., if home, would be too cautious to answer a blocked call. So if anyone picked up, we figured it'd be William. Either way, Richard would ask for Mr. B. If unlucky enough to actually reach him, the plan was to simply fall back on the truth and say he was calling regarding Wendell Platt.

A few moments later my phone rang. "Saunders answered," Richard said. "When I asked for Mr. B. he told me to call back after eleven."

"Thanks." I snapped my phone closed and checked my watch. "It's ten thirty," I said to Jeannie. "He's supposed to be back in a half hour. Call if there's any sign of him."

I climbed outside, immediately assaulted by unforgiving furnace-blast heat, and flung my door shut hoping to spare her. Behind my sunglasses I was squinting; everything seemed to be hyper-illuminated by the oppressive sun.

At Saunders' door, I rang the bell and surveyed dead bugs on his porch while I waited for an answer. His arrival on the other side of the platen glass was sudden, almost like he'd been standing out of view waiting to pounce.

"It's me, William," I said. "Emily. We met on Tuesday."

The dead bolt clacked and he cracked the door. There was the eye again. "Joseph Daniel H-Hennessey the third liked the Houston Oilers."

I couldn't help but smile. "Good memory. How have you been? Everything going okay?"

"You looked p-prettier the last time."

Quite a bit so, I imagined. Leave it to an innocent teddy bear like William to say so. On Tuesday I'd been made-over, had styled hair, and nicely filled out Jeannie's Armani mini-dress. Today it was back to jean shorts, a faded tank, sneakers, and minimal make-up. "It's really hot out here. Could I come inside for a glass of water, please?"

"No."

"Is Mr. B. here? Maybe we could finally talk about your neighbor, Dr. Platt."

"No." He moved to close the door.

I stopped it with my toe.

It was tricky for me, this line between respect and persistence.

"What are you up to today? Anything fun?"

He stared at me a moment, but with the kind of far-off look that made me wonder if he'd heard what I'd said.

"Would you like to go for a walk?" I was running out of ideas. Down the street, all I could see of Jeannie's car was a blinding white glow reflecting off the windshield.

"I don't like people looking at me," he said. "And can you w-work a glue gun?" In the crack between the jamb and the door he produced the stub of a glue stick. "It's hard."

"Sure," I said. "I can do that. What are you trying to do?"

He shifted his weight back and forth, resulting in the disappearance and reappearance of his single eye. "I'll be in trouble."

"Are you making something?"

He swayed faster. "Fixing." His anxiety was palpable. "Nobody's allowed inside."

"Look, William. I'll fix whatever's broken and then leave. You won't get in trouble."

He moved away from the door and vanished, leaving me on the porch with a mostly closed door and no invitation. I pushed it forward a few inches and peeked into the empty foyer. The place smelled like burnt toast. "William?"

He reappeared from a space beyond the entryway stairs carrying the pieces of some kind of ornamental pitcher and I got my first full look at him. In sweats and socks, with a Texans tee, he looked like any other grandfatherly sports aficionado, except for an inconsistent limp that seemed to change sides and a slightly wild look resulting from hair that wasn't thoroughly combed.

"I'm not supposed to cook when I'm by m-myself." He thrust the pieces toward me and stutter-stepped away again.

The pitcher had broken cleanly. Fixing it would be nothing.

William stopped after a few paces and turned back. "Hurry."

I followed him to the back of the house where we turned into a kitchen best described as Late Seventies. Wood grain Formica counters and an old-style stainless faucet reminded me a little bit of my father's house. A lower cabinet door was missing and its absence revealed jumbled Tupperware lids and a discolored roasting pan. I felt uneasy spotting a mess that was supposed to be hidden from view.

The first thing I did was turn on the vent hood. Its noise agitated William even more.

"This will help with the burnt smell," I said. Glancing toward the toaster, I added, "You should clean up those crumbs so Mr. B. won't know you were cooking."

Red sauce was dried around one of the burners on the stove and something grainy, either salt or sugar, coated the countertop next to it. I assumed both were left over from something William's caretaker had prepared so I didn't bother cleaning them.

William lumbered toward the sink and wetted a dish rag. "Mother's p-pitcher was next to the plates. I didn't mean to."

"I break stuff all the time," I said. "We'll fix it, don't worry."

He'd left the glue gun plugged in, lying on its side on the counter. A pool of congealed glue had formed under its hot tip and threads of glue criss-crossed the countertop in all directions, advertising several failed attempts. I set the gun upright again and fed it another glue stick.

"You'll be our look-out," I said. "Wait by the front window and tell me if Mr. B. comes back."

His eyes widened. I tried not to think about what might have instilled so much fear of his caregiver.

"Where is he, by the way?"

William turned and left but I was certain he'd heard me. I stepped around the corner behind him. "William?"

"With Sandy," he said.

"Sandy who?" I said to his back.

"Sandy Diaz. She doesn't like orange juice and w-won't eat bacon."

I let it go. There wasn't time.

My new acrylics made short work of cleaning up William's disaster in the kitchen. I used them to pick at the countertop and separate voluminous strands of dried glue from its Formica surface. After moving them to the trash, I turned my attention back to the repair. The gun had suitably softened the fresh glue stick and it only took a few minutes for me to press the three large pieces back together. Cracks were visible, and it would never be serviceable again, but I doubted Mr. B. served up much iced tea or lemonade anyway. At least William wouldn't have to explain an empty spot in the cupboard. I unplugged the gun, wrapped its cord around the handle, and as quickly and silently as possible, made for the stairs. They were carpeted but hadn't seen a vacuum for a while. I bounded to the second floor, thankful for the padding.

Upstairs, I felt like the wind had been knocked out of me and it wasn't from the hasty climb. Straight ahead was a work room like I'd never seen.

A series of tables had been arranged around three walls of the room, each serving what appeared to be a specific purpose. On the one nearest the door, two desktop computers hummed side by side, their monitors turned off. The tabletop behind them was thickly coated in dust.

A small basket nearby was filled with a variety of thumb drives and a watch. I turned the watch over and found a non-descript panel above the twelve o'clock position. When I peeled it back, a USB interface was nestled inside.

On my left I recognized a key grinder and an open leather pouch with eight slender metal tools inside, each crafted to a unique point. It was a lock pick set. Beside it, a box of fifty key blanks and a container of various blank pin-on name tags had been stacked on top of a tackle box. I opened the box and found several keys, some labeled indistinguishably, some not at all.

Coveralls and work shirts, none matching each other, hung in the closet: Baxter's Automotive, CenterPoint Energy, Comcast, Wayne's Heating and Air, AT&T, Burt's Landscaping. Two button-ups, one garage brown and the other utilitarian blue, were unlabeled, but the brown one still had a nametag pinned near its pocket: "Manny," from Herrera Cleaners. On the floor, wigs, various glasses, and a stash of ball caps had been tossed in a laundry basket.

I closed the door, horrified.

Piano notes, slow and detached, like those of a child practicing, drifted up from the first floor. I hadn't noticed a piano on my way inside but I hoped its position afforded William a view of the street. Nervous, I crossed the hall and checked the neighborhood through the front window of an opposing bedroom. When I pulled the curtain back, I found more dust in the sill, and two dead flies, but no sign of Mr. B. Above the window, an irregular plank of wooden paneling had been nailed to the ceiling. It was the type of random repair I might expect from my neighbor Florence.

Back in the work room, I continued my search. Inboxes, like those typically used in offices, were aligned along the table on the far wall. On the floor underneath, two bottles of acetone and a single bottle of bleach had been jammed into a corner beside a stack of small plastic buckets and a pile of newspapers. White arcs in the carpeting told me that the person who used this room either worked in a hurry or had little regard for the home. I riffled through the paperwork in the boxes, disbelieving.

Xeroxes of about forty employment applications for a local electronics superstore filled the top bin. Below were a stack of pre-paid VISA gift cards held together by a thin rubber band. Beside those was a MasterCard, still stuck to its letterhead, with an activation sticker pressed across its front. I knew the routine—call the 800 number printed on the card from your home phone to activate the card. When I read the name on the card I shuddered: Daniel Gaston.

I shoved it in my pocket.

There was more: an embossing machine, plastic stock, solder irons, and some kind of machine that looked like it was made for running credit cards. I pulled out my phone and took a few pictures, astonished the camera function still worked. A clock on the wall said 10:49.

I dug through the wastepaper basket next, removing its contents haphazardly in my rush, and found more copies of employment applications, some from the electronics store, others from a bank. Envelopes—stamped but not postmarked—and associated bill payment stubs for half a dozen men and women with names I didn't recognize were mixed among them.

Then I hit paydirt. A single e-mail printout was wedged in the bottom of the trash.

Dated nine days earlier, it was written from Claire to Platt:

I won't be ignored, Wendell. Keep it up and I'll make you sorry.

Out of time, I shoved the papers, all except the e-mail, back into the trash can and went downstairs as quietly as I could, folding the note as I went. Anything sent from Claire's account nine days ago should have turned up in my search of her account, yet the address on the header was the same one she'd given me.

Disconnected notes from *When the Saints Go Marching In* drifted from the front room, where I found William seated on a piano bench that he absolutely dwarfed. Afraid of startling him, I coughed before joining him in the room.

"It's finished," I said. "Remember to put the pitcher and the glue gun away, okay?"

He only cocked his head and repeated the same measure he'd just finished. I caught the faint scent of rancid water and turned to find a wilted bouquet of mixed wildflowers decaying in a vase near the window.

"William," I said. "Where does the blue pitcher belong?"

"In the c-cupboard next to the sink."

"And the glue gun?"

"In my mother's desk drawer." He pointed to an antique secretary piece in the room and then returned his attention to the sheet music propped open in front of him. The songbook he used was yellowed and its binding had been poorly mended with Scotch tape.

I went to the kitchen and put away the pitcher, then brought the gun back to the front room.

"Which drawer, William?"

"The s-second."

At the desk, only steps behind William's back, I examined mounds of paperwork and notes. Significant documentation, some organized, some not, crowded the limited space and I couldn't help noticing that most of it looked like medical records. I slipped the glue gun into the second drawer and allowed myself a moment to take in all the forms. A series of brightly colored sticky notes, most lime green, dotted several piles. I glanced at William, who seemed to have forgotten me, and ran a finger over the papers.

A bold, black pen had been used on all the sticky notes. Judging by the identical handwriting on each sample, they'd been written at the same time:

Bathes every other day. Allow privacy. This was stuck to a list of William's preferred soaps and shampoos.

Absolutely no unsupervised cooking. Sandwiches and cereal were okay, but apparently William was not to use the microwave or toaster oven without help. Knives were off-limits so any fruits or veggies should be pre-sliced.

His payments sometimes lapse because he forgets about due dates. Please promptly remit any utility bills. Call me before paying anything that comes from the insurance company. This one was stuck to the vinyl cover of a checkbook. I flipped it open and was surprised that the account belonged to William. Then I felt ashamed for assuming he could do nothing by himself.

One note, stuck to the edge of the desk, seemed to be a catch-all for instructions that didn't fit elsewhere:

Has trouble matching clothes but can dress himself.

Does poorly on the phone. May need help making therapy appointments.

Likes help with reading his mail.

Likes game shows.

The last one had a series of asterisks beside it:

Sometimes locks himself out. Be careful!

Below, a careful hand had signed, "Call anytime. VS."

I slipped the top layer of instructional papers aside and attempted to decipher what looked like a bunch of insurance codes on medical invoices. The numbers and abbreviations meant nothing to me.

At the bottom of one stack, a three-ring binder, thick as a phone book, caught my attention. Its pages were separated by dividing sleeves labeled in reverse chronological order by year. I started at the back, with the oldest records, because that section was the thickest.

William stopped playing his song mid-measure and I stepped away.

"Do you know the hand position for middle C?" He stared at the piano keys, fingers lightly resting there, and tried to remember.

I placed a hand gently on his shoulder and left it there until he looked at me, then shook my head. "I'm sorry, I never learned. You sounded good. Will you play it again?"

"I like that one too." He started from the beginning, and I returned to the binder and skimmed newspaper clippings, medical reports, and patient care instructions until William's situation started to make sense.

The first article I found, dated four years earlier, said that "a 63-year-old male" had been the "front seat passenger in a traffic accident and suffered a severe closed head injury with frontal lobe impairment" and that "surgeons performed a right-side craniotomy." At press time, authorities had not determined fault.

Medical records indicated that William required total assistance after his accident and a thick stack of invoices and insurance forms showed that his family had arranged for long term facility care and rehabilitation. One file note said that any dysfunctions that remained two years post injury would be permanent. I paused and stared at that one. It seemed wrong that anyone, even a medical professional, could so confidently write off another's future.

A pamphlet about traumatic brain injury, tucked inside the binder's front pocket, outlined William's struggles: difficulty concentrating, trouble organizing thoughts, easily confused, often forgetful, unable to perceive social cues, adversely affected judgment, slow or slurred speech, overestimates abilities, unrealistic future planning.

I tapped the brochure in my palm and glanced at my watch, horrified to notice I'd lost track of time. I closed the binder and replaced the papers.

"I'm leaving now," I said. "Everything's back to normal. Come lock the door behind me."

He pushed back the piano bench and its feet, obviously padded, made a soft whispering sound as they glided over the hardwood floor. We walked to the front door, and I stepped outside into the sweltering day.

"Thank you for helping me," William said. "Don't tell Mr. B. you were h-here."

"No chance."

"I liked your hair better the first time."

Before I could get in a goodbye, the door closed abruptly and I heard the now familiar sound of the Victorian's deadbolt sliding into place. Jeannie pulled up, and as I made my way down the steps I caught the faint notes of William's song playing in the great, lonely house behind me.

"Change of plans," I said, sliding into the passenger seat. Our original idea had been to ask nosey questions at the apartment complex where Daniel was murdered. "I need to see the police."

"Sweet. You found something." She rolled through a stop sign. "Which way do I go?"

"I have no idea. Pull over and ask somebody."

She produced her cell phone—a model that made mine look as ungainly as a brick—and began using its GPS function to get directions to the nearest public safety building. Jeannie navigated its screens easily, despite her long fingernails, whereas my new fakes were much shorter and I couldn't even accurately select a radio station.

"I need Richard's help," I said. "Just drive. I'll explain in a sec."

I dialed him on my own cell and described everything I'd seen at Saunders' house.

"The evidence of identity theft you found is compelling but not urgent," he said. "Under the circumstances, there's not probable cause for a warrant and it may not get followed up for days. That e-mail and credit card, though…different story. Those are potentially linked to a homicide. Your report will go into the system and when a detective downloads it, you'll probably get a call within hours."

"There's more," I said. "Mr. B. was with somebody named Sandy Diaz. Can you follow up on that?"

"You bet."

We hung up and Jeannie and I exchanged a hopeful look. Inwardly I felt torn, wondering what this new lead would eventually mean for William.

Chapter Twenty-seven

We'd heard on the news where Daniel had been shot. While she drove us to that apartment complex, Jeannie grilled me about my police report and seemed morbidly excited about visiting a crime scene. But when we passed the bustling Rice Village shopping district, offering everything from boutiques to artisans to booksellers to coffee shops, I lost her attention without warning.

"Look at all these stores," she said at a stop light. "Sorry, girl. I can't resist." Before I knew it, the car was in park and she'd left with her purse. "Call me when you're finished. I'm going shopping."

She joined some crossing pedestrians in the crosswalk and a car honked behind me. I scurried out of the car and hustled to the driver's seat. As I rolled forward, Jeannie gave a spirited double thumbs-up and I reached for my notes to the address I wanted.

The complex was subdivided into multiple courtyards, each surrounded by red brick three story buildings with black shutters and beige balconies. One of the courtyards had a streaming yellow crime-scene ribbon cordoning off five carport spaces. I parked in a nearby reserved spot and got out of the car. The place smelled like magnolias and cut grass.

No one answered at the apartment I'd seen flashed on the news, so I went to the unit directly below and banged its ornamental knocker in hopes of catching somebody at home. Opaque window sheers provided enough privacy that I couldn't easily see inside. I made out two vague silhouettes in a kitchen nook, though, and it looked to me like maybe a card game was underway.

A man inside hollered. "You a reporter?"

"No," I called back. I wanted to explain, but my voice was unlikely to make it through the door as crisply as his had.

The door opened, but not much.

"Yeah?" It was what Jack would have called a Whitehead—his catch-all term for white-haired retired guys. Something in this man's apartment smelled divine, a mix between fresh dinner rolls and seasoned meat.

"Sorry to interrupt," I said, now unsure whether I'd interrupted cards or a meal. "I heard about the murder on the news and I'm trying to figure out whose apartment that is?"

"Why?"

No suitable lie sprang to mind. "The guy that was killed. Did he rent that apartment?"

The old-timer shook his head. "He's a Johnny-come-lately. It's a gal that rents that place, not a fella."

"Oh. Do you know her name?"

"Think it's Marcy or Margo, something like that. Works at a framing store over on Rice Boulevard."

"Thanks," I said, and he nodded and closed the door.

I stepped out from the landing that was the bottom of Marcy or Margo's porch and stared up at her apartment, wondering what the heck was going on.

On Rice, finding the framing shop was way easier than finding a parking space. I backtracked on foot past three blocks of shops before opening a glass door that jangled with bells. Inside, I suffered the most frigid blast of A/C I'd endured in recent memory. It was triple-digit hot outside and I was so sweaty from my walk that the cold air against my wet skin and clothes gave me a sudden chill. The shop smelled like artificial citrus. I made my way toward the counter and tried not to look too confused.

Behind the desk, an alert-looking hippie-type with shaggy hair and round spectacles conjured the image of John Lennon in an apron. He dropped a pen into the apron's pocket and leaned forward on the counter, waiting.

"I'm looking for Marcy. Or maybe Margo." I grinned, hoping levity would head off any questions.

He held my gaze a moment and his lips curled into a conspiring smile. When I didn't offer more, he stood up again and winked at me. "I think you mean Marta."

I chuckled, not sure it sounded sincere. "Bet you're right."

He took a few steps back from the counter and opened one of two swinging doors that reminded me of old Wild West saloons. This set had been upgraded with bumper stickers depicting recycle signs and peace frogs. He called into the back room and a woman, significantly younger than I'd expected, emerged. She was *maybe* twenty-five if having a bad day, which she probably was, judging by her saggy eyes and the stray wisps falling out of her ponytail, not to mention the fact that Daniel had been shot dead in her carport last night.

"Hi, Marta," I said. "I'm looking into the death of Daniel Gaston." I cut a glance to the hippie, who seemed to be in charge. "Can you spare her for a few minutes?"

"Are you a cop?" she asked. "I've already given a statement."

I shook my head. "Private investigator." Not entirely accurate, but easier than explaining the real situation. Neither of them asked to see a license, which was lucky.

Her boss waved us off and she untied her apron and laid it across the far end of the counter before coming around to join me.

I still had a ten dollar bill in my purse. "Can I buy you a cup of coffee?"

She nodded and was first to the jangly door. The heat outside was almost a relief as we took a left and made our way into a Starbucks two doors down. I ordered an iced Cinnamon Skinny Latte and she ordered a Caramel Skinny Latte with no whipped cream.

We settled into seats near the window at the front of the store and I noticed she had trouble looking at me.

"What do you want to know?"

"Could you start with what happened last night? I only know what I heard on the news and that wasn't much."

She looked at me cautiously. "You said you're a private detective. Who hired you?"

"It's complicated," I said. "I'm actually working on a different case but I think Daniel's murder is connected."

"What's your other case?"

"Also a homicide."

She took the lid off her coffee and blew on it. "So you think it's a serial killer?"

It occurred to me then that Marta might be Daniel's murderer, and that she could be having coffee with me to figure out what I knew. *No*, I decided, *you're being paranoid again. The police left her alone.* Surely, they knew more than I did.

"I suspect it's the same killer, yes, but I think it's more cover-up related. I'm trying to figure out what, exactly, is being covered up. Did you see the person who killed him?"

She took a tentative sip, shook her head. "He went out last night to get some wine. Around eleven thirty I heard the shot. By the time the EMS arrived, he was dead." Her tone was remorseful but matter-of-fact. "Shot before he was even out of his car."

"He was staying at your apartment?"

She nodded.

"Were you two a couple?"

Another nod, this time with a sip.

I thought of Claire, Daniel, and their impending divorce. "How long had you been together?"

"About a month."

"And you came to work today?"

Suddenly, she checked her watch. "I should get back. The only reason I came in at all is because I'm taking a trip in two weeks and I can't afford to lose the hours."

That seemed strange, considering her boyfriend was newly dead, but I reminded myself that her definition of "boyfriend" and mine were most likely quite different. What Marta called a boyfriend, I called a sugar daddy.

"Okay," I said. "But before you go, this other case I told you about...I think it has something to do with a con artist and credit card fraud. Has anything weird like that been going on with you or—"

Her eyes flashed and I stopped talking.

"Daniel had weird credit card charges. He said he didn't think much of them before, because his divorce wasn't final and his wife was still using their cards. I guess she was a big spender."

If only you knew.

"Except, last week she went to jail—he didn't say what for—and the charges kept coming so they couldn't have been hers. One was a recurring charge for fifty-eight dollars every Monday night at Brewster's." She drew in a breath and exhaled slowly through her nose, deliberating. "This next part sounds bad." She raised a hand in the universal plea for me to reserve judgment. "He really was a nice guy, but had kind of a short temper. We went down to Brewster's together and Daniel got a little obnoxious, wanting to know who came in there every Monday and spent fifty-eight dollars. The manager didn't like it at first, but after Daniel calmed down and explained it better, the guy gave in and described this person."

"And?"

"Said he was a tall, good looking guy who came in by himself every Monday, had a nice steak fillet and two glasses of old-vine Zinfandel. Same meal, same tip, every week. Anyway, Daniel hands this man a hundred and says, 'Next time that guy comes in here, call me.' He left his number and we went home. Sure enough, three nights ago, he calls."

"Then what?"

"Daniel went down there. He made me stay home, which turned out to be lucky since that's the night we had the big storm. He couldn't make it back that night with all the flooding, so he ended up staying at his wife's house because it was closer." Marta shrugged, unbothered. "She wasn't there."

But I'd been. I remembered Daniel's swollen jaw that night and the pieces began to fit.

"How'd it go at Brewster's?"

"They got kicked out."

"Fighting?"

She nodded. "Daniel never got the guy's name but he wrote down his license plate number."

"You have it?"

"No. I never saw it, don't know what he did with it."

"He say what kind of car it was?"

She thought for a moment, then shrugged. "I don't know. Something sporty I guess because he mentioned fancy rims."

"I think that guy killed Daniel so he couldn't report any of this."

She crinkled her nose as if smelling something horrid. "You think he got killed because of a dumb fight?"

"Not the fight. I think he knew something."

She checked her watch again and stood. "I have to go. Rob's nice but he has limits." She lifted her cup. "Thanks for the coffee."

"Thanks for the talk," I said. "Sorry about the circumstances."

We walked outside together, she peeled off into the frame shop and I continued to my car. Jeannie and I reconnected by cell phone and I collected her at a nearby accessory boutique. She emerged resplendent in a new flowing orange summer scarf.

"How'd that go?" she asked. "Anything good?"

"Real good," I said. "We have a lead."

"I love it when you talk dirty to me."

"We're going to Brewster's."

"What's that?"

I told her the fifty-eight dollar steak story and about how Daniel had confronted his credit card abuser and come away with a bruised face last Monday night. Before I finished, she had her cell phone out again, this time mapping our way to Brewster's.

In Midtown, I pulled alongside a curb and parked the Altima. "I'm so lucky you're here. Or rather, so lucky your phone's here." We'd found the place without so much as a wrong turn or a panicked lane change.

We got out of the car, her sheer scarf blowing in the summer wind. "Admit it. Technology's a beautiful thing."

Inside Brewster's, I felt underdressed even though we hadn't come to eat. Shutters at every window had been permanently closed, giving the place a dim look that made it feel hours later than it really was. Each table, even the vacant ones, had been pre-set with nice crystal and meticulously arranged silverware. A stoic greeter met us near the door and I asked for the manager. Moments later an athletic thirty-something arrived, smiling. The guy was ready to please.

"Oh yeah," he said, after I explained my reason for coming. "No forgetting those two. Had to ask them to leave, then they were carrying on in the parking lot." He shook his head. "Not what you want customers to see."

I looked toward the ceiling, scanning for cameras. "Do you have surveillance here? I'd like to get a look at the one who was passing bad cards."

He shook his head. "Sorry, no."

"Can you describe him?" Marta's "tall and good-looking" report was unlikely to get me very far.

"About six-two," he said, "Maybe two hundred pounds, two-ten. Probably my age. Blond hair, sharp clothes." He paused. "Before this mess he came here a lot, always alone, and the ladies sure did like him."

"He picked up women here?"

"Oh no," he said. "We're not that kind of place. I only meant to say that he turned some heads."

"Shame I missed this guy," Jeannie said.

The manager gave her a fleeting once-over, seemingly unsure what to think.

"You happen to see his car?" I said.

"We all did. I mean, those of us working that shift who could slip outside for a gawk." He chuckled, but probably noticing my anticipation quickly added, "Blue vintage Mustang. Very nice."

I nodded.

"Hey, Em," Jeannie said, surveying the empty tables. "How about something to eat?"

The manager perked up. I'd have rather eaten somewhere cheaper, especially with my personal finances now in such flux, but I appreciated the guy's help and having lunch there seemed an appropriate way to express our thanks. It'd also soothe my nagging conscience about leaving Jeannie alone during so much of her visit.

He showed us to a corner table near one of the boarded up windows. White sunlight sneaked through the shutter chinks, diminishing the illusion that it was evening, but I didn't mind. The case was finally moving forward.

I didn't particularly like the track we were on, but at least we were inching away from the station.

Chapter Twenty-eight

"You know," I said. "I'm starting to get a feeling in the pit of my stomach."

"Nothing a salad and fettuccini can't fix." Jeannie drizzled raspberry vinaigrette over a bowl of baby spinach, walnuts, and feta cheese.

I used my knife to scoot a cherry tomato to the edge of my plate and rephrased. "No, I mean things are adding up."

"Good!"

"Yeah, for the case. But it feels gross to me. I know somebody's out there watching everything I do, or at least making me feel like he's watching everything I do. I hate that he's been in the apartment, and I can't help but wonder what else in my personal life he's screwing around with."

"Hey, that reminds me about Vince—"

I raised a hand. "We'll come back to him."

She pushed a forkful of salad into her mouth and nodded. When she finished, she set her fork down and sipped from her water glass. "How do you figure things are adding up?"

"Monday night when I got stuck at Claire's during that storm, a guy stopped by. Later Claire told me he's a hanger-on ex-lover."

"Bummer," she said. "We've all had those."

No, not all of us. I let it go.

She angled her head down slightly and gazed up at me from under perfectly tweezed brows. "Why didn't you tell me about that?"

I squinted at her. "Maybe I would have if you'd have answered any of the phones that night when I called."

She grinned, apparently pleased I was still annoyed.

"Anyway," I continued. "This guy who stopped by had a key, knew the pass code, and made his way around the kitchen like he owned the place. He was completely adorable and a real looker—" She grinned and her eyes crinkled. Any mention of handsome men got this response from her. "—But don't get excited yet. The creepy part is that he looked like that manager's description."

Her smile vanished. "Ick."

"Exactly. And it gets worse." I took my own sip of water.

A waiter brought a fresh loaf of warm bread over and Jeannie began slicing it immediately.

"Did you tell the guy your name?"

"Of course," I said. "At the time I thought maybe he was her live-in boyfriend. I mean, a guy walks right into the house, helps himself to a beer and offers you a drink. Doesn't that seem like somebody who lives there? The entire encounter was bizarre. Totally awkward."

She grabbed a saucer from my side of the table and put two slices of bread on it before passing it back. I buttered them and tried not to get ahead of myself in the story.

"He told me his name was Kevin Burke. When I asked if he lived there, he said it was Claire's house."

"Suitably vague."

"Yeah. And then he walked over to the freezer…"

At this, Jeannie twisted her face into an expression best described as repulsion. "Stop. Just stop now."

"Well it's relevant, I think. He went to the freezer for you-know-what and tossed one into the sink and said he was doing Logan a favor by feeding the snake while the kid was at his grandmother's house."

She closed her eyes and turned her head away, presumably letting a wave of nausea pass. I was pretty sure this was all for show.

When she turned back, she took a bite of her own buttered bread and thought for a moment while she chewed. "The kid was there earlier in the day," she finally said. "You suppose he forgot?"

"*Thank you,*" I said. "At the time I wondered the same thing. The weather was horrible...you remember." She nodded. "You'd think an errand like that one could wait a day, until conditions cleared. I mean, can't snakes go weeks without eating? What's another day or two?"

"Please stop with the snakes and the eating."

I smiled. "*Then,* when he pulled down the driveway, I remember watching his tail lights go and I'm positive he drove a Mustang."

She brightened. "Like the fifty-eight dollar steak guy."

"Yes, but there's *more.*"

"You're killing me. You're like Nancy Drew today." She chuckled. "Must be the clothes. I think she dressed frumpy too."

"Just because an outfit isn't skin tight and cut to my navel doesn't make me homely."

"Maybe we should get you a little pillbox hat to go with your sensible shoes."

"I hate you."

She laughed. "Tell me the rest."

"No."

"Come on." She went back to cutting her salad.

I returned my attention to my own salad and ignored her. Why pick the middle of the story to insult me?

She tried again. "So he drove a Mustang *and. . .*"

I couldn't help myself. "But I don't think it was blue. Or vintage."

"Weird."

"When I went to the Heights on Tuesday evening to talk to Platt's neighbors, William, the one who's afraid of strangers, was wearing a shirt with a Mustang logo on it."

"How do you remember this stuff?"

"I thought it was sad. He seemed to like cars but probably couldn't drive."

She shrugged, stabbed a bite of lettuce.

"Then I went to Platt's house later, after Diana gave me the key, and somebody came home to William's house as Vince and I were leaving. I saw the garage door going down."

"Let me guess," she said, "A Mustang."

"Yep."

"Blue vintage?"

"No. I think it was a later model."

"Someone in this mess has a penchant for Ford, I guess."

Two waiters came, each with a plate, and set steaming dishes of pasta in front of us. We were offered fresh cracked black pepper and Parmesan cheese grated off a huge block. I declined, wanting to be left alone, but Jeannie asked for both.

When we were alone again, I added the last detail. "The guy that takes care of William is called Mr. B."

She twirled angel hair around the tines of her fork. "Mr. Burke?"

"That's what I'm wondering." Maybe I'd had too much bread and salad. My appetite was gone.

After the meal, Jeannie drove us toward Claire's house in River Oaks while I tried to get through the convoluted phone system at the Harris County Jail. I needed to ask Claire where I might find a photograph of Kevin Burke to show the manager at Brewster's. If I couldn't reach her, or if no photos were at the house, I still wanted another pass through her records. Now that I knew what to look for, I hoped something new would come to light.

After a transfer and what felt like a half hour on hold, I learned that offenders in jail can't receive incoming calls. Frustrated, I asked when visiting hours ended, figuring that maybe there was still time to go ask her in person.

"Attorneys on record can visit around the clock, seven days a week," the attendant said. "Everyone else has until nine." We still had a few hours. Computer keys clacked on the other end of the line. "Unfortunately, it looks like she's already had a visitor. Only one visit per day."

Of course. Young had sent her mother to break the news about Daniel.

I took an extended breath and exhaled slowly through my nose, letting my head fall back into the headrest.

An idea formed. I thanked the attendant and hung up.

"I can't call her or see her. Young's going to have to do it." I opened my phone again. "I really don't want to make this call."

"Don't call him yourself. Have Richard do it."

I swiveled my head, still on the headrest, and looked at her. "That's the call I don't want to make."

"Read it back to me," I said.

Richard played along, but he wasn't pleased. "You want to know if there are any pictures of Kevin Burke and where they are. You want to know how long she and Kevin were together. You want to hear all about the break-up, and whether anything sketchy was going on with her credit cards."

"Right," I said, a little louder than was necessary. "The break up's the most important part. Make sure Young gets it right. I need to know *everything* she would have told me if they'd let me come see her. He'll have to explain why I'm not there."

"When are you going to tell me what's going on?"

"Tell him to hurry too. He needs to go right now, no matter what. We're almost to Claire's house. Call me back after you've talked to him and I'll fill you in."

He hung up on me, his normal thing when I got too bossy.

I turned to Jeannie. "Claire holds stuff back. Sometimes she leaves out the most obvious details."

Jeannie kept her eyes on the road. "Self-destructive?"

"Not sure. When I talk to her it's like pulling teeth. This morning Young told me I got further with her than he did."

"Weird."

"I'm worried she won't tell him what I want to know. She has a knack for glossing over the big points."

Jeannie checked her mirror and changed lanes. "You're doing everything you can with what you have."

I looked out the passenger window and idly watched sidewalks, cars, and billboards stream by while thinking about that. She was right.

"Now about Vince," she said, with a stern edge in her voice that meant there'd be no more avoiding the topic.

I rolled out my neck, its tension suddenly oppressive. With my chin still on my chest and the muscles at the base of my skull stretching, I took a deep breath.

"Here's the thing," I said, chin down, thankful to avoid her steely eyes. "Staying with Vince would be too awkward."

"Because I'm there? Because I'll get a hotel room, no problem."

"No," I said, aware my pulse was elevated. "Awkward because of tons of other stuff."

"Richard was right, though. It's a good idea to stay elsewhere until we figure out what's going on with your cyber stalker."

I didn't know where to begin. "It'd be different if we were, um—"

"Sleeping together."

I nodded.

"Because then you'd be staying over at each other's places already."

"Right."

"Has there been any talk of this?"

"No."

"You're waiting each other out?"

"I think so. I don't know."

"Do you want to sleep with him?"

I hesitated, aware that my face was frozen in confusion. "That's complicated too."

She looked at me funny, like I'd just admitted that I couldn't spell my own name. "Well, either you do or you don't."

"There hasn't been anyone since Jack," I said. "That's a long time."

Her lips curved into a wan smile. "It's like riding a bike."

I wanted to shrink and disappear into the space between my seat cushions. "So there's that. And dealing with sleeping arrangements would be uncomfortable. I don't want to put us in a position where we both have to pretend we're not thinking about it."

"He'd do anything to help you." She nodded toward the phone in my hand. "When we get to Claire's you can call him when I'm not around. I know how you are." She let go of the wheel with both hands for a moment and wiggled her fingers in the air in a bewitching sort of way. "Wanting *privacy*, and all."

I smiled, and the moment was interrupted with a vibrating buzz from my cell phone.

"Damn."

I'd set it to vibrate *and* ring, but it was past making any noises at all now and Caller ID was still offering only garbage.

I flipped open the phone, determined to replace it within hours.

"Young's headed to the jail now," Richard said. "He'll call when they finish. Guy's keen to know what brought all these questions all of a sudden. I was a little hard-pressed to explain that I didn't know myself."

I checked the dashboard clock. "Can you meet us at my apartment in a couple hours? I'll take care of dinner. We can go over everything."

"Do I have a choice?" He didn't sound put out. I figured the dinner offer had helped.

"Do me a favor," I said. "Bring your laptop."

"Sure," he said. "See you then."

Jeannie and I rode the remaining ten minutes in silence. I tried to mentally review what I remembered of Burke, but my thoughts kept returning to Vince. Our relationship needed definition but I'd been too distracted to take the lead and he'd been too polite. Between Annette and the new job, I'd been overwhelmed, neglected to do the normal new-romance womanly things. In three months, all I'd given Vince were pleas of confusion and mixed messages.

For weeks I'd told myself that once things settled down at home and work, I'd do my part to get us on a straight path. I'd imagined us sitting together one night, coming clean with everything. Maybe it would take a few talks.

My new problem was that I hadn't laid the framework to seek any favors, particularly of the sleep-over-at-your-house variety. The undertones that had bothered me before would be nothing compared to what was coming.

Chapter Twenty-nine

There'd been no word from Mick Young by the time Jeannie and I arrived at Claire's house. We used the hidden key and pass code to get inside, same as before, but this time I had an uneasy feeling when I walked through the door.

"Is it me or is something different here?"

Jeannie paused midway between the kitchen and foyer and sniffed lightly. "You mean that stale, empty house smell?"

"No." I tapped a thin stack of mail waiting on Claire's counter. "This is new."

Jeannie shrugged.

I walked the perimeter of Claire's wide kitchen, dragging a finger over her cool granite countertop. At the sink, I stopped in front of a window-sill herb garden. "Somebody's watering these plants."

"Sure," Jeannie said. "Probably her mom."

I recalled my earlier conversation with Claire and her uncertainty about the number of people who may have had access to the home. The memory made me restless and I wandered into the living room, vaguely aware that Jeannie was following.

A remote control, left on the arm rest of the couch, waited beside two throw pillows now compressed into a spot where there'd originally been only one. What had seemed like a sterile house before now showed signs of life.

I looked at Jeannie. "Surely, her mom doesn't come over here to watch TV?"

"You're forgetting the boys. We know they still come home."
She picked up the remote, examined it. "All kids do anymore is
sit in front of the tube."

I relaxed a little. "Do me a favor," I said. "The extra room
upstairs where we saw those photo albums..." I pointed overhead
in its general direction. "Bring down any pictures in that stash that
might be Kevin Burke...ones that match the description from
Brewster's. I'm going to have another pass through her folders."

Jeannie headed for the stairs and I stepped across the foyer
into the home office and flipped on the light switch, which also
turned on a ceiling fan. I sat in Claire's desk chair for the third
time and it occurred to me that I should be the one looking for
pictures of Kevin. I was the only one who'd seen him.

I called after her. "Be up in a sec!"

I pulled open a filing cabinet drawer again, this time paying
special attention to anything financial. Separate folders had been
designated for specific credit cards and for bank statements,
but as I thumbed through their contents I found that the dates
reflected records that were several months old in some cases,
and over a year old in others. Why had Claire or Daniel kept
meticulous records for years and then suddenly stopped?

Above me, fan blades whirled and little ornamental pull
chains tapped the light fixture in irregular beats, giving the
momentary impression that drizzling rain was falling. Realizing
the source of the noise, I leaned back in the chair and took in
the room again from ceiling to floor, stopping to think about the
unplugged mouse, forgotten on its pad, and the disconnected
printer, with its cord draped loosely over its top. For once, a
conclusion arrived in my mind, clean and uncluttered, like
the room I was sitting in. *Of course there are no recent records,* I
thought, *The Gastons use on-line bill pay, same as me.*

Without use of their missing computer, I'd never be able to
figure out when the spending habits had first changed on their
credit cards. I lingered in the quiet, dim study, thinking. Spotting
the handset on the corner of her desk, I wondered if anything
useful might be in her Caller ID log. Platt's had been a windfall.

I pressed the arrow that took me backward in time through sixty incoming calls and noticed that three in June and July had come from "Financial Card Services," a familiar term after having spent so much time sorting my own credit hassles.

"Emily!" Jeannie thumped down the stairs. When she reached the bottom of the carpeted steps her footfalls changed from muffled thuds to loud clacks on tile. She came around the corner, breathless.

"Her jewelry's gone."

I set the phone down and dropped my chin into my hand. For a moment I felt like I'd reached the point where nothing could surprise me.

"When we were here on Monday," she said, "There were rings and bracelets. All of it's gone."

I was too frustrated to move.

"My favorite was her blue topaz cocktail ring. You should have seen the *size* of that baby…" She frowned. "*Gone.*"

"I sent you up there to look for pictures in a different *room*. This isn't dress-up time, Jeannie. A woman is sitting in jail and a crazy computer freak is after me. You're worried about her jewelry?"

I ran my open palm upward over the right side of my face and then down the left, as if the face-washing pantomime might wake me up, conjure some ideas. With my head still low I grabbed my temples and squeezed. For the life of me, I couldn't *think*.

I raked my fingers through my hair and sat up. "Her mom might have taken those things for safe keeping, but somehow I doubt it."

Jeannie lowered her chin and stared at me, her skepticism evident. "There's a painting missing too."

I stood and followed her upstairs. The coincidence of Claire's apparent jewelry theft in the same week as mine didn't sit well.

"I don't get to be around nice things like hers every day," Jeannie said without apology. "Had to take a second look."

She peeled to the left, where the door to the master bedroom had been left open. The room was as I'd remembered, and if Jeannie hadn't pointed out the empty nail along the wall where a painting had once been, I wouldn't have noticed it missing. She led me to Claire's bureau. The jewelry box still had a few nice costume pieces, including an oval pendant embossed with delicate paw prints, but it was nowhere near full anymore. I was about to go look for photos in the guest room when my phone buzzed.

Expecting Richard, I flipped it open with a curt, "Yeah?"

"*Yeah* to you too, lady." It was Vince. I mouthed his name to Jeannie and she gave me an encouraging nod before leaving the room and pulling the door closed behind her. "What kind of trouble are you girls up to tonight?"

"Funny you should ask," I said. "Because you might get dragged into it."

He chuckled. "How so?"

I sat lightly on the edge of Claire's king bed and focused on my reflection in the mirror mounted over her dresser. "We need a favor."

"You always need favors."

"This one's big."

"Okay, let's hear it."

"It's fine if you want to say no." When he didn't say anything, I continued. "I've been getting some…creepy e-mails and somebody broke into the apartment—"

"What? When?"

"Yesterday."

"Were you there? What happened?"

"No. I didn't figure it out until today. It happened when we went out for dinner." On his end, a horn blared. "You're driving?"

"On my way home. Did you call the police?"

"I don't want to go into everything while you're in traffic," I said. "Can you come over for dinner?" Before he could answer, I clarified. "Richard'll be there. We're going to brainstorm the case."

"Sure," he said. "I'll head over in a little bit."

I told him to drive safely and we hung up. My phone buzzed again.

"You never told me what the favor is."

"Richard doesn't think my apartment's safe anymore. He wants Jeannie and me to find a place to stay for a few days, starting tonight."

Vince was quiet. I thought he was probably doing mental iterations of sleeping arrangements, stressing about the implications of each potential set-up the same way I had.

"I'll have to get food," he said.

Or maybe he was thinking like a guy.

"I'll stock the fridge," I said. "Don't worry about it."

"And you won't like what's behind the shower curtain."

"I'll take care of it."

"No. Make Jeannie do it."

I laughed. "Never happen."

"There's the dog hair," he said.

"I get it," I said, trying to find balance between being playful and reassuring. "It's not like I've never been there." *It's only that I've never slept over.* "We'll be low maintenance, I swear." I paused. "At least I will."

"And there's a condition," he added, as if he hadn't heard me. "This is short notice so you can't hold anything against me."

"I love that you're worried about making a bad impression."

"Is it a deal?"

"Thank you *so* much."

"I'm always bailing you out of trouble." His voice made it sound more like a compliment than a complaint.

I grinned. "See you in a little bit."

After the call, I found Jeannie sitting cross-legged on the bed in the guest room, going through photographs in a series of boxes and albums.

She looked up expectantly. "All good?"

"Yep."

"Told you so." She replaced the lid on a photo box and moved it to an empty spot on the quilt behind her. "These pictures are old. Unless she knew the guy ten years ago, he's not in here."

I shook my head. "He's new. A short-timer." I checked my watch and wondered how much Claire might be telling Mick Young. "Where else can we look?"

"If he was a short-timer, there might not *be* pictures." A devilish smile crossed her lips. "At least...not of his face."

It made me wonder how many summer flings Jeannie had had. Her point about not having pictures hadn't even occurred to me. I shook my head in distaste and dialed Richard.

"Any word?"

"Pictures aren't the least of it," he said, "but we can talk about that in person later. She thinks there's a snapshot in one of her handbags. Something juicy."

I glared at my over-sexed friend. "I'm not going to find an x-rated photo, am I?"

"Huh? Oh. No, I meant the purse, not the picture. She told Young the purse is something juicy. I don't know what that means."

"Hold on."

My face twisted into an impatient expression, the result of getting half-information from a totally clueless man. I looked at Jeannie. "A juicy purse?"

She nodded serenely, as I imagined the Dalai Lama might. "Juicy Couture. Claire has three." Jeannie stretched her legs over the side of the bed and pushed herself up. "Be right back."

I watched her disappear into the hallway. "Jeannie's on it," I said into the phone. "So did Claire talk? Did she say anything about Burke?"

"Young said the meeting was a test of his patience."

"I don't care what Young said. What did Claire say?"

"She gave him a bunch of flack but eventually acknowledged that they'd been together a couple of months before she broke it off. It wasn't a cold turkey break, either. One of those long, arduous break-ups. She didn't want to cut Burke out of her life entirely because she thought he was a positive influence on her sons."

"Yeah," I said. "She told me something similar."

Jeannie returned, waving a snapshot. "A hottie!"

I snatched the photo from her and stared at it.

"We have his picture," I said to Richard. "Head over to the apartment and remember your laptop."

◇◇◇

We swung by Brewster's on our way to meet Richard. The manager confirmed my hunch with a single definite flick on Burke's impossibly handsome face. "That's him."

He passed the photograph back with something like a remorseful shrug, perhaps sensing my mixed feelings about finally knowing who we were dealing with.

Forty-five minutes later, Richard sat at my kitchen table studying his computer screen while Vince and I lounged on the couch sharing mine. We were tapping keys, clicking links, buried deep in Google and Wikipedia.

I'd printed the last e-mail from my cyber spook and Richard busied himself with biographies of all the famous people Burke had cited in that message. He aimed to figure out what they had in common. Vince and I tried to learn what we could about William Henry Saunders the third so we could determine how he'd gotten unwittingly tied up in this mess.

We only found his name once, in a caption. He'd been photographed with his mother, the late Judith Saunders, a decade ago at a Houston Rodeo fundraising event. Apparently she'd been an avid volunteer for thirty years.

Vince pointed mid-way down the list of search results. "Click that one."

An obituary from the *Chronicle* came up and I read it aloud so Richard could hear too.

> JUDITH SAUNDERS, age 80, passed away on Thursday, April 2 at her home. A long time resident of Houston Heights, she was born in New Braunfels, Texas, on December 22, 1920 and was preceded in death by her husband, William H. Saunders II. Judith will be remembered for her tender heart and iron will, traits that served her for decades of commendable volunteerism in her community. For thirty years she and her husband sponsored scholarships for local children with intellectual disabilities. They were instrumental in raising community awareness of these underserved children.

```
She leaves her loving son, William Henry
III, and sisters Claudia and Violet. Judith
touched the lives of everyone who knew her
and will be greatly missed. The memorial
service will be Sunday, April 5, at 11
a.m. at Grace Family Fellowship. In lieu of
flowers please send donations to help fulfill
Judith's dream: Saunders Scholarship Fund,
c/o First National Bank, Houston Heights.
```

"That's scary," Vince said when I'd finished. "A rich old lady died and her estate went to her mentally challenged son?" He rested an arm on the back of the couch. "Hardly makes sense. A reasonable person would have put it into a trust."

I considered the timeline and shook my head. "He wasn't always this way. It's from a head trauma. When his mom died, he was perfectly fine, so it makes sense she'd leave everything to him."

I started to tell Vince what I'd read in William's medical records. The front door knob rattled and Jeannie battled her way inside with a precarious arrangement of soft drinks and too many sacks of Chinese take-out. I'd sent her out for dinner while waiting for the guys. They stood to help her and she closed the door with a bump of her hip.

"Hi, Richard," she said, passing him the drinks. "Hey, Cowboy." She handed off a wayward sack.

I headed to the kitchen for plates and heard them pop lids and arrange entrees behind me at the kitchen table.

"Smells good," I said. "You bring me anything that wasn't fried?"

I already knew the answer.

"Where would be the fun in that?" Jeannie said. "Did I miss anything?"

"Not yet," Vince said. "Richard's trying to figure out what that list of famous people was supposed to mean. So far, all we've found is an obituary for the neighbor's mom. Seems she left her son quite a haul."

I pulled some forks from the silverware drawer and joined the others. Richard helped me pass out plates and then stacked his high with fried rice and mandarin chicken. He returned immediately to what he was doing on the laptop. The rest of us filled our own plates and fit where we could in the remaining space around him.

"So the guy next door to Platt is loaded," Jeannie said. "And his caretaker's skimming."

Richard glanced at her. "Understatement."

"Platt must have noticed and tried to report it," I said. "But since Saunders didn't know better than to give Burke everything he asked for—"

"There's no crime." Richard said. "Everything Saunders gave Burke is probably legally considered a 'gift.'"

Vince shook his head. "That makes me sick."

"Platt must have confronted him." Jeannie dipped an egg roll in sweet and sour sauce. "That's the only way Burke could have known he had suspicions."

"Makes sense," Vince said. "Then Burke got paranoid because Platt had his number. So he killed him."

"Sure," I said. "But not at that confrontation. It would have taken planning to pin it on Claire."

We stopped talking momentarily, all too busy thinking or eating.

Jeannie, not one for silence, tapped her fork on her plate. "That's a good reason to want Platt dead. For a long time Burke had been living carefree in a fancy house, driving nice cars and using a bottomless supply of cash."

I remembered Burke's recent e-mail to Claire, the one I'd found in her closeted curio box. "He told Claire he was an artist, working on an important sculpture or something, and that's why he never had her over at his place—because he needed the solitude for his art." I took a sip of the Coke Jeannie had brought me.

Vince reached across my plate for more soy sauce packets. "Framing Claire to get even for breaking up sounds extreme."

Jeannie was chewing but waved a finger to reserve space to comment. She swallowed. "Getting dumped might be even tougher on a sociopath's ego than it is for the rest of us. And let's not forget there's more to the Claire thing. He was swindling money from the Gastons too."

Vince looked up. "Really?"

"Oh yeah, big time," she said. "Daniel had a girl on the side and she told Emily all about it."

Richard looked up from the monitor. "A girlfriend?"

I took another pull on my Coke. "We went to Rice Village to check out the murder scene. I tracked down the woman who rents the place where he was shot. Daniel had noticed extraneous charges on his credit card statements for a while, but since he and Claire still shared those accounts, he assumed the charges were hers. When she went to jail, the charges didn't stop, so a few days ago he started asking questions."

I took a bite of cashew chicken and Jeannie relayed what we'd learned from the manager at Brewster's. She explained how the Mustang coincidence had made me suspicious enough to re-visit the Tone Zone parking lot footage from last week. Sure enough, a car by the same description had been in the lot Thursday morning.

Vince glanced at me with a subtle smile. I wasn't sure if he was impressed or amused.

"Then Platt wasn't the only one onto Burke's ruse," Richard said, scrolling down his screen without looking at us. "Daniel confronted him too. And they both ended up dead." He punctuated the statement with a double mouse click.

Jeannie dipped her egg roll again. "I wonder how he met Claire in the first place."

"Through Platt, I'm sure." Vince emptied the last of the ginger beef from its paper container.

I shook my head. "Claire and Platt didn't know each other. At least not according to her."

"She met Burke at Tone Zone months ago," Richard said, glancing up for an instant. "He was helping a friend move a piece of furniture to the club one day. Claire was there working out. The rest is history."

Inexplicably, I suddenly felt sorry for Claire. "More likely he was helping a *neighbor*. Platt was an older guy, not many friends or relations. I wouldn't blame him for asking the young, athletic caretaker next door for a hand. And Burke and Claire are both charismatic flirts," I said. "So Richard's right. All they'd have to do is meet."

"How she met Burke isn't important," Richard said. "What we need to know is how he set her up. The murder weapon came from her garage."

His comment conjured the image of a dark stain on the floor in Platt's study and, without meaning to, I imagined a bloody screwdriver lodged in the dead surgeon's neck. Appetite lost, I set down my fork and reached for a napkin.

"With Burke at her house all the time, it's easy to see how he got the screwdriver," I said. "And we know he got her to the crime scene with that bogus note about a neglected dog. Having lived with her, Burke would know she was a sucker for critters and that she'd respond to a situation like that. That's how he got her prints at the scene. But how'd he get them on the screwdriver? She hardly seems the fix-it type."

Richard must have finished his drink because he started stabbing his straw up and down through its plastic lid, moving around the ice that was left behind. Still focused on his monitor, his attention was obviously divided between our conversation and whatever he was reading. He went through another series of mouse clicks and then, with apparent effort, finally pulled his eyes off the monitor and glanced around the table. He stopped at me.

I suffered through an awkward moment while it looked like he was remembering something he'd wanted to say. He scratched his cheek the way men with stubble sometimes do and said, "I'm starting to wonder if Burke isn't way smarter than we're giving him credit."

Personally, I'd been giving Burke lots of credit but I didn't interrupt Richard to say so.

He continued. "You wanted to know when they broke up."

I nodded. "Because I thought that's when the weird credit card charges would have started."

"Young says it was a slow, languishing separation. Not a clean break."

Jeannie made a disgusted face to convey that, like Claire, she'd been there. I assumed it was for Richard and Vince's benefit because I already knew and didn't care.

Richard continued. "Claire thought she'd finally found a decent role model for the boys and was reluctant to cut him loose, despite her instinct that things weren't right." Without picking up his cup, he fiddled with his straw again. "What if she'd tried to break it off a few times, but Burke was tuned in to her reluctance? Maybe he was sweet talking her, or promising to change."

"If he was siphoning money from her, I'm sure he'd exploit any weakness he could if it meant he could stick around longer."

"Exactly," Richard said. "And I think he was successful to a point. But when Platt figured out the scheme with Saunders, and Claire kept talking Splitsville, suddenly Burke's castle in the sky began to crumble. The on-again, off-again break-up might be what saved him and ruined her. Surely he saw the writing on the wall. What if he got her prints on the weapon before she kicked him out for good?"

Jeannie snapped her fingers. "Maybe when she was sleeping."

Richard shrugged. "If he's as shrewd as I think he is, I wouldn't put anything past him."

"So I'm being electronically stalked by a practiced con-man and meticulous killer." I looked at Richard. "I should be earning hazard pay."

He didn't look up from his screen.

"I'm scared," I continued. "He knows who I am and why I'm asking questions. He's warned me several times to stop. He's been here and he knows about Annette. What if he comes back and goes after her?"

My breath caught.

Vince put a hand on my arm. "She's safe with Betsy and Nick," he said. "And you'll stay at my place for a while like we talked about." He wrapped his arm around me and pulled me into him sideways, trying to be reassuring.

A new idea came to me and I straightened. Burke had tracked me down on-line, broken into the apartment, and stolen some jewelry—all scary things, but hardly anything life threatening.

"Burke's a pro," I said. "He knows I'm suspicious. When Platt and Daniel got suspicious, they ended up dead. All I got were e-mails. Why?"

Richard pushed back from the table and stood. "I think I've figured that one out," he said, wiping his hands on a paper napkin. "Printed something." He walked through my little kitchen toward the printer in the laundry room and returned with a sheet of paper that he passed to me.

It was a list of excerpts, all in different fonts and formats, that he'd obviously cut and pasted from various websites while we'd been eating.

"The theme was clear," he said. "I only copied from a few of their bios." He nodded to the paper in my hand. "You'll see."

Vince faced me and I read aloud from Richard's haphazard list:

"Bach's mother died in 1694 and his father in 1695, when the boy was only ten years old.

"Tolstoy's mother died when he was two and his father died when he was nine.

"Aristotle, whose parents died when he quite young, was raised by a guardian who later sent him to Plato's academy in Athens.

"Born Norma Jean Baker to an unmarried woman, Monroe was in foster care until she was nearly seven.

"Malcolm X's father was murdered by white racists in 1931. Years later social workers removed him and his siblings from his mother's care and put them into a children's home.

"Fitzgerald never knew her father and her mother passed in 1935."

I could hardly believe it. When I glanced up from the page, Richard was the only one watching me. Vince stared at the table and Jeannie at my front window. Both seemed lost in somber thought, same as me. I stepped backward and felt for the couch. Finding it, I took a seat and exhaled. "He's telling us he was orphaned."

"That's not all," Richard said. "What's frightening is that he counts himself among great people in history who grew up without parents. I think he views himself as some sort of…overcomer."

I squeezed the back of my neck, thinking. "I wonder if he found out about Annette when he broke in here," I said. "Or maybe he knew about her already, from looking up articles about me on-line."

Richard shook his head. "Impossible to know, but I think Annette saved you. He knows you're her only parent and he has a soft spot for orphans. He's anxious, though. I don't think he'll hesitate if we cross him again."

"Me either," Vince said. Then, turning to Richard he added, "I suppose you're taking it from here then? Emily can't stay involved now."

Richard shook his head. "Not me," he said. "Homicide. When the detectives download her report there's going to be an instant follow-up." He looked at his watch. "They're probably at the Saunders house right now."

I wanted nothing further to do with Kevin Burke and his twisted schemes but couldn't help thinking about William. No matter how much care was taken, detectives would confuse and frighten him. There was no getting around that and William had nobody left to soften reality for him.

For my part, I didn't like the way Richard and Vince were suddenly making decisions for me as if I weren't in the room. But the rational part of my brain, where my maternal instincts lived, told the willful, independent remainder to sit down and shut the hell up.

So while they talked about packing bags and coordinated plans for Jeannie and me to relocate, I didn't say a word.

Chapter Thirty

I'd been to Vince's house plenty of times but it felt strangely foreign when I stepped inside carrying an overnight bag for the first time.

Jeannie brushed past me with her bag-on-wheels and over-sized tote and stood in the middle of his vast living room to have a proper look around. "Nice place, Cowboy. I especially like this vaulted ceiling."

I flipped on his porch light and closed and locked the door behind us. Vince's Yellow Lab, Cindy, was in the back yard scratching at the glass door, whining to be let inside. I dropped my bag beside the couch and left Vince to enumerate all his recent home improvement projects for Jeannie. When I opened the back door, Cindy rushed to greet me and nearly took me out at the knees. Her tail wagged so violently that the back half of her body twisted with every swing. She followed me to his couch where I sat down and coaxed her into rolling over for a belly scratch.

Vince told Jeannie to make herself at home. "Emily knows where everything is." He walked past the dog and me on his way to the kitchen. "Beer?"

"Yeah, thanks." Jeannie paced the room's perimeter, inspecting shelves and photos.

"Emily?" Vince said from the kitchen.

"None for me," I said. "Not in the mood."

As if she understood, Cindy licked the back of my hand. I leaned close to her face and ignored the dog breath. "What am I supposed to do here tonight?" I whispered.

She only thumped her tail. Glasses clinked in the kitchen, the familiar sounds of a warm, inviting house. Exhausted, I slipped off my shoes and curled up under an afghan Vince kept draped over his sofa. Mostly reclined, I scratched Cindy's ears with my free hand.

Vince returned with the beers and tapped me on the leg with a cold bottle of Shiner Bock as he passed. I pulled myself further under the blanket.

"You look tired."

He passed a bottle to Jeannie. I nestled into a throw pillow and let my silence speak for me.

"Can I get the five cent tour?" Jeannie said. "Or do guys not do that?"

"Sure," he said. "Let's start back here."

I listened to them chat as Vince led Jeannie down the hallway. My eyes closed and I made no effort to keep them open. Sleep was near and I was weak for it.

When I awoke, I had no idea how much time had passed. The house, dark now, gave no hint about where Vince or Jeannie might have gone, but judging from its stillness, I could guess. I sat up. Someone had laid a quilt over me. I pressed the Indiglo button on my watch and saw that it was 11:21.

Going comatose on the sofa had solved the problem of sleeping arrangements, but I wasn't sure if I was relieved or disappointed about where I'd ended up. I thought about Vince, only a few yards away in his room, and felt lonely without him. I leaned back onto the pillow and pulled the quilt over me again. In the dark, all I could see was a green, blinking LED on the ceiling. I assumed it was a smoke detector and stared at its persistent little light, asking myself on a scale of one to ten how ridiculous it was to be sleeping alone on Vince's couch with him so near that I could almost smell his cologne.

Jeannie was right about him. He was too polite for his own good. And I'd made so many big decisions, so fast, lately that the prospect of initiating another huge life change was terrifying. With this much self-doubt it was no wonder I couldn't send consistent signals. I wondered what was keeping him around.

Well, I knew. We both knew, didn't we? We could just never find the right words.

In our short history, we'd always said more when neither was talking. There'd been our first dance. Surrounded by hoards of mostly drunk people, I remembered the way he'd pulled me close and how I'd eventually rested my head on his shoulder, eyes closed. Despite the noise and hullabaloo, while we were dancing it had seemed we were having our own private conversation. In the time between the beginning and end of that song, something between us changed. Maybe something inside me had changed as well.

Once, he'd found me crying. He hadn't said a word then either, just held me close and kissed my forehead. That was special, too.

I pushed the quilt back and sat up a second time, listening to nothing and staring into virtual blackness. The ice maker in the kitchen rumbled, then stopped. My chest felt a little bit tight, but when I stood, anxiety faded into resolve.

His door had been left partially open, which I hoped was a good sign. I entered slowly, unsure if he was asleep, and silently closed the door before walking toward the bed. In the shadows, I made out the form of his silhouette but couldn't tell whether he was facing toward or away from me. For a moment I stood over him, wanting to crawl in but scared of screwing everything up.

I needn't have worried. Blankets rustled and shadows changed as Vince slid the covers back.

I slipped in with him and my feet felt something solid at the end of the bed. Cindy's collar jangled as she gave up her spot and slinked to the floor. Vince's arms enveloped me under the sheets with him.

The bed was already warm.

He was shirtless, nearly motionless, and his touch was talking in that silent way I cherished. I couldn't find his eyes, and it didn't matter. He ran a hand lightly up my arm to my shoulder and barely squeezed, enough to reassure me we were having the same conversation.

He kissed me slowly then, deliberately, and retraced his path down my arm so tenderly that the gesture was incredibly seductive. I gave myself fully over to him then for the first time, feeling everything coming back—his vulnerability, desire, all of him.

Even though no words were said, in the morning I awoke beside him, comfortable in knowing we'd finally talked it all out.

Chapter Thirty-one

Friday morning, Vince climbed out of bed while it was still dark, showered, and got an early start. I stayed behind, mostly asleep, and smiled when he kissed me before sneaking out the door. It seemed only moments later that Jeannie was bumping around in his kitchen, but when I finally opened my eyes, light was streaming through the window.

Still in pajamas, I shuffled out to meet her and propped myself on a stool along the bar. Grinning, she passed me a just-poured cup of coffee that I assumed was originally meant for her. "Blankets on the couch this morning," she said. "But no Emily."

"I'm not going to talk about it," I said. "Thanks for the joe."

Without looking at me, she turned and pulled four eggs from a carton on the counter and cracked them into a bowl with surprising precision. "That's fine," she said. "Because I'm trying a new thing. Respecting boundaries."

"How very mature of you. Need some help?"

"With the boundaries or the omelets?"

"Either."

She found the silverware drawer and produced a fork. "No."

She used the fork to whip the eggs, then pulled a knife from Vince's cutlery set and cubed a block of cheddar cheese, her back still to me. "So what's the plan for today?" A skillet, I noticed, had already been positioned on a front burner. She turned the knob to start the gas.

"I didn't feel guilty," I said.

She faced me, cheese cubes in hand. "What?"

"Last night. Does that make me bad? Should I have felt guilty?"

She tossed the cheese in the skillet and poured the eggs in too. As if she hadn't heard me, she pulled open a series of drawers before finding a spatula and stirring the mixture. Finally she said, "What would you tell Annette?"

"If she asked about Vince?"

"No. If, twenty years from now, she were you and you were me and the same thing happened to her."

I felt my face scrunch. Jeannie snapped her fingers at me. "Just answer."

"I'd want her to be happy, and not to be alone. I'd tell her there was nothing to feel guilty about."

Jeannie opened her hand and motioned as if to say "there you go."

"Of course," I said, "It's different when the person in question is me."

She turned the heat down on the burner and leaned backward on the counter, still within arm's reach of the pan. Her expression softened. "I can absolutely guarantee what Jack would say."

I tapped my nails on the ceramic mug. The coffee was too hot.

Her point made, Jeannie redirected her attention to the stove and used the spatula to test the edges of the omelet. After all the months of haranguing and unwanted advice regarding my tardy milestones with Vince, her new restraint flummoxed me.

I let it ride.

"Diana King deserves to know what we learned yesterday," I said. "I'll try to catch her at the club this morning. Not sure if she'll see me, but either way the day is ours afterward. I'm sorry your whole week here revolved around the case. What do you feel like doing?"

"Laying out on the beach." She folded the omelet over onto itself and then maneuvered it clumsily onto the reverse side. "How much time do you need at Tone Zone?"

"Not more than fifteen minutes."

"Enough time to tan. Hand me the phone. I'll see if I can get in."

I grabbed Vince's cordless off its base and tossed it to her. "Why tan in a coffin if we're going to the beach?"

She shook her head as if I had the intelligence of a plank of driftwood. "No tan lines."

Jeannie pulled her temporary club pass from her purse and, finding the club's number, placed the call. With the phone squeezed between her shoulder and ear, she made an appointment while sliding a giant cheese omelet onto a plate and dividing it in halves. She passed me a plate but no fork, so I watched her talk tans with someone on the phone and rinse utensils absently. Her multitasking was mild, but watching it tired me.

Too lazy to get off the stool and find my own fork, I tore a piece off the omelet and ate it. Jeannie caught me and rolled her eyes. She hung up the phone and opened the silverware drawer, drew a breath as if to say something, and then didn't.

She carried her plate to my side of the bar and sat down beside me, slid me a fork, and then, with apparent effort, returned her attention to her omelet.

"What?" I finally said.

"Nothing."

"Tell me."

She shook her head.

Respecting my privacy was killing her.

"Thank you," I said, not looking up from my plate.

"You'll be fine, Em. He's a good guy."

I lifted my mug with both hands, reassured by its warmth, and almost didn't notice the tremble.

"We never know what the day holds in store," Diana King said from the other side of her desk, "but I confess this is a shock."

She'd been writing when I showed up and held her pen barely over the page as if any moment she'd continue her written thoughts. I stayed in the doorway, partly afraid to go inside but mostly not wanting to give the impression I cared either way. I smelled apples, and wasn't sure if it was air freshener or Diana's fragrance of the day.

"I figured you'd want to know what we've learned."

Her posture relaxed and she pushed back from the desk and moved her hand to her lap, the pen casually resting between long fingers. Huge rings, one silver, the other a shimmering amethyst, momentarily distracted me.

"My boss had a guy on you." I said. "We know you were the one who left the key to Dr. Platt's house."

She cut a glance to a chair beside her desk and I slid into it.

"I used it. Found your old letters and the other half of this." I pointed to the impressive geode on the corner of her desk. "It's pretty clear you cared for each other."

Diana's lips tightened. Something in her expression morphed toward determination.

"I wondered why you'd let me inside, and why you'd have that key in the first place, but—"

"He traveled," she said. "To conferences and such. I kept an eye on things when he was away. Picked up the mail."

"You forgot the fish."

"Excuse me?"

"After he died. No one took the fish."

Her gaze fell to the desktop and flitted over it.

"I gave it to my daughter," I said. "Hope that's okay."

"Poor thing," she said. "I'd completely forgotten."

Diana's bauble necklace and matching bracelet, both with ridiculously oversized beads, made me wonder if some part of her depended on these external distractions to ignore whatever was going on inside.

"Why didn't you just tell me?" I said. "I spent a lot of energy this week trying to convince a jackass attorney and a control-freak private-eye that you didn't kill Platt. It was harder than you'd think, too—I couldn't tell them how I knew it."

"Why on earth not?"

"Because I didn't have permission to be in his house."

"Nonsense. I let you in."

"Unless you're the property custodian, a judge isn't going to care."

She frowned. "I couldn't have investigators calling the house and dropping by to see me about Wendell," she said. "My husband thinks all that ended years ago, before we met."

"It never ended?"

There was the slight tensing of her jaw again. She was apparently unused to personal questions. Good thing for me that the case was as good as over. The only one who stood to lose anything now was Diana.

"Wendell was honorable," she said. "Nothing in our history disrespected our spouses. Still…" She seemed unable to find suitable words. "We shared a friendship that my husband would never understand. Some in our social circle might deem its nature inappropriate for a married woman. But 'friendship' remains the best description for what it was."

Her expression drooped, much as it had Tuesday night on my front steps. I suspected Burke had taken away Diana's only real friend.

Silence lingered between us while I considered how to continue. Diana caught me off-guard with a discreet yawn.

"It looks like it was Dr. Platt's neighbor that murdered him," I said. "Not Claire. A phone number in his Caller ID log led me down that path. I thought you'd want to know that your help getting me into his house made a difference."

"His neighbor?"

"The caregiver, actually."

"That man that lives with William?" She looked stricken.

"You know him?"

She nodded, almost imperceptibly. "He helped Wendell here at the club once or twice."

"That's Kevin Burke. Guy's been scamming William for all he has. By the looks of it, he's taken plenty of other people too—including Daniel and Claire Gaston." I debated telling Diana about Daniel's murder and decided not to. "It seems

Doctor Platt found out what was going on. I gave a full report to the police yesterday. They'll take over from here."

Diana raised her heavily ornamented fingers to her lips, visibly affected by my story.

I stood to go. "Take care of yourself. I'm sorry for the loss of your friend."

She nodded. I was nearly to the door when she found her voice again.

"I'm the property custodian for that house," she said behind me. "Tell me if there's more I can do."

"Somebody will call," I said. As an afterthought, I pulled a card out of my purse and walked it over to her. "Thanks for not kicking me out of the club again."

She pursed her lips, not quite a smile. I took it as my sign to leave.

Chapter Thirty-two

Jeannie, in glittery platform flip-flops, crossed Richard's parking lot with her face lifted toward the late morning sun. She stole a glance at her watch. "We're getting into prime tan time now. You promised to make this fast."

A hot pink bow from her string bikini lay over the back of her fitted tee and bounced with each step.

Richard had phoned as we were leaving Vince's neighborhood. I'd agreed to stop by the office—briefly—on our way to the shore.

"You and tanning," I said. "I don't see how you spend so much time in the sun and don't have leather skin."

"For one thing, I don't buy cheap moisturizer at Walgreens."

Her cover-up clothes were so tight they left nothing to the imagination.

"And how can you be ten years older than me with a body like that? I hate you."

"Surgery," she said. "Make it your friend."

I opened the door to a community lobby Richard shared with a massage therapist and a financial planner. The transition to air conditioning gave me goose bumps.

Jeannie followed me down a hallway that led to our offices. "You're such a Debbie Downer about women who have work done." Behind me, her shoes were flipping and flopping. "Like Claire and that Diana woman…it doesn't make us lesser people, you know. Just better looking than you."

"Exactly." We rounded a corner and found Richard at his desk. "More power to you."

Richard perked up when he saw us. "Those employment apps you found at William's house? I went to that store and asked if Sandy Diaz still worked there. It was only a hunch, but sure enough."

"You talked to her?" I slid into a seat opposite his desk.

Jeannie tapped me on the shoulder. "Don't sit." Then to Richard, she added, "We can't stay."

Richard ignored her. "Add Sandy to the list of people Burke screwed over."

I stood and jangled my keys. "What's her story?"

"She was his girlfriend until about forty-five minutes ago. Works in Human Resources. Said Burke went back to school at U of H—totally false, I checked it out. He told her he was working on a telemarketing project for a class and asked if she'd copy applications for people the store didn't hire. He wanted to recruit them for his project…they could earn easy money from home, and all that. She figured they were looking for work anyway and it helped him with his class, so every couple weeks she brought him a few more."

"What'd he use them for?"

"Employment applications are a goldmine. Full name and address, birth date, Social Security Number, driver's license number…all he has to do is apply for credit and have the cards sent wherever he wants. Scammers do this all the time. Max out the cards and pay the minimums on the bills."

Jeannie looked incredulous. "What an ass."

"I also went to the Heights and asked the neighbors about Saunders. The homeowner whose property backs up to his is the only one who knew him before his accident. Said he spent three years in brain injury rehab, most of it at a deluxe residential place." Richard rubbed his fingertips and thumb together in the universal sign for "big bucks." "Guy was lucky," he continued. "Eventually he improved enough to come home, but he'll always need supervised care."

"How'd Burke get his hooks in?"

"Home care staff came in shifts for years until the hospital program was dropped in April. When that happened, he had a string of bad luck. His aunt, who coordinates his care, found a private agency, but most folks that came didn't speak or understand English. Others couldn't cook. Some missed shifts, leaving him alone for blocks of time throughout the day. Right now she's torn between overseeing William's care and looking after her sister in New Braunfels…end-stage cancer."

I had a soft spot for William and didn't like where I thought this was headed.

"Imagine her peace of mind when she found a charming, enthusiastic live-in replacement to bridge the gap for a few months while she tended to her sister."

I felt my pulse quicken. "Are you kidding me? What about credentials and licensure?"

"Not sure. She's juggling ailing relatives two hundred miles apart, all by herself. That's a tall order for someone like you or me. Imagine doing it at eighty-four."

Jeannie shook her head. "It sounds like Burke was a temporary solution. If she trusted him—"

"He could rob her nephew blind and get a paycheck for doing it." The realization nauseated me.

"Anyway," Richard said, "When I mentioned what was going on with Burke, this guy said two people on his street have been victimized by check washing this summer."

"I have no idea what that means," Jeannie said.

"I didn't either." Richard motioned toward his computer, where I figured he'd looked up the details. "Turns out, scammers steal outgoing mail—anything that looks like a bill being paid—and remove and alter the checks. They hold the signed check upside down to preserve the signature and dip it in chemicals to remove the ink everywhere else. Then they write in whatever amount and payee they want."

I remembered the bleach and acetone in Burke's work room. "Is there anything this guy didn't try?"

"He knows a few tricks, that's for sure. There's also the cars. William Senior kept two vintage Mustangs. After he died, the cars never came out of the garage again until last spring."

"When Burke moved in." With each new detail, I felt angrier and more defensive about what this leech had done to William.

"Yep. He even added a new one, the car you saw in the Tone Zone footage. Neighbor says it came into circulation in May, a few weeks after Burke arrived on the scene."

"How do you suppose he staged that e-mail from Claire to Platt?" Jeannie said.

"That was probably easy. I don't think Claire was tech savvy."

"She wasn't," I said. "Her son set up her e-mail. He told me she couldn't do much on the computer without help." I thought back to our Monday meeting in their River Oaks driveway. "Come to think of it, he said that her boyfriend helped her, too."

Richard nodded. "You saw all that computer gear at Saunders' house."

"Yeah, and the bizarre spy watch with the USB port."

"He's slick, I'll give him that."

The events were adding up, yet one detail bothered me. "How do you send an e-mail from your account and make it look like it's from somebody else?"

"My guess is he did it from her account," Richard said.

"But he wasn't living there anymore when the message was sent."

"I think he installed remote access software on her machine. As long as the computer stayed on, he could access it from anywhere."

I didn't buy it. "He wouldn't have known her Yahoo password."

"*You* knew it," Jeannie said.

I paused, stuck. She had me.

"Somebody with those skills might even have used keylogging software," Richard added. "I wouldn't put anything past him."

I thought about it. "If he knew how to do that, he'd have access to all their on-line passwords and accounts too."

"You bet."

"Okay," I said. "So he sends threatening messages to Platt from Claire's account to make it look like Claire's an obsessed crazy woman. Say he deletes them from her Sent folder too. That would explain why I couldn't find anything when I went through her e-mail on Wednesday. But surely Platt would be confused when he received these notes. He didn't know her. Wouldn't he respond? At least once to tell her she had the wrong guy? Burke couldn't camp at her computer twenty-four hours a day. He'd be taking a big risk that she might receive something back from Platt."

Richard leaned back. "I thought about that. He might have set up her account to treat mail from Platt as spam. It'd give him a little time to check and delete anything. I don't know. He's obviously smart. Been getting away with this, and worse, for a really long time."

"The police have her computers now," I said. "They'll know whether remote access software was found."

"It wasn't."

"Then why'd you bring it up?"

"Because it can also be *uninstalled* remotely."

I did a little mental calendar work. "You're suggesting he uninstalled anything incriminating before the search warrants were issued?"

"That's one way he might have done it."

"He obviously wasn't afraid to come back to the house," Jeannie said. "Balls of steel."

"Emily solved that one for us yesterday when she found the Gastons' new credit cards."

His reasoning had passed mine and it took a moment for me to catch up.

"Of course," I finally said. "The phone. Burke intercepted Daniel's replacement cards in Monday's mail and then hurried inside to activate them—a task he could only accomplish from the Gastons' home phone. No cars were in the driveway so he thought the coast was clear. When I showed no signs of leaving, he acted like he'd come to feed Logan's snake."

Jeannie picked up my line of thought. "That explains what happened to the missing gym note too. With free access to the house and its computers, he could erase anything, paper trail or electronic."

"Gotta hand it to the slime," Richard said. "He had it all worked out."

We paused, each mulling the new information.

Jeannie pounced. "Don't take this the wrong way," she said to Richard. "But if there's nothing more, we're late for the beach." The look she gave me said she expected my full support.

"Fair enough," he said. "Surf safe."

We said goodbye to Richard and this time I followed Jeannie down the hall. Ninety minutes later, she worked on her tan while I walked ankle deep in froth, glad for a break from the case. It felt nice to finally have a quiet moment to think about the other things on my mind.

I listened to waves and gulls, watched light glint over the seas, and reflected on my paradoxical shortcomings as a mother and a girlfriend.

With Vince, it would be easy to share my emotions once I understood what they were. With Annette, the opposite. My boundless love for her was unequivocal, but the challenge was how to express it in a way she'd understand.

Warm ocean water rolled over my feet and, somehow, soothed me. For the first time since moving to Texas, I didn't even mind the sun.

Chapter Thirty-three

After the beach, we stopped at a Sonic because Jeannie didn't believe me when I told her there were still roller skating carhops. The issue settled, we sipped grape and orange slushies for the remainder of the trip, most of which we passed in contented silence, except for the occasional announcement of a brain freeze. By request, I'd left the windows down so it was too loud to talk anyway. And despite the highway wind rushing through the car—whipping my hair into tiny, unforgiving knots—it was still inhumanly hot, so I also left the air conditioner on. If a Hell existed for the ecologically calamitous, my name was on the list.

Exhausted from our day in the sun, I recognized the slight warmth and tightening of my skin, especially my face, and knew that soon I'd be pink. A cool shower and fresh clothes topped my list of Stuff I Want Right Now.

At the house, we split in different directions, slogging with only half our usual energy. Jeannie headed for the guest room and I turned for Vince's. Cindy circled excitedly at my feet, stepping on my toes, and I knew she wanted to go out. So before cleaning up, I found a leash and clipped it to her collar. We headed out the front door for a jaunt around the block.

I checked my phone, an upgraded replacement the sales guy talked me into the night before.

There were no new messages, but I did have a few e-mails, only one of interest.

Emily,

It's about Wendell. The gym closes today at 6:00. Could you come by after? I'll be here until eight. The main entrance will be locked but I'll leave the south door open.

Diana

Her interest in talking to me again was compelling. I hated typing on my phone so Diana got a quick "OK." It seemed that no matter which way I angled the phone, its display was now dim and washed out. Exasperated, I shoved it into my pocket and hoped the condition was only a product of bright sunlight.

Cindy and I finished our walk and Jeannie was out of the shower when we returned. With a towel twisted on her head and another bound around her curves, she declared that her shower had been marvelous and that it was time for a nap.

"You smell good," I said. "Peaches?"

She smiled. "More to life than Irish Spring, Em."

Soon her hairdryer whirred. I took my own shower, longer than usual, and pulled on clean khaki shorts and a fitted tee. It was barely past five so I had time to kill before leaving for the club. I hauled my laptop to Vince's bar, propped myself on a stool, and connected to his wireless network. Days had passed since I'd answered my e-mails and, with nothing else to do, now seemed the perfect time. But ten minutes in, fatigue overtook me. I rested my head on my arms at the bar and next thing I knew it was 6:15.

A quick peek down the hallway revealed Jeannie's motionless legs on top of the quilt. I let her sleep, jotted a note, and left for the club.

◇◇◇

Daylight was fading when I arrived. Westheimer's traffic fumes were as thick as the humidity and, even though I'd parked near the familiar front entrance, I was in a mild snit because I didn't know which way was south. I tried the side of the building to my left but there were no doors. I backtracked to the opposite end, which shared a wide alley with a running store. As promised, the door there was unlocked. I stepped into what must have been an employee lounge and weaved around tables as the door closed behind me.

The gym was partly lit. Though the corridors remained lighted, exercise rooms and spa nooks were dark and abandoned, doors closed, only black showing on the other side of their glass panes. Walking though the quiet passages reminded of my old job at BioTek and the times I'd stayed after hours to work alone. It'd freaked me out then and was still uncomfortable, similar to how I'd felt during the storm when I was stuck in Claire's massive house all alone.

At the top of the stairs, faint but recognizable jazz music played in Diana's office. The track leading to her door was in shadows but a wide triangle of light spilled onto its rubberized surface.

I stepped into her office and knew right away I was in trouble.

Nobody was inside, but Georgina—Annette's faded, stuffed giraffe—sat propped on the desk's front edge. An open ring box had been left beside the toy. Confused, I edged forward for a closer look, then felt the sick adrenaline rush of a trapped idiot. My wedding rings were inside, glinting under the overhead lights.

I didn't reach for them, just turned and ran, but Burke was waiting at the top of the stairs. The sight of him brought me up short.

"Your friend is hard to miss." He was ten yards away, blocking any chance of escape. "I saw her parked on my street yesterday."

"You mean William's street."

He glared at me. "Because of you, I can never go home again." His empty hands should have been a relief. They weren't.

He stepped toward me and I backed up.

"Your scheme was so important that you killed innocent people to keep it going?" I glanced at the reception area below and considered jumping.

"I left you and your kid alone. You should have done the same for me. Now I have to move and start all over. It's your fault." He took a confident stride forward.

I turned and ran to the far end of the track. Burke surprised me and charged.

Behind me, his footfalls were muffled thuds on the rubber. They grew closer, and I knew that if I didn't get off the track fast, he'd catch me before I reached the stairs. I thought about what he'd done to the other two people who'd caught onto his scam and knew I'd have to do something. Now.

I stopped, swung my legs over the steel banister and...dropped.

I seemed to hang in the air and, for that single instant, I thought I'd escaped.

Then I slammed into the floor below. My landing on the unforgiving marble was violent and I was too hurt to move right away. When I finally did, my knee and hip throbbed.

He looked down and shook his head. "That had to hurt."

I didn't see a gun.

Scrambling up, I re-oriented and bolted for the alley, trying to ignore the pain.

"You're fooling yourself, honey," he yelled. "Papa's got the good doctor's keys."

I tried to control my rising panic. If he'd dead-bolted the exit, running to the lounge would leave me cornered. But he might have been bluffing.

I doubted it.

Ahead, the hallway ended in a T—weight room to the left, locker room to the right. The weight room was another dead-end, so I veered right, remembering that the locker area connected to the indoor pool, which in turn opened to the lobby. I silently slipped into the locker room's darkness and tried to steady my breathing. My purse was gone, probably lost when I'd crashed on the lobby floor, and that meant I had no phone.

No matter where I hid, Burke would find me eventually. He had all night and I couldn't leave. My only chance for survival was to get help to come to me.

I squeezed back into the hallway and ran for the short corridor Kendra had shown me. A fire alarm box had been by the water fountains.

I dashed for it and broke the glass. Bell-style clanging erupted throughout the building and didn't stop. I scooped a shard from the floor and barely registered the sting when it cut me. I stood and turned back for the lockers and Burke was *right there* watching me. He reached into his pocket.

I didn't wait to find out why.

Barreling through the serpentine halls, my left knee and hip throbbed and it felt like my lungs were on fire. With the alarm, I couldn't hear him behind me and I knew better than to look back. The corridor dumped me in the lobby, right next to the natatorium, and I heaved open a glass door and hurried toward the corner of the pool. Burke entered as I reached the first turn and paused as if calculating his next move. I rounded the second corner and didn't stop until I was exactly opposite him. Four pool lanes separated us.

We stared at each other across the lane ropes, both breathing hard. Burke pushed hair from his forehead and said something that I couldn't hear over the alarm.

He reached into his pocket and withdrew a metallic object. In the half-light, I couldn't see what it was. He raised his hand and pointed it at me. A stiletto blade sprung out and I knew—just *knew*—he'd slit my throat if I let him get close enough.

I glanced at the far end of the pool, gauging the distance to the locker rooms. As if reading my mind, he produced a set of keys, spun them around a finger and laughed. He moved to the exit behind him, took his time to find the right key, and locked the door. Then he tested it to make sure.

Ignoring me, he moved to the far end of the pool toward the locker rooms. I shuffled painfully sideways to keep directly opposite him across the water.

Burke disappeared behind a partition that led to the changing areas, and then quickly reappeared. I was locked in, no doubt. The switchblade was gone, I assumed replaced in his pocket, and even from twenty-five yards away, his cold, tired stare bored into me. I mirrored his movement as he paced the perimeter of the pool, never looking away from him. He glanced at me only occasionally and seemed to be talking to himself. It went on like this, in a clockwise pattern, him walking and talking and me limping opposite him on my increasingly painful left leg, until we'd changed places and I was in front of the glass lobby door.

I pushed the handle and it was locked, as expected.

I looked around, desperate for something to break the glass. Working through the pain, I balanced on my left leg and kicked the door with my right foot. The glass cracked, but didn't give, and when I turned around, Burke was headed toward me in a full sprint.

I ran away from him as hard as I could, around the short end of the pool. Already short of breath and with my hip and knee smarting with every step, I wasn't sure how long I could keep the pace. The pool deck was slick, and I lost speed in the turns. By degrees I knew Burke was gaining. He was charged, jacked on adrenaline, and got closer on the second lap.

Finally, I turned a corner and he wasn't in my periphery.

It was the upstairs track all over again; I'd have to jump or be slashed.

I leaped wide and landed on the nearest lane rope, immediately maneuvering backward in the splash because I knew Burke would come right behind me. He pushed off the deck with the power of a cheetah and landed on top of me. I swiped at him with the glass shard and caught his cheek below the eye. A thin red line discolored the water streaming down his face. I tried again and caught his shoulder, but the glass also sliced my palm. Reflexively, I let go and the shard splashed in the water between us.

I pushed myself backward across the width of the pool, kicking to keep him at bay whenever I could. But Burke was stronger and taller; the water only came to his chest. It was over my shoulders and I could only move in what felt like slow motion. I angled for the shallow end and ducked under the second rope. Even underwater, I heard the fire alarm's tireless clang.

I splashed furtively, trying anything to slow him down. I thought I'd gained some distance, but then he surged forward and clenched my hurt right hand.

I pushed off the bottom and caught him with a left hook. He didn't even flinch. He responded with a back fist I never saw coming and, in the time it took me to reorient, grabbed my hair and forced my face to the water. He was too strong, so I grabbed a big bite of air and knew I'd have to use it wisely.

Underwater, I focused on his jeans. He'd shown me twice now that he carried the knife on his right. My left hand was still free. If only I could close the gap.

Burke pressed harder on my head, his finger span wide enough to cup the entire back of my skull. I grew hungry for air and flashed to Annette. She'd lost her dad to the water and I'd be damned if she'd lose me too. I swam further down, nearly beyond Burke's reach, and used my feet to push off the bottom toward his hip. My fingers snaked into his front pocket and I groped for the switchblade while he tried to step away. He let go of my head and reached for my hand, but it was too late. I had it.

I wrenched it from his pocket and thumbed the switch. The water resistance prevented a solid drive into his hip, but I dug and twisted its point until the water between us turned pink, then red.

Out of air, I drew an involuntarily breath and choked. At the surface I coughed and gagged and nearly threw up.

Burke still had my right wrist so I twisted away, holding the knife as far from him as I could. I dipped under the third rope and came up with a fast swipe at his arm before turning away again. The blade connected, but he didn't let go.

We were in the last lane now, an arm's length from the ladder. If I got an arm through its handrail I'd have leverage. I thrashed again with no effect. Splashing at him would put the knife within his reach, so all I could do was kick. But drag made each attempt slow and ineffective.

I kept my eyes on Burke and tried to shove him off with a foot while I felt behind me for the ladder. Finally the knife scraped against something hard and I took a quick look at the wall. Looping my arm through the metal handrail, I was careful to keep the blade high. Then I shoved my back into the foot rungs, pulled my knees to my chest, and with all my strength, swung my feet above the water's surface where they met Burke's face. His neck snapped back and my wrist was finally free.

I turned to the ladder and started to pull myself out, but he lunged toward me. He wrenched down on my collar and slammed my chin into the cement pool deck. My mouth filled with the metallic tang of blood, and I when I tried to move my jaw, my tongue ran over something hard and loose—a broken tooth.

Behind me, Burke angled to push me under again, but it was clear that what he most wanted was the knife. I had no chance against his greater size and leverage, so I made the decision. I'd have to give in.

I let him pry my arm from where it anchored me to the relative security of the handrail. Using all his furious strength, Burke spun me to face him and groped for my left hand to protect himself from the switchblade I'd been holding there.

His focus was so intense that he didn't notice when I moved my other hand underwater and scooped the knife from where I'd placed it on the ladder's top rung. Clutching the switchblade like the last chance I knew it was, I drove it deep into his shoulder. The crimson rush that followed assured me I'd finally slowed the monster down.

I raised the knife again but my arm was intercepted in midswing. Before I knew what was happening, I was hoisted to the deck and dragged backward through the shattered glass door, then pushed forward across the lobby and outside into the sticky night. Red and blue lights flashed everywhere, spotlighting uniforms and glass, and assaulted my eyes, already stinging from the chlorine. Fire trucks and squad cars lined up for blocks, and someone wrapped a blanket around my wet shoulders. Later, Burke was shoved down the stairs past me, his hands shackled. At the bottom step he looked over his bleeding shoulder and spat words I didn't understand because, thanks to the fire alarm, I couldn't hear for shit.

Epilogue

"When can I have my own cell phone?"

Annette and I were huddled on our sofa playing checkers on my new iPhone. Richard, feeling guilty about landing me in the E.R. again, and pitying my misfortune with the cell phone upgrade that wasn't, had sprung for something…less cheap than I'd have ever picked out for myself.

"Maybe when you're a teenager," I said. "What would you do with a phone anyway? You haven't even started school."

"I could call my friends."

I nodded.

"And get you unlost when you drive bad."

I gave her a wry half-smile and shifted her off my swollen side. The bruises were still morphing through all manner of disgusting shades.

"Also I could take pictures and watch movies."

I brightened. "We can watch movies on this?"

She nodded and opened her hand. "Let me see it."

I passed her the phone and watched her tiny fingers tap its screen. She was probably only playing, but I felt marginally concerned that she already knew what she was doing.

It was Sunday evening and I'd been unable to find a dentist to see me on the weekend. My broken tooth was so sensitive to air that I didn't want to talk much, but that worked out fine because Annette picked up my conversational slack.

The only problem was that she did it all with questions.

"Can I see your stitches again?"

I unwrapped the gauze around my palm. The wound was clean; it had taken five sutures.

"Gross. Does it hurt?"

"Not much anymore."

"I'm glad you were wearing your helmet."

Saturday, after dropping Jeannie at the airport, I'd retrieved Annette from the Fletchers. Pressed to explain my pronounced limp and bandaged hand, I told them I'd had a bike wreck. Betsy looked at me sideways but didn't push.

I kissed the top of Annette's head and pulled the gauze back into place. She raised my good hand to her little mouth and kissed it. "Maybe you should stick with running."

I had Jeannie and her nosey snooping to thank for my aquatic rescue. She'd used my laptop Friday night to print Saturday's boarding pass and, as usual, the browser opened up my webmail application by default. Seeing the note from Diana in there, she read it and then mentioned my impromptu meeting with Diana to Richard when he stopped by with a check to reimburse her Tone Zone fees. But Richard had just left Diana at Mick Young's office, where she'd shared her story about Platt and the reason she'd slipped me his key. Richard put together that Burke had staged another bogus e-mail. He tried to call and stop me from going to the club, but we figured out that, by that time, I'd already jumped the upstairs track railing and lost my phone. When he didn't reach me, he'd sent the police.

"Hey," Annette said. "Why are your eyes closed? It's not dark yet."

I opened them, unsure whether I'd zoned out for seconds or minutes. She'd started a new game of cell phone checkers.

"Tired, sweetie. Little bit of a headache."

Annette's bedtime wasn't for another hour, but I could have easily called it a day right then.

She regarded me. "What's a headache?"

I searched for a parallel she'd understand. "Like a belly ache, in your head."

She giggled. "You're messing with me."

"It's a throbbing, hurting feeling behind my eyes."

She frowned a little and I wished I'd lied.

"Hm." A soft, tiny hand smoothed back my hair. "Maybe one of your thoughts went down the wrong pipe."

I laughed. A wave of cool air rushed over my tooth and made me wish I were dead. Only, not really, because I was totally and completely in love with my child.

"You know, I met a new friend this week," I told her. "His name is William. He's unusual because his body is old but his mind seems very young."

"Like my mind?"

I nodded. "He's lonely. I thought we could visit him when I'm feeling better."

"Does he like Legos?"

"I don't know him well enough to say."

"Why do you want to be his friend?"

Her question stopped me. Like William, I realized, I still felt in many ways alone, kind of on the outskirts of normalcy, and was unsure how to make life go forward smoothly. That part of him resonated with me.

Annette waited. I knew I'd never find the words to explain what I was thinking, so I changed the subject.

"Hey, let me get your opinion about something. Vince invited us to take a trip with him before you start school next month. He thought maybe you'd like to visit Sea World."

"What's that?"

"A giant park with whales and dolphins and lots of fish and things that live in the ocean."

"Octopuses?"

"Probably."

"Sting rays?"

"Yeah."

"Tuna?"

"Anyway." I sighed. "How does that sound?"

She shrugged. "I'd rather go with just you."

I pulled her close and squeezed, thankful and happy in our moment, and privately celebrated the best No I'd ever heard.

To receive a free catalog of Poisoned Pen Press titles, please contact us in one of the following ways:

Phone: 1-800-421-3976
Facsimile: 1-480-949-1707
Email: info@poisonedpenpress.com
Website: www.poisonedpenpress.com

Poisoned Pen Press
6962 E. First Ave. Ste. 103
Scottsdale, AZ 85251